E.D.F Chronicles - Eye of the Dracos

When a lone, unarmed survey ship drops out of plasma drive on the
fringes of the far flung Auriga system, they chance upon the remains of
a once great civilization. A gigantic facility is re-activated by accident,
and suddenly a race that the galaxy thought long dead, are not as dead
as they were led to believe.

A new evil emerges, and will stop at nothing to reclaim a planet that
they believe is theirs by right. Plunging Michael Alexander, Nikolai
Vargev, and Kathryn Jacobs into a nightmare they will not soon forget.

First published in Great Britain in 2012 by Ian J. Smethurst.
ISBN#978-0-9574705-2-1

Typeset in Garamond by the author.

E.D.F Chronicles - Eye of the Dracos

Ian J. Smethurst

For Rachel,

For being a very dear friend, and for being there through the good and the bad times.

Contents.

1. A new dawn.

Lieutenant Commander Kathryn Jacobs stared out the viewport of the Copernicus, a civilian survey vessel chartered by the E.D.F research division to investigate the Auriga system for potential new colony worlds.

Auriga was, by and large, an unremarkable system. Situated in the far south west of the Bryant sector, right on the edge of E.O.C.A territory, and about eight light years from the nearest E.D.F facility at Gamma Aurigulon, which happened to be Charlie Echo base, a small research facility conducting experiments into a new higher definition space telescope.

Five years had passed since the great Krenaran war, five long years, hard years, where humanity had toiled and dug itself out of the ashes that were the war torn outer colonies. It was now 2076 and humanity had set to repairing the damage done during that colossal war admirably. Some of those devastated colonies, were now thriving trade and commerce centres, while many others where still being rebuilt, such was the ferocity of the fighting.

Like a great many people, Kathryn held an intense distrust, bordering on hatred of the Krenarans for what they had done. For the damage they had inflicted on humanity, and for the scale of wanton slaughter visited upon them. She tried to forget about those times, of the time when she barricaded herself inside the medical bay of Delta base, scared half mad by the horror of what she had witnessed. Until a dashing man by the name of Michael Alexander came and rescued her, held his hand out in friendship when many had thought her insane. She tried to forget about the evil Krenaran and their empire, however, the scars ran deep.

Michael was now a decorated war hero, and the captain of the Liberty, Kathryn however, was one of the few that really knew how he felt inside, his pain had almost destroyed him.

She brushed her long brunette locks, now streaked with the very occasional grey strand, she was only twenty three, and a fresh faced ensign, when Michael had rescued her. Now she was twenty eight, a lieutenant commander, and she still often thought of him.

E.D.F Chronicles – Eye of the Dracos

Lieutenant Ayella approached her, "Commander, you are wanted on the bridge."

"Understood, lieutenant."

She pushed her wayward thoughts to the back of her mind for the time being, duty called.

Although originally a nurse, Kathryn re-trained shortly after the war. The horrors she faced on the triage table on so many embattled worlds eventually proved too much for her. She did, however, discover a love of planetary geology, and so joined the E.D.F research division as a planetary geologist. She never quite understood how this interest manifested itself, she suspected it was a kind of defence mechanism, as she tried to blot out the memory of those soldiers and naval personnel, blasted apart by Krenaran weaponry that she had to patch back up.

Captain Akimbe was a middle aged man of dark African descent, a noted geologist himself, although he was mostly known as one of the foremost minds on interstellar phenomena anywhere in the E.D.F. Kathryn regarded him as a quiet, gentle, thoughtful man, whom she had come to regard highly over the years.

She strode onto the bridge, and took her usual position at one of the myriad science stations dotted liberally around the command centre.

"We are approaching the Auriga system, Captain." A male voice announced behind her.

"Understood, drop her out of plasma drive gently ensign, the old girl is not as spritely as she used to be."

"Yes, Captain."

The Copernicus was an old Trojan class frigate, once the mainstay of the E.D.F fleet, before the faster and more advanced Mandela class superseded it. The Trojan class was over twenty years old, and was one of the first frigate sized vessels built by the E.D.F when it had first formed.

Ian J Smethurst

The Copernicus was the last of these old warhorses still operating, its sister ships were all decommissioned shortly after the Mandela class light cruisers replaced them. The Copernicus was originally named the Achilles during its tenure as a warship, it too was briefly decommissioned.

However, after spending years floating in a gigantic starship scrapyard, in a wilderness area of space between the Levius and Sicarius systems, the Achilles was re-commissioned after the research division put out a petition calling for new science and survey vessels to replace its own ageing fleet.

The Achilles was stripped of its weapon systems, targeting arrays and military hardware, and was instead packed full of the latest, most powerful sensor suites available. New ultra high definition scanners were installed, and it had a completely re-designed computer system, doubling the amount of data its computers could process. Eventually, after all the work was finished, they re-commissioned the ship, the Copernicus, after the great explorer.

For the past four years it had served as home for Kathryn, it had an air of quaint nostalgia about the place, as though the ship was like a very old friend, a totally different feeling from the uber modern, ultra high-tech, yet dark and brooding interior of the Liberty.

The ship shuddered slightly; the deckplates began to vibrate and creak as the vessel dropped out of plasma drive, lighting up its sloped forward section, studded with delicate sensor antennae, its long rectangular hull with its giant triangular shaped sensor boom, raised above it from tall fifty-metre pylons jutting out from the aft dorsal section of the ship, and chock full with all manner of sophisticated sensor systems.

Two giant inter-system booster engines roared into life, blazing a trail of super heated gas which slowly began to propel it on its long journey into the Auriga system.

As the small ship left the giant swirling plasma wake it had just emerged from, the wake collapsed in on itself in another blindingly bright flash that lit up the silhouette of the vessel once again.

The first planet it passed was the barren, frozen ice world of Auriga VII, the furthest planet out in the system, a routine scan of the small planetoid had revealed that the surface was far too cold, at minus one hundred and fifty seven degrees, and the atmosphere too thin to support human life. It was removed as a suitable candidate for habitation rather quickly.

The Copernicus passed close to the blue-green noxious soup of the gas giant Auriga V, noting the violent storms constantly whipped up across its surface for further study later.

They continued further into the system, towards their ultimate objective Auriga III, the planet was located in this system's 'habitable zone.' Far enough away from the Auriga star so that it would not be too hot, yet close enough that it would not be too cold. A few hours later and the ship had reached its destination. Taking up a geo-stationary orbit above the deep beige coloured planet, it began taking detailed scans.

"It looks like the rocks on the surface are made up of silicon carbides and molybdenum, scans of the core show an unusually hot molybdenum-tungsten mix. It points toward the planet may have once been very close to the Aurigan star, some kind of spacial incident may have forced its orbit further away." Kathryn said as she turned towards Akimbe.

The captain considered this, stroking his gently grey stubbled chin thoughtfully, "Try a full geological scan of the surface, see if we can find any craters, or evidence to explain why the planet was pulled so far out."

"Solar flare?" Lieutenant Pryor suggested.

"Could be, although there would be some scorching on the surface, I'm not picking up anything." Kathryn replied, "Something has pushed it out this far, and the planet has settled into a new orbit." She studied her screen intently, Kathryn loved little scientific mysteries like these, it allowed her to play detective.

"The atmosphere has a high concentration of carbon dioxide and methane, if we go down there we'll need environment suits." A junior scientist from the opposite side of the oval command centre announced.

Kathryn's screen suddenly blazed into life, almost taking on a life of its own as huge amounts of data and recordings streamed across the display.

"What in the blue hell, is that!" She said, peering wide eyed at her screen.

"Show me," Akimbe said in excitement, moving as fast as his body would allow.

Kathryn brought up a high definition scan of a gigantic metallic looking structure, pointing skywards from the planet surface, towards the Copernicus. It closely resembled that of an enormous eye, looking up at them. The sight gave Kathryn a shudder down her spine, she didn't know whether it was excitement at this new discovery, or fear.

"My god," Akimbe gasped, glancing over Kathryn's shoulder, "that thing must measure some three kilometres wide, any power readings or signs of life over there?"

Kathryn glanced over the readings again, "Nothing, the whole structure seems to be abandoned. Although whatever it is made of is throwing off my scanners, it appears to be some sort of new metal, it isn't even on the periodic table. Although judging by the level of corrosion, it's been defunct for around three hundred years."

"Could be the remains of a dead civilisation," Akimbe offered.

"If so, why isn't there any other structures or traces of habitation, just this one giant structure."

"Maybe they were swept away or buried in some natural disaster?" Akimbe didn't have any real answers, he was as befuddled as Kathryn.

"We'll have to send a team to investigate, if we are to know for sure."

"I agree, prepare a landing shuttle."

"Pryor, Gomez, your with me," Kathryn announced as she left the command centre with the junior scientists in tow.

"Kathryn, I don't have to tell you to be careful down there, we still don't know what we're dealing with," Akimbe said with a warm but ever so slightly concerned smile, just as he sank himself back down into the command chair.

Kathryn returned the smile as she turned back to face the aged captain, touched by his concern for her welfare, "Don't worry captain, I will."

With that, the science team left the bridge and made their way down to the shuttle deck. Kathryn had picked some other scientists she thought would be useful in the exploration of that strange place. In total, the science team was made up of six members, Dieter Kalschacht the noted German physicist. Mira Romaine, a talented chemist; a fellow geologist by the name of Matthew Broadhurst, Lieutenant James Pryor a specialist in both spacial and planetary meteorology, and finally Pablo Gomez a Mexican scientist trained extensively in xenoarcheology.

The science team was escorted by a ten man squad of troops from the thirty seventh black falcons infantry division, assigned to the Copernicus to safeguard the scientists onboard when exposed to potentially threatening environments, such as this.

The sixteen strong group all boarded the long shuttle, vaguely resembling that of a 20th century executive jet. Although in spaceflight mode its wings and tail were retracted inside its elongated bullet shaped fuselage.

Inside, it was cramped, in part due to the press of bodies. Typical E.D.F shuttles normally carried a maximum of ten men, this one was being asked to carry sixteen and their equipment as well.

The shuttles powerful solid fuel boosters roared throughout the empty shuttlebay, its anti-gravity motors gently lifted it clear of the bay floor, just as the bay doors fully opened. With a loud roar the boosters increased to full power, and the tiny craft accelerated out from the rear shuttlebay of the Copernicus and out into the inky blackness of deep space. Leaving the comparatively enormous survey ship far behind it, before banking gently and heading for the beige hued planet below.

Matthew, piloting the shuttle, deftly made some slight course corrections, so that the craft could enter the planets atmosphere at just the right angle, the small vessel began to heat up as it began its descent through the upper atmosphere of Auriga III. Increasing in speed as the planets gravity took hold, pulling the small craft closer to its surface.

The shuttle punched through the roiling carbon dioxide and methane clouds in the atmosphere, and deployed its delta wings and tail for normal atmospheric flight.

Kathryn ventured a look from out of the port side viewport next to her seat, as the craft sped towards its destination. She could make out deep rocky, windswept valleys, and tall jagged mountains rising up from the surrounding flatlands, although there was nothing in the way of habitation, the planet seemed barren, forlorn, bereft of life.

That was, until the occupants got their first glimpse of the gigantic, strange structure they had glanced from orbit.

E.D.F Chronicles – Eye of the Dracos
2. Discoveries.

It was absolutely enormous in size, six massive dull metallic pylons seemed to reach up, high into the sky. Looking like great claws spouting out from the planet. These 'claws' surrounded what appeared to be a giant cannon-like aperture in the centre, a massive sinkhole that extended into pitch darkness.

The shuttle circled the massive dark installation, its sullenness gave Kathryn a second gentle shudder down her spine.

"My god, that structure must be almost three kilometres in diameter." Romaine said awestruck of the sheer scale of the defunct installation.

"It looks like nothing we have ever seen before," Kalschacht added

To Kathryn though, the structure looked as bereft as its surroundings, lost in the mists of time. Even here looking upon it from the safety of the interior of the shuttle, the sight gave her goose bumps. Nevertheless she had a job to do, so she swallowed her fears. "It resembles Solarian architecture with it having a grand, almost organic like form, with lots of flowing curves, instead of our own rugged utilitarian style."

"There are some notable differences, however." Gomez replied, "Take a look at the tips of the pylons, they are not curved gently like traditional Solarian designs, instead they appear to be sharp, almost blade-like."

"And it's dark, the metal is like some sort of non-reflective anthracite, I don't recall the Solarians ever using a material like that." Broadhurst pointed out, as he gently manoeuvred the shuttle in for landing, deploying the landing legs as he did so.

"Either way, we'll know more when we get inside," Kathryn added.

The shuttle gently touched down on a small area of flat ground not far from the edge of the pylons. The occupants all donned their environment suits, clicking their helmets into place and checking the hermetic seals on the suits were all secure and not leaking, before disembarking from the shuttle.

The guards all fanned out, forming a small hemisphere around the site of the shuttle and the scientists. The shuttle behind them continued gently humming, as the turbines of the boosters slowly came to a rest.

The wind had certainly gotten stronger, everyone could feel the chill in the air through the outer layers of their suits. It was all Kathryn could do to prevent herself from being blown over, hearing the howling winds through the glass in her helmet, she ventured a look across auriga's mountainous landscape, in the sky the planets single moon was approaching its zenith high in the night sky, the moonlight cast upon the surface was perfectly bright enough to see by, due to the fact that this moon was almost twice the size of Earths moon.

She tried to shout into helmet mic. over the winds that whipped by them all. "We need to look around, see if we can find some sort of entrance to the structure!"

"Understood," the other scientists all said in unison.

The group began to split up into teams of two, and started combing the derelict surface. The giant pylons loomed over them, reaching up well over two thousand meters into the night sky.

Kathryn ran her hands over the various panels and indents, carved with such a precision, such an intricate attention to detail, E.D.F scientists could not better it. The wind that blew through this place gave off an eerie howl as it whistled by the metallic surface of the pylons.

The ground was perfectly smooth, and even gave off a slight sheen as the moonlight glanced across it.

Despite the ferocity of the wind battering against the tall pylons, not a single one of them swayed so much as a millimetre. Whatever these were made from, they were immensely strong, and incredibly weather resistant Kathryn thought as she continued to explore the surface. As she moved her hand across a portion of one of the pylons, it came back wet, the whole surface of the pylon was damp with condensation, yet there was very little rust or oxidisation. She wondered how the Copernicus's sensors could have dated the structure to be three centuries old, with such scant evidence. The pylons looked as though they had been built here recently, although that could be mostly due to the exotic metals used in their manufacture. This was getting weirder by the

9

minute, she thought as she looked across the base of one, it was easily a hundred metres wide.

Kathryn abandoned her search and headed towards the massive aperture in the centre, she reached the edge after a moderately short walk. Surprisingly there was no hand rail, the smooth floor just seemed to stop, and form this perfectly smooth borehole.

"What do you think is down there?" One of the soldiers asked as he approached her.

"I've no idea," She replied honestly as she knelt down to peer over the edge of this massive abyss. "The Copernicus sensors, could penetrate much more than a few metres."

The wind howled and blew again, the soldier took hold of her, in case the wind should blow her in.

"Thanks," she said as she leaned over to peer into nothing but a dark inky blackness, the aperture itself looked bottomless.

"Pass me your torch," Kathryn asked, still peering.

"Sure thing," the soldier unclipped a small torch from an accessory rail under the barrel of his pulse rifle and passed it to her.

She switched it on and shone it down into the darkness, the beam only went so far, and could not show the bottom, however it did show that the sides of the giant hole were filled with small but lethally sharp concentric rings that ran as far down as she could see.

Footsteps were approaching from behind, she spun around startled, lost her footing and began to fall backwards into the aperture. She screamed, flailing wildly, panic flooded through her. She felt a steely grip clamp onto her wrist, and pulled her steady again. The torch, flung from her flailing hands, disappeared into the gloom, without so much as a clatter to indicate any sort of depth.

"Godamnit Kalschacht, don't sneak up on me like that!"

"Err, sorry. Hey we found the entrance," he replied with an excited nod.

"Excellent!" Kathryn replied, equally excited. Now she was going to have a good look into this place, she followed Kalschacht to a relatively small hatch, slightly sunk into the smooth surface.

"There's no keypad, or discernable means of entry." Romaine said.

"We'll have to find some way to prise it open." Kalschacht replied.

"Are you kidding me, those hatch doors must weigh a couple of tonne apiece." Pryor argued.

"We have a set of pneumatic prise bars in the shuttle, in the emergency kit, used for forcing an exit in an emergency, can't we use those?" Kathryn said, turning to Kalschacht.

The German nodded an affirmative.

"Okay you and Pryor go get them, take a couple of guards with you in case you need help, we'll be waiting here."

"Understood," Kalschacht replied as the two scientists made their way back to the shuttle, waving to a couple of bored looking guards to accompany them on route.

"So what do you think so far?" Mira asked, as she and Kathryn stood over the dull metallic hatch.

"We are either looking at the greatest scientific discovery since the formation of the E.D.F, or the greatest threat since the Krenaran invasion, I'm not sure yet."

"It certainly is mysterious, strange metals impervious to scans, who knows what we'll find down there."

"The whole place gives me the creeps, I can't help thinking that maybe we are disturbing something that wasn't meant to be disturbed," Broadhurst cut in.

"Me too," Gomez added.

"Will you two stop. We're scientists, where's your sense of adventure, figuring out things like this is what we do." Kathryn chided them both sarcastically.

"Well, you're the project leader." The two of them nodded.

At length Kalschacht, Pryor, and the two guards returned, hefting the heavy looking prise bars, they looked like long thin cylinders with a powerful magnetic clamp at either end. In the centre was a bulky panel containing a pneumatic pump, and a laser energy pod, that powered the thing.

The four men gradually lowered the heavy pieces of equipment onto the hatch surface, with a 'thud' the magnets gripped the hatch surface.

Kalchacht and Pryor both looked at one another. With a silent nod, they each flicked a switch at precisely the same time on their respective pryzors, as they were called. This activated the attached laser pod, which in turn powered the pneumatics that slowly, but with tremendous force pushed the telescopic bars inside, away from one another, thereby gradually opening the hatch.

A loud scream of tortured metal greeted them, as the hatch doors, not opened for three centuries slowly parted. Allowing the assembled scientists their first glimpse of, and access to, the mysteries contained within.

The group shone their torches down what appeared to be an immensely deep shaft, there were a set of metal rungs forming a ladder, etched into the sides of this shaft, their torches however could still not illuminate the bottom.

Kathryn looked down with a sense of nervous trepidation, more to do with the fear of the unknown than of anything else. However, she knew she could not stay up here with the howling gales that threatened to blow them all down this great shaft, so she elected to make her way down into the dark gloom, one rung at a time.

The other scientists all gradually followed her, beams from torch lights cast eerie shadows as the team descended into the darkness.

"Hey Kathryn, I wonder if we'll find the facilities inhabitants when we get down there?" Gomez said into his helmet mic.

"What like some subterranean city?" Pryor cut in.

"Who knows?"

Kathryn was silent, she was trying hard to contain her breathing, although all she could hear, were her own shallow, nervous breaths. She did not like this; her nerves were increasing.

The wind from the open hatch howled above, filling the empty chamber with a strange dull whine, it resembled that of a wild animal in pain. The further they descended the fainter the whine became.

Kathryn's arms began to ache from the descent, and she looked back up the shaft, she could make out the other puffing forms of the scientists all slowly descending, as well as the soldier escorts, although she could now no longer see the hatch above them, she was enveloped in the darkness, and this added to her nerves. Jesus, she thought, this must run hundreds of feet down, it was almost like being entombed.

She swallowed her nerves for the second time, and resolved to continue down the immense shaft.

"Jeez, how far down does this thing go?" Pryor asked, as though reading her thoughts.

"No idea, but we just have to keep going until we reach the bottom."

"That's if my arms, don't fall off first," Broadhurst piped up.

"Pussy!" Kalschacht replied from further up.

Kathryn chuckled as they all continued their descent into the black abyss. After about an hour of descending Kathryn's torch glinted off of something, as she climbed down a little more, more of the surface was revealed to the torch light.

"Hey, I've got something down here!" She shouted up to the others.

A myriad of torchlights all flickered across to where her own beam was pointing.

"It looks like the roof of some kind of ancient elevator," Gomez said.

They neared the structure, and Gomez's assessment was proved to be correct, whether it still worked after all this time, was anybody's guess.

"You see, what did I tell you," Gomez said smugly.

"Okay, smartass." Kathryn replied.

They managed to inch their way around this elevator, groping in the pitch darkness as they did so. They found that the elevator was stopped at a rather large room. The stale air stank, they could all smell it, even through the filters built into their suits. Casting their torches over this gloomy looking room, they quickly found it was abandoned. There were no bodies here, everything looked pristine, as though it could have been built yesterday.

Mira looked over the walls of the room, as she cast her torch upon it, she could make out strange alien writings in places, etched with incredible precision into the walls themselves.

"I really wish we had a linguist with us, to study these symbols."

"Well, I'm no language expert, but I'll try to give it a shot," Gomez replied as he peered closer to the etchings, his forehead furrowed in thought.

"It looks a lot like Arabic writing that we see on Earth, but where Arabic uses lots of curves and dots. This is sharp, angular, very incisive."

Kalshacht also looked over the writings, "It takes one hell of an advanced laser to make etchings this fine, this precise, our best scientists don't have lasers anywhere near as sophisticated as that what made this."

"Who then, professor?" Kathryn asked.

"My guess would be the only race we know of with this kind of technology, Solarians."

"But the writing doesn't match the script Solarians typically use," Gomez offered, "at least none that I've seen."

Kathryn thought the writing looked sharp, aggressive. Just like the sharpness of the giant pylons on the surface, the warning signs were beginning to mount, still she pressed on.

They continued to explore the dark, eerily silent room, their beams came across a corridor that extended into the blackness beyond. They slowly, nervously made their way down the tall, but rather narrow corridor, Broadhurst and Kalschacht began to speculate amongst themselves.

"This place is getting weirder by the second," Kalschacht said.

"You're telling me."

"Let's look at the facts, the architecture we've seen so far and the writing, rules out Solarian architecture. The laser etching is so fine, it rules out Krenarans, plus we don't have any evidence they use lasers in anything anyway, so who the heck built this place?"

"That's just one more piece of this puzzle, perhaps it is an entirely new species, one we've never encountered before."

"That's the only conclusion I can come to right now as well."

Gomez interjected, "and look at the writing, the structure, it so sharp, so angular, almost blade-like, could this be an aggressive species?"

That is just what worries me, Kathryn thought as she overheard the other three men's conversation.

"Who knows? Who knows if they are even alive or dead? If they are alive, it seems a terrible waste to build a structure of this scale, and then just abandon it."

Kathryn continued listening into the conversation with interest, this facility, the events surroundings it were creepy, there's no doubt of that. But they were also intriguing, here was a three hundred year old mystery to be solved, and she was determined to solve it.

She checked the status panel on her suit, realising she hadn't done so for quite some time now. She had plenty of air left, the display also registered that it was an oxygen environment, albeit rather stale. Gingerly she pressed a control on the display to activate her re-breathers. Acting like tiny vacuum pumps, sucking in the surrounding oxygen as she walked, filters inside her suit screened out any harmful microbes, and purified the air, making it breathable again, it was akin to the smell of a slightly polluted city. The re-breathers came in handy from time to time, as it allowed her to switch off her air tanks, only using them when she absolutely needed them, thus extending her mission.

In theory at least, the re-breathers allowed her to work indefinitely, within a suitable nitrogen/oxygen atmosphere, in practice however, filters got clogged up, and equipment failures meant otherwise.

She also checked over the temperature on the display, it was showing 31 degrees, the temperature had gone up four degrees, since she last checked it on the surface. She thought it might go up by the occasional degree or two, but not by four, that was odd in itself.

"Let's see if we can find some sort of power source, or command facility for this place." She said into her helmet mic.

"Kathryn's right, the sooner we get the lights on, the less creepy this place will look," Broadhurst replied.

The gathering of troops and scientists, began to venture down this long dark corridor, the torchlight cast shadows off the exposed supports that ran down its length in even sections, even these looked sharp. Like metallic fins, ready to slice open the unwary, they ran down the entire corridors length.

Their torchlight illuminated what appeared to be a doorway, there was more of the alien writing around it, the door itself, however, did not open. Instead two of the burly Sicarian guards stepped forward, and with an almighty heave, managed to open the door just slightly. The door itself, was again unlike anything the E.D.F had known, it opened diagonally. After another great heave, it was opened sufficiently for people to step through.

What they saw, horrified and intrigued them in equal measure, casting their torches around the long, wide room, there were dozens of cylindrical tanks all arrayed in rows, filled with clear liquid, inside these tanks were the rotting corpses of long dead aliens, the shadows cast across their grisly forms, almost made it look like they still moved. Several times Kathryn found herself involuntarily flinching as she looked over the grisly menagerie. There was a spider-like alien in one, in another a millipede looking creature, six feet long, with hundreds of hook shaped legs and possessing of five yellow, unblinking eyes. Kathryn shuddered as the team passed by the grotesque assortment.

They came to a final pair of tanks, the team immediately recognised them, they contained the half-decayed bodies of Solarians.

16

"Why are Solarians here?" Kathryn whispered nervously into her helmet mic.

"I'm not sure, they could have been captured and brought here." Kalschacht replied.

"Not an end I would like," Pryor said solemnly as he looked up at the half-rotted carcasses.

"The Krenaran's took prisoners all the time, it's not unreasonable to suggest that other races do so as well." Gomez pointed out.

Kathryn circled the containers, looking closer, "Look at the scarring on the bodies, the open wounds, the lacerations, this was done while they were alive, like they were tortured. Except the cuts are so clean, so fine, A great deal of care was taken to cause maximum pain to the victims.

"Some of them have had organs removed," Mira said as the studied the spider-like alien, her torch revealed a perfectly cut hole in its back.

"This place is beginning to creep me out," Broadhurst said, "if you guys need me, I'll be outside." The sight of the half-rotted bodies had made him sick to his stomach. As he turned to leave, something flapped at his face, panic shot through him, he screamed out in terror. "Get it off me! Get it off me!"

The guards hearing the commotion whirled, and immediately readied their weapons. The panic spread through the other nearby members of the science team too, they spun around, to see Broadhurst fighting with a dead alien arm.

The team all looked up to see what the arm was connected to, their flashlights revealed the bodies of more dead aliens. Their rotten stomachs and chests sliced neatly open, entrails and viscera hung in grisly clumps, unseeing eyes stared down blankly at them. Yet more horrific body parts adorned work benches, where experiments must have been conducted upon them, although now these body parts were little more than withered husks, long since dried out, just like the bodies suspended above them.

The air stank, the reek of death and decay was everywhere, aged blood had gathered in dried up pools that gave off a sickening crunch when one of the scientists accidentally stepped upon it.

The scientists, terrified and disgusted at the horrific display, left the room in a hurry, and regrouped in the corridor outside. The Sicarian guards, used to seeing maimed bodies on horrendous battlefields during the Krenaran war, casually regrouped with the panting, nervous, sweating scientists.

"That was not a laboratory, that was a slaughterhouse," Kathryn said, trying to get her breath back in an effort to calm herself. Her heart pounded in her chest, she could hear the other's breathing through their helmet mics, all trying to take deep breaths to calm their shattered nerves.

"The sooner we get these lights on the better," Kalschacht said between breaths.

The team continued onward, past two other doors, which also contained grisly mockeries of Laboratories, what appeared to be a toilet facility, and a storeroom, before hitting a dead end.

Inside the storeroom, however they had discovered some intriguing clues as to what might have built this structure in the first place. They found a rack of black bodysuits, all of which were a similar size to a man, yet much taller. Kathryn considered that the wearers must be around seven feet tall, which is very similar to the height of a Solarian.

They also found a myriad of different bladed weapons, curved blades, serrated blades, blades sharpened so fine, that their edges were microscopic. The evidence was mounting, Kathryn thought. Whoever these people were, they were an incredibly aggressive race, who seemed to take great care in torturing their victims. Dare she think it; are these perhaps even more aggressive than the Krenarans?

After a walk of about an hour, they had made it back to the elevator shaft.

Captain Johnatan Akimbe was pacing the bridge of the Copernicus uneasily, as the small survey ship orbited the planet far above the science team. The sophisticated sensor suites on the ship had been tracking the landing party for almost half an hour, the conditions down there weren't ideal, winds had picked up on the planet surface, and his sensors were showing a storm surge coming in from the north east that looked pretty nasty. On top of this, they had lost contact with the landing party once they had begun to descend into that alien facility due to the effects of the metal the whole thing was constructed from. That was almost two hours ago, he had no idea if his people were alive or dead.

"Anything yet?" He asked Ensign Strandzhar, the relief geologist onboard.

"Nothing," He repeated for the umpteenth time.

Sensor images from the surface was showing that the shuttle was still intact, there was no signs of a fight, or movement down there. So Akimbe reluctantly had no choice, but to wait, and hope that someone would be sent up to give them a status update soon.

He relaxed into his old, worn leather captain's chair. Secretly he wondered why E.O.C.A had any business wanting to colonise a world as inhospitable as Auriga III, it didn't even have a nitrogen/oxygen atmosphere. Yet the powers that be, labelled it as one of their top priorities. He wondered whether they knew something he didn't about this world, the Auriga system itself was close to the south-eastern tip of Solarian territory, and with the discovery of these new structures, no doubt scientists from the E.D.F research division would be clamouring all over the place, like a flock of wild geese in the years to come. The thought amused Akimbe, and he smiled gently to himself.

Kathryn and the rest of the science team had found that the lift shaft extended much further down than where the elevator had stopped. It was a very tight squeeze, but they just barely managed to climb down past the elevator to a second floor.

It had a similar configuration as to the first, opening out into the same type of room, with similar etchings daubed across its walls, and an identical unmanned desk.

"These first rooms are all alike," Kalschacht said, stating the obvious, "I wonder if they are some kind of security checkpoint."

"Makes sense, anyone coming down that elevator would have to go through one of these security stations, before venturing further into the facility." Broadhurst replied.

At length Kathryn stopped, "we'll need someone to go up to the surface, to give the Copernicus a status update, let them know we're okay."

"I'll do it," Broadhurst said.

"It will be a lot faster if I do it," one of the guards suggested, he bore corporal's stripes on his arms, it was Corporal Jankov, a rather young, stout man who was Sergeant Rachthausen's number two. Jankov had the rare honour of being born and bred on Sicarius, where the sixty ninth were based.

With the outer colonies only being settled over the past thirty five years, many could still remember the day they left Earth, searching for a new home that wasn't as crowded or polluted as Earth had become.

Jankov shouldered his weapon, and began the long climb up to the surface, while Kathryn and the rest of the team continued to explore this second floor.

Although laid out in a similar manner as to the floor above it, the rooms where different, there was a huge, wide hall on this floor, all sectioned off into tiny cubicles. Inside each cubicle was a bed and a locker, at least these guys slept similar to what humans did, Kathryn thought with a wry smile.

"Well, if we ever do get stuck down here, at least there is somewhere we can crash," Gomez said with a slight chuckle.

Kathryn checked over her wrist display again, and found the temperature had risen again, by another two degrees, it was now showing thirty three degrees, this caused her a little alarm. This was strange, the temperature had now risen by six degrees from the surface.

"Anyone noticed how the temperature keeps rising?" she asked, betraying a slight hint of concern.

The other scientists had not really noticed, they were all too engrossed in the riddle of this facility to check their own status displays, however upon Kathryn's prompting they all checked them immediately.

"To tell the truth, it is getting a little warm down here, we must be a couple of hundred feet down by now," Pryor replied.

Unbeknownst to the scientists, they had descended over four hundred feet into the planets crust, as they continued down the dark, slightly humid corridor, they came upon a large communal toilet block, and a large dining area big enough to seat two or three hundred people, all of which was deserted.

This floor must house those scientists that worked in the floor above, Kathryn figured. They continued exploring until they came to the familiar dead-end.

With a dejected sigh at not finding the all-important control facility, the team headed back, once again, to the elevator shaft.

Corporal Jankov had reached the surface, his arms ached and burned from the long climb, the winds had increased significantly since the descent, he scrabbled his way out of the elevator hatch, the howling gale lashed at him, and it was an effort for him to keep his feet in the onslaught. The roiling methane clouds overhead blocked out the moonlight, casting everything into almost pitch-blackness, flashes and rumbles lit up the darkness as forked lightning arced across the sky in terrific bursts of blindingly bright light.

Rather than be caught out in the storm, he staggered his way to the silhouette of the shuttle, lit up by the lightning flashes overhead, once inside he used its own subspace transceiver to contact the Copernicus in orbit.

"We've got a message, sir. It's from the surface, it's pretty garbled though, the storm on the surface is interfering with our sensors, I'll see if I can clear it up," Strandzhar announced.

"Shunt main power to the sensors, give it everything you've got, ensign."

"Yes, sir." Strandzhar worked the controls for several seconds, as he diverted power to the giant sensor boom.

"Much better, putting it onscreen now," Strandzhar said with a hint of relief to his voice.

Corporal Jankov's slightly flushed face appeared on the screen, "Jankov to Copernicus are you receiving, over."

"Copernicus here, we are receiving you, we've had some difficulty due to the storm." Akimbe replied.

The corporal looked visibly relieved that his arduous journey was not after all, for nought.

"Are you okay?" Akimbe asked, slightly concerned for the corporal.

"Yes captain, the storm has increased in its intensity, the winds are approaching gale force now, I have taken shelter in the shuttle until the storm abates."

"I can see that, what about the science team?"

"They are okay, and continuing to explore the interior of the facility, whatever the structure is made of renders communication all but impossible."

"I know, it's the same reason why our sensors cannot penetrate it, how are the guards?"

"They are all fine captain, the facility runs for hundreds of meters underground. The science team are trying to locate a control room of some kind, so they can get power back online."

"Understood," Akimbe nodded.

"With your permission captain, I would like to ride out the storm here, before re-joining the landing party."

Akimbe chuckled, "of course corporal, Copernicus out."

The message ended and Akimbe was at last able to rest back in his seat, his fingers pyramided in thought. If the facility does extend that far underground, then this thing could be much bigger than we originally thought. The question still remained however, why build an enormous underground facility on this scale, and then just abandon it, without a fight. It made no sense, hopefully the landing party could uncover the mystery surrounding this thing.

Kathryn and the rest of the science team climbed down onto a third floor, by now they were beginning to tire, and frustration was beginning to set in, they had been down here for hours.

"How many floors does this place have?" Broadhurst asked.

"The shaft ends just below this floor, so I guess this must be the last one," Kalschacht replied matter of factly.

"Lets all just keep calm, and find this goddamned control room," Kathryn cut in, their earlier assumptions have proved to be correct, as was the case in all of the others, this floor began with a security room also.

"It does make you wonder though," Gomez said, "with all the security around this place, what were they protecting? What was this place really built for?"

"Somehow I don't think it is bodies in the attic," Pryor said remembering the grisly science labs.

"Anyway, that's what we're here to find out," Mira cut in, in answer to Gomez's question. Mira was normally the quietest of the whole team, typically keeping herself to herself, and only rarely mixing or joining in conversations. Though her work was first rate, which was why Kathryn had chosen her in the first place.

Their spirits arose as they explored this third floor, passing what appeared to be a rather spacious, yet spartan office, another store room, a huge briefing hall with enough seating inside to easily accommodate one hundred people. However it was the next two rooms that proved to be the most interesting, these piqued the scientists curiosity immensely.

They were like nothing they had seen before, walls were lined with sophisticated looking consoles, work surfaces lined with yet more controls. These were definitely control centres for something, but for what?" Kathryn thought, the first of the two rooms was completely shut down, no monitor or terminal was functioning. So the team checked over the second room, again they found all the controls and monitors had been shut down.

How the hell where they supposed to get this place powered up again, the frustration at coming so close, and then not finding a way to activate this command centre was palpable. Kathryn could hear the curses and mutterings through tiny little speakers inside her helmet.

"Wait!" Of all people it was Mira, who called out. "I think I've found something."

"What?" everyone else asked in unison as they hurried over to her position.

She was stood at a small console taking up a corner of the slightly rectangular room, there were a myriad of buttons, small displays and dials, all of which were defunct. That was, all except for a single button, which flashed irregularly, as though clinging on to some last vestiges of power remaining.

"It could be an activation switch," Kalschacht said enthusiastically.

"Or it could be some sort of self-destruct," Pryor replied, "there's no way to know for sure."

"Well we've come this far, it would be a waste to go back without at least finding out what this place is built for, and all because we are scared to push a button," Broadhurst said, as he reached down, and pressed the gently flashing control.

3. The Beacon alights.

As Matthew Broadhurst pressed that tiny flickering control a deep low hum began to reverberate throughout the installation, everyone heard it. A low-pitched thrumming noise, that felt like it was pounding the insides of their skulls, almost as if an ancient and powerful forgotten relic was coming to life once again.

Kathryn began to get very worried, "What have you done!" she shouted over the increasing din. The deep thrumming steadily grew in its intensity, roof lights began to gradually flicker as they awoken from their three hundred year slumber. Console lights slowly blinked and came to life, the awakening of this ancient facility had begun.

"Oh god!" she shouted nervously into her helmet mic, as she saw lights begin to dance across slowly activating consoles, the roof lights flickers more fervently as power grew. Suddenly Kathryn was rather scared of what they had awakened.

The deep thrumming noise now took on a kind of rhythmic, pulsating sound, as though something truly massive was beginning to rotate in the heart of the heart of the facility, this was made all the more clear as they could feel a gentle vibration in the ground all around them.

Broadhurst had definitely awakened something, something so unimaginably powerful, they could neither comprehend nor control.

Kalschacht desperately searched the displays, muttering Germanic curses, as he looked for some way to shut the infernal thing down again, everything was written in an alien language that none of them could understand. Wall mounted displays began showing data streams no one could decipher.

Ensign Strandzhar, sitting at the sensory officers station on the Copernicus orbiting far above, studied his screen, oblivious to the usual noise of people coming to and fro, and working at consoles. Suddenly he almost jumped out of his seat, "Holy moly! Err....captain, I think you might want to take a look at this."

Akimbe turned in his seat, towards the startled young ensign, "What is it?"

"Something's happening on the surface, sir. I don't know what, by my sensors just went crazy."

The captain made his way over to look at Strandzhars findings, to judge for himself. "Hmmm…It looks like it is coming from the alien structure, a massive energy surge, and its already off the scale and it seems to be increasing even further, Jesus Christ!"

Akimbe tried to make some sense of what he was reading, "What in god's name can generate that kind of power? any change we can find out what type of energy source it is?"

"negative, sir. Our sensors still can't penetrate the structure."

Akimbe breated himself for his oversight, he already knew this, then wide eyed with shock asked, "the science team?"

"There's no way to tell."

Akimbe had only one option open to him as he raced back to his command seat, "full alert status, break orbit." He had to assume the science team was dead, nothing could withstand an energy surge of that magnitude, even a ship.

The bridge of the Copernicus took on a darkened tone, a ruddy glow played across the various consoles and surfaces as the ship went on red alert, panicked officers hurried to their positions all over the ship.

Just as the Copernicus was powering up its mighty engines, to break orbit, a colossal incandescent orange beam of raw energy, shot out from the enormous aperture in the centre of the structure. Blindingly bright, like a ray of pure fire. The strength of the beam instantly atomised the methane clouds in its path, and raced through the planets atmosphere with all the fury of a rail-cannon shell. Within milliseconds, it had shot through the upper atmosphere and straight past the Copernicus, coating the ship in an intensely bright orange glow as it careered past it and hurtled out into deep space, before shutting down again.

It had missed vaporising the tiny Copernicus by a matter of feet.

"What in the name of god was that!" Akimbe shouted over the warning sirens, and wailing of the red alert klaxon

"A beam of pure energy captain, of what type, I have no idea," Strandzhar replied.

"Is the alien structure still intact?"

"From what I can tell, yes sir. It seems as though the entire facility was designed to emit a beam of that magnitude."

"A weapon?"

"If it is, it would be a clumsy one. It could only fire in a single direction, and only then at a stationary target."

"True, but if that beam did hit, nothing would be able to withstand a direct hit from that kind of power."

On the surface, Kathryn and the rest of the panicked scientists were desperately trying to find some way to shut down the facility, to prevent a repeat of what had just happened. So far they could find nothing they could understand.

The loud thrumming had diminished into a low barely audible groan, the station was definitely awake now, it had awoken with an almighty scream too.

"Guy's, come take a look at this," She heard Gomez say from across the room, she and Kalschacht came over to join him.

"That is it?"

Gomez pointed towards a display, now fully lit, it was showing power readouts throughout the base, it also showed a three dimensional cross section of the entire facility.

"My god," Kalschacht exclaimed in wonder, "the place is like a huge underground city, we haven't even explored half of it." He peered in closer, studying the three dimensional map in more detail, "If I'm looking at this right, the whole facility is built over a massive geo-thermal vent. The thrumming noise is a giant rotating collider, collecting the energy and increasing it, thereby turning the immense heat and pressure underneath into massive amounts of raw energy."

He stepped back a moment, stoking his chin in contemplation, "This whole facility is nothing more than a super advanced, geo-thermal power station. Kathryn have you any idea of the amount of power a facility of this size can produce?"

Kathryn nodded blankly, "rather a lot, I guess."

"Rather a lot is the under-statement of the decade, this facility can generate virtually unlimited power. If we can find a way to replicate this technology, we would have virtually solved E.O.C.A's power needs overnight."

He turned back to the display, "It must have some kind of collector, somewhere, a means of storing the energy it produces."

The physicist touched the display in an effort to find a control to zoom out of the facility, he quickly found that he could manipulate the representation by touch. Gradually managing to pan out, he could not see anything, he panned out further and further until he had zoomed out all the way to the upper atmosphere of the planet itself.

There it was, in orbit. What appeared to be a large collector, faintly resembling a mushroom, its under surface was wide, in order to collect as much energy as possible from the beam that shot toward it. It was full of small energy cells, all of which must transfer the accumulated energy to a storage facility in the centre of the mechanised 'mushroom'.

"This is showing that there is a collector," Kathryn said, stating the obvious, "But our scans did not detect anything in the atmosphere when we entered orbit."

"It's showing there *was* a collector," Gomez corrected for her, "Don't forget, the data is three hundred years old."

"And no doubt in that time, the orbit of the collector would have decayed and burnt up in the atmosphere long ago." Kalschacht replied

"But the facility still believes it is there, so is transferring its energy to it, as it would normally," Broadhurst said.

"So what would happen to the beam of energy, now that the collector was burnt up?" Kathryn asked, fearing the answer to her question.

"It would simply continue on its journey through space," Kalschacht answered.

"Possibly hitting the Copernicus in the process?" It was the answer that Kathryn had most feared; the realisation of the enormity of what had just happened hit all of them. "We need to get a message to the ship, see if they are okay up there."

Kalschacht warned, "If a beam of that power has hit the Copernicus, the entire ship would be vaporised in a split second, nothing could withstand it."

The entire team exited the small control room and strode back out onto the adjoining corridor, hurrying towards the elevator, it was easier going now as the lights were fully on, and they could all see in front of them, without having to resort to the flashlights. Even though, all the ceiling lights gave off was this soft, eerie, almost twilight like glow.

"Perhaps the inhabitants are sensitive to light," Gomez offered as though reading Kathryn's thoughts.

"Could be," she replied breathily as she hurried.

They got to the end of the floor, and strangely enough the elevator appeared right in front of them, fully operational now. Inside their were several strange buttons within a panel near to the door. It consisted of a button for each floor, written in a form of roman numerals, although sharper as though each number was a weapon, like a dagger. There was a separate symbol, and this was completely alien, none of them understood it.

Using a process of elimination, they found that this symbol represented the surface, and so they pressed it.

The small elevator whipped them up to the surface at a speed of several hundred miles per hour, yet the occupants felt nothing, just the gentle sensation of the device picking up speed as it left off, together with a gentle deceleration as they closed with the main hatch itself.

They had to climb the few remaining steps to the hatch, and once back out to the howling winds of the surface, it was a struggle to stay on their feet.

Kathryn gingerly touched her wrist comm. as a powerful gust of wind buffeted her. "Jacobs to Copernicus, are you receiving?"

There was no answer.

"We'll need to get to the shuttle and perform a scan to see if she is still in orbit!" Pryor suggested, shouting over the noise of the intense howling winds.

"Okay let's go!"

It was only a short walk to where the shuttle was landed, but it felt like a trek battling against the prevailing winds. Strange we haven't heard back from that corporal yet, Kathryn thought to herself.

They made it to the landing site, she flipped open a small cover on the shuttles fuselage and pressed a control secreted within, slowly a side hatch opened, Kathryn gasped at what she saw, "my God!"

The reason they hadn't heard back from Corporal Jankov was due to the fact that he was unconscious on the floor of the craft. His entire face was horrifically burned, his nose none existent, just a mound of seared flesh, his lips nothing more than a cracked and scorched parody of a mouth. Worst of all his eyes had been completely burned out of their sockets, miraculously though, he was still breathing through that charred mouth of his.

Kathryn immediately rushed into action, tiptoed past the corporals prone body and opened one of the overhead storage lockers onboard, picking out a large med kit.

Being a fully trained triage nurse, meant Kathryn had experienced all manner of traumatic scenes like this throughout the Krenaran war, silently she cursed that she had to experience one more.

While Kathryn tended to the greviously wounded Jankov, she asked Kalschacht if he could get a message to the Copernicus, a far higher sense of urgency to her voice now, they had wounded, it was now an emergency.

30

Sergeant Rachthausen quietly helped her with his fallen number two. She noticed that Rachthausen was immense. A big, broad, muscular, burly sergeant, although his blue eyes hinted at a gentleness, that his quiet nature confirmed, it was slightly odd to find these traits in an E.D.F trooper, normally they were aggressive, go out there and get the job done types. Rachthausen was thoughtful, calm and serene however.

She thought that if the sergeant was a little more aggressive and forthright, he would make an excellent commando. Though they only other commando she had met personally was Nikolai Vargev, and the Russian colonel was the sergeants match in both size and strength, and much more aggressive.

Kathryn bandaged the corporals face with 'synth-flesh' bandages, and tied a strip of cloth over the man's ruined eye sockets, other than giving Jankov morphine injections, there wasn't a lot more she could do for him until she got him back to the ship.

"Shuttle alpha-zero-four to Copernicus, are you receiving, over?"

There was a tense pause, and Kalschacht thought for an instant that the Copernicus had indeed been hit.

"Copernicus to shuttle, are you alright down there, that was one hell of an energy surge."

"We're fine captain, but we have wounded down here, request permission to return to the ship."

"Granted, but you'll have to hold out a little while, until we re-enter orbit."

"Understood Copernicus, just don't take up an orbit that puts you anywhere near the structure."

He communication was suddenly broken. "Copernicus…..Copernicus, are you receiving? Damn I've lost contact with them."

"Keep trying," Kathryn said as she continued to try to help the wounded Jankov.

"Shuttle to Copernicus, do you read, over?" Kalschacht tried again, "Shuttle alpha-zero-four to Copernicus, are you receiving." He waited for a response, then with a hint of frustration said, "all I'm getting is static."

"what the heck is going on up there?" Kathryn asked, her own frustration was beginning to show, she is the mission commander, and this whole thing is going to hell and a handbasket.

Unbeknownst to those on the planet, another craft had detected that gigantic energy release. It bore a striking resemblance to a Solarian cruiser, with its crescent shaped hull, however instead of the gleaming silver of the Solarian ships, this was dark, almost completely black except for the faintest of light given off by its portholes. It had a raised command structure, like its Solarian counterpart, though not beak-like, this was swept forward, sharp and angular like a snake darting forward to strike at its prey. Along the port and starboard sides of its gently curved hull, were a series of blade like fins.

Right now, just like a snake, it was stalking the Copernicus, its crew had identified the energy signature from the surge as being one of their own.

One of the aliens onboard, turned toward another sat atop a dark, raised, almost throne like command chair. "ship is rigged for silent approach, one quarter sub-light speed, their communications are still being jammed."

"Good; very good." Drax replied to his subordinate, "close to within weapons range, then load dark matter torpedoes in tubes one and two, fire on my command."

The Copernicus, still on full alert after that near miss from the energy surge was on-course to re-enter orbit with the planet, it had not detected the dark predator sneaking up behind it.

"See if you can isolate the source of the interference," Akimbe said to Strandzhar, the captain was delighted his science team was still alive. After a surge of that magnitude, he had feared the worst. However, he was also frustrated that his communication link to the shuttle had been cut off.

Strandzhar worked the controls furiously, "It seems the source of the interference is coming from behind us, captain."

Akimbe stood instantly, wide eyed with horror, "What!"

Ian J Smethurst

That alien ship continued to close, "Steady..........steady." Drax whispered as he stared at the image of the Copernicus getting slowly nearer.

"We are within firing range, we have target lock."

Drax silently allowed a couple more seconds to pass by, just to be absolutely certain.

"Fire!" He shouted; fist clenched.

Twin torpedoes shot forth from launchers secreted each side of its angular command hull, and raced toward their target.

The tiny Copernicus had no time to react, as the two warheads slammed home with horrifying force, one tore its primary sub-light engines to pieces in a violent explosion. Flames and shattered debris were flung out into space. The second smashed headlong into the starboard side of the vessel, blasting a gigantic fiery hole in the starboard side of the ship.

Onboard the stricken Copernicus, it was carnage, bodies lay bloodied and burned everywhere. Smoke hung like a pall in the air, choking those that still lived. Flames licked out from half a dozen smashed consoles on the bridge. Delicate wiring hung limp, with only the occasional spark and crackle to give any clue that power still ran through those severed conduits.

Akimbe struggled to his feet, a nasty slash to his forehead that bled profusely down the right side of his face. "Status!" He half-shouted half-choked, under the intense heat and acrid smoke that filled his command centre.

A young navigation officer, one of the few men left alive on the bridge managed to make it to an intact computer terminal. "Main engines are destroyed, we have a breach from decks four through eight, and fire is spreading through decks five and six!"

"Get to the escape pods, everyone abandon ship!" Akimbe ordered in desperation, as he rushed to the only functioning sensory console left intact on his bridge. He had one last duty to perform, and only seconds to do it in. He quickly performed a computer core dump into a distress beacon, and punched the launch key.

E.D.F Chronicles – Eye of the Dracos

The beacon containing the Copernicus's computer core records and sensory data shot out from beneath the vessel, and out into the inky blackness of deep space.

Akimbe switched the crackling, barely functioning viewer to rear view in order to glimpse his assailant. He could only barely make out its shape against the blackness of space, its dark hull glinted as the light from the Aurigan sun reflected from off its surfaces. The monstrosity blotted out the very stars themselves, poised like a great black bat, ready to snuff him out of existence at any moment.

Akimbe sighed, safe in the knowledge that the distress beacon was away, and that the E.D.F would eventually learn of what had happened here.

That was the last thing Captain Johnatan Akimbe of the Copernicus ever saw.

"Ready laser lances, fire at will, finish that thing!" Drax called out, not hiding the distain in his voice for such an unworthy foe.

The twin wingtip mounted laser lances at either end of the ships main hull, flashed out and instantly blasted the Copernicus apart in a bright fireball. Torn pieces of the ships shattered hull where thrown out in all directions due to the force of the now dissipating explosion. Some of the fragments hurtled through the atmosphere of the planet below, looking like a faint meteor shower blazing across the sky.

Some of those now stranded on the surface spotted the myriad streaks shooting past overhead, following their trails with awe, unaware that they were really witnessing the deaths of their friends and co-workers.

"Contact our other ships nearby; let them know we have found one of the long lost halo worlds." Drax said with a wide grin.

4. The darkness descends.

"Kaeleth, have two units of my elite Kallan warriors form up in the main hangar bay. I want two assault landers ready to launch immediately, you are in command of the ship until I return; see that she remains in one piece." Drax added, with a malevolent grin.

"But, sir," Kaeleth made to protest. A simple wave of the hand had convinced him that his commander had made up his mind, it was useless to try to change it.

With a final nod, Drax left his dark, brooding, ominous command centre and headed straight for the hangar bay. This will be an interesting hunt, he thought to himself, the thought amused him.

Drax gave off the air of a consummate and powerful commander, a brutal disciplinarian, he was not above executing even his own people if they dared challenge him. In fact he had done so once, several years ago, a young second officer began to conjure up thoughts above his station. As commander of his ship, Drax could not tolerate that, and so tore open the throat of the upstart on his own bridge, before tossing the body out of the nearest access hatch. It took quite some time to clean the gore afterwards, if he recalled.

Drax and his people all shared the same mottled white and grey skin tone, an incredibly pale complexion. They looked remarkably like a shortened version of a Solarian, in that they were tall, and yet dainty, slim and awkward looking.

Although Drax was indeed not as tall as a typical Solarian being normally seven feet high, he was not short either, standing over six feet in height himself. He had large almond shaped eyes similar to the Solarians, and predominantly black irises. Solarian eyes tended to give away a hint of calm serenity, his eyes were tinged with a kind of dark malevolence, a wickedness that despite his best efforts, he could not hide.

He made his way over to a small yet wide hangar bay, lined with two rows of assault landers, facing each other, two to a row, and with a wide aisle in the centre. The dark craft where tiny in comparison to his ship, but looked immense and powerful here. His ship was equipped with four of these in total, together with half a dozen attack shuttles, which he used from time to time to hunt down weaker prey. Seeing as he didn't really know who this new enemy were, it was more prudent to use the assault landers.

Twenty of his finest Kallan warriors were stood in two perfectly formed rows ten men to a lander. They held their weapons silently aloft, their barrels pointing to the roof in the traditional Kallan salute as he neared. They were already wearing their black environment suites, and dark helmets, that only ever reflected the bright scarlet of their sights. The Kallan were his races finest fighting men, feared across the galaxy for their ability to go unseen, and strike when least expected, they were famed for their brutality, savagery, and above all else for their love of torturing their prey.

Drax addressed the assembled men in his native tongue, ""Men, tonight will be a glorious hunt, against a new and unknown prey. We have never encountered this race before, and that makes them dangerous. Below us lies Auriga III, until recently a forgotten world, however on this world lies the remains of one of our peoples greatest achievements, the eye of the Dracos, an underground facility with the capability of producing almost unlimited power."

He paced up and down his men; each ones stare fixed upon him in rapt attention. "A facility built when our people were at the peak of their power, and we, the chosen few shall re-claim it and restore the Dracos to their rightful power once again!"

A loud roar came back at him, as the Kallan voiced their approval and thrust their weapons forward in salute.

"Tonight the screams of the dying, will fill our ears once again!"

There was another wild roar, before the men fell out, and strode up the inclined ramps on the underside of the landers. They had no need to strap themselves in for the flight to the surface, all Dracos environment suits were moderately magnetic, allowing them to cling to walls and ceilings in order to launch deadly surprise attacks. Thus in the lander, they were sat perfectly still, clamped to the metallic seating and walls as the two craft powered up their primary Ion engines, coating the interior of the hangar bay in a bright green light. The hangar bay doors opened revealing a stunning vista of the starlit backdrop of deep space. The two craft gently rose from the floor of the hangar bay, their delicate landing gear slowly retracted inside their elongated bullet shaped fuselage. The ailerons on their angular, sickle like wings pitched the craft anti-clockwise so that they now faced the hangar bay doors themselves. With a deep 'thoom' the Ion engine of the craft increased power, and they gently accelerated out of the hangar bay.

The two craft were not large, although they did share some features with old Earth military jet aircraft. Most notably the bullet shaped fuselage, and small winglets below the fully enclosed cockpit, that and the two huge tail fins which jutted out from the twin bulbous secondary engine pods sat atop the main fuselage. There the similarity ended, as halfway along the fuselage, it widened noticeably, forming a type of bulge on its underside. This was where the Kallan were gathered, ready to burst forward from the boarding ramp at the front, and attack their prey.

The crafts main Ion engine was lit an intensely bright emerald green as it manoeuvred toward the planet, the engine itself was nestled in-between the two giant engine pods. The most curious thing about these craft were their strange, forward swept sickle shaped wings, giving it the appearance of some kind of giant mechanised bat, made all the more appropriate by its dull black coating, designed to make it all but invisible during night attacks, the Dracos's favourite form of attack. At each wingtip, a vicious laser lance was mounted, often used by the pilot to clear a bloody path through the enemy, before offloading the troops contained within.

The two small craft dove into the beige coloured atmosphere of Auriga III.

Kathryn looked up at Kalschacht with a hint of sadness on her normally gentle features, "We have to assume the Copernicus has been destroyed. Night is closing in, our best shot is back inside the base."

They carried the prone form of corporal Jankov in a portable stretcher with them.

It was the second night, Kathyn had barely slept all day, the mission should have been wrapped up hours ago, however despite how tired she was, she knew she had to keep going for the sake of the others.

Kalschacht turned to the other scientists, "Quickly, grab whatever we can use from the shuttle, we may only have a matter of a few minutes, if the Copernicus has been destroyed, they may know we are here also."

The assembled group all began looting the shuttle, taking food supplies, water purification kits, anything of any use.

Kalschacht worked the communications console one last time, so that it would emit a continuous distress beacon, before the entire science team exited the shuttle and made their way as quickly as they may, toward the main hatch of the facility, carrying the wounded Jankov with them.

As they neared the hatch, just on the horizon, they could just about see the faint forms of two black shapes heading towards them.

Rachthausen looked back to see them also, "everyone inside now!"

They barely made it inside, as the two craft swooped down over their position, intensely bright flashes of violet laser energy shot forth from the Dracos craft's twin wingtip mounted laser lances and tore the shuttle apart in a gigantic explosion, debris rained down around the immediate area.

Rachthausen was the last to make it inside, after making sure everyone else was safely within the structure. As he himself dived closed the hatch all he saw as the doors closed was the fiery remains of the shuttle, billowing out into the night sky, he cursed to himself silently.

The assault landers both gently touched down nearby the flaming wreckage of the shuttle, the boarding ramp quickly opened, its end slamming into the ground as the Kallan poured out of the craft, all donning their advanced black environment suits, even Drax had donned his in the flight. Only rarely did he get the chance to wear one, yet when he did, he savoured every moment.

The Dracos environment suits were a marvel of his people technology, constructed of a lightweight, yet immensely strong carbon fibre weave, it was wearable and also extremely tough. In addition to the advanced construction of the suit, it could be configured with additional accessories for each individual mission, Drax had opted for a set of razor sharp blades jutting outwards from his left lower arm, so that he could make slashing attacks yb simply swinging his arm. On his right wrist he had concealed a weapon favoured by many of the Dracos. A devastating weapon, known only as 'the silencer', it consisted of a tiny monofilament line attached to a spool that shot the line out at several thousand revolutions per minute through a small barrel. At the end of this line was a viciously sharp metal spike, barely larger than his thumb, within this spike, there were four tiny barbs that flicked open once it passed through its target. Then all the user had to do was press a small switch to reel the line back in, tearing the barbs straight through the victim causing immense pain, and in many cases death, hence its macabre moniker, it was one of Drax's favourite weapons.

In-case things got a little ugly, which he doubted they would, he carried a typical dracos eviscerator pistol as a sidearm.

His men mainly carried eviscerator rifles, some wore wrist blades, others had equipped silencers, like his. For now they kept their main weapons attached to their suits via magnetic strips of the weapons casing, allowing it to be stored on the body. Many had them attached vertically across their backs for easy retrieval.

Drax switched his helmet to infra-red nightvision mode, so he could see better in the dark, not that he needed to. Most Dracos had adapted to living in dark conditions over the last three hundred years, hence why their skin had become so pale and grey.

He cycled it again to thermal imagining mode, and did a quick sweep around the area, the flames of the shuttle can up as brilliant whites and yellows on his display, however there was no sign of any form of body heat for a quarter of a mile in any direction, which was as far as the range of the onboard thermal imaging processor.

"Let the hint begin," He said into the comm. link.

Rachthausen and the other guards used the pryzors to help seal the top hatch shut, and also make it more difficult for whoever those aliens were to access the facility, he could feel the gentle thrumming of the facility begin to increase, it was about to release another gigantic blast of energy, he hoped it would immolate those aliens on the surface as well.

"It won't hold them for long, we need to get as far away from here as possible."

"I agree, let's all form up on the third floor," Kathryn said to the group.

They all hurried inside the elevator, pressed the button for the third floor, and the contraption shot them to the lowest point on the facility. The group all jogged along to the briefing hall they passed earlier, dropped their supplies, and rested the badly injured Jankov.

Everyone was panting considerably; Kathryn turned the re-breathers back on within her suit. "Hey I'm getting clean air through, it's no longer stale."

"Some sort of automated environmental system must have kicked in when the facility was activated," Kalschacht replied, gradually removing his helmet, " that's better, it was getting rather stuffy inside."

Everyone else followed suit, all laying their helmets on the ground, Kathryn's long dark hair flowed out over her shoulders, "okay, so now what do we do?"

Rachthausen turned to face her, "we hold out for as long as we can, Hobbs, how much food and water do we have?"

Private Hobbs a rather short, stocky soldier came forward, "we have enough food to last four days. We might have enough water, and we managed to gather a couple of filtration kits from the shuttle also."

"What about weapons?"

"We have the weapons we carry, and we also managed to gather a few pistols from the shuttle."

"Okay," Rachthausen said pausing in thought, then turned to his troops, "everyone give your sidearm to the scientists, they'll need a weapon."

The guards unclipped their holsters, housing their pulse laser pistols and handed them over to the scientists, together with the weapons they had gathered. Each scientist now had a weapon.

"Here, take this, you'll need it," the sergeant said gently as he handed her his own sidearm.

Kathryn took the weapon, and smiled back up at him tenderly, "thanks."

"Gather around for a demonstration," he said to the arrayed scientists, who all gathered around the big, burly sergeant.

He held a pistol out in front of them, pointing to a circular indent in the underside of the barrel, about an inch ahead of the trigger. "This is the laser pod attachment port. To place a new laser pod, insert the top of the pod inside the port and twist anti-clockwise. You'll feel a click, that means it is housed properly. Each pod is good for thirty shots; we use the new high yield pods now instead of the older ones, which were only good for ten."

The sergeant pointed to a set of two buttons on the side of the weapon, just above the trigger. "The first one, is the priming button, press this once, when you click in a new laser pod, the other is the safety switch."

He then proceeded to point to a series of four rather scorched looking holes either side of the outer wall of the weapon, just below the barrel. "Do no touch these at all, they are heat dispersion holes, used to vent off excess heat from the barrel after firing."

The surrounding scientists all nodded their understanding.

"I've lost count of the number of cadets, who have had their finger ends melted by playing with these holes." He proceeded to show the assembled group the top and the underside of the weapon, "This is a laser sight, it automatically comes on whenever the weapon is ready for firing," he said point to a bulbous protrusion from just under the barrel opening of the weapon, "and this is an accessory rail, normally used for attaching a flashlight to it, any questions?"

There were none, the sergeant had given a pretty thorough demonstration of how to use the weapon, all the scientist had managed to clip in the laser pods with little difficulty, and pressed the priming button.

Thank God, for small mercies at least, Rachthausen thought as he watched the assembled scientists all ready their weapons successfully.

"Okay, we don't know how many of them there are out there, and we have no idea what they are capable of. So everyone be extra careful, myself and the guards will try to draw most of their fire, if you do have to use your weapon, try to make your shots count, once these are used up we only have five spare laser pods for the pistols."

Drax and his Kallan warriors approached the main hatch. As they looked over the hatch, they saw a small-lit panel. They keyed in the control to enter the facility, and were greeted with a loud noise and some small jerking movements. The doors wanted to open, but something on the other side was blocking them.

Locked themselves in, Drax thought. A shame really, they are only delaying the inevitable. He took a few steps back from the hatch and pressed a tiny control, secretly embedded on a unit around his right wrist.

"Drax to the Flame of Celthris."

"Kaeleth here, sir."

"I want a full layout of this facility, search the ships main database, then transmit it to my suits augmented reality uplink."

"Understood, I'll do the search now."

The communication ended, Drax could feel the ground shaking from beneath him, it wasn't violent, just a gentle rhythmic thrumming, although increasing in its intensity. The wind was blowing but not to this degree.

He eventually realised what it was, and screamed with all the urgency he could muster, "Everyone down, now!"

No sooner had the Kallan flattened to the ground, than the station released a second massive burst of energy through the atmosphere, the whole facility briefly turned a bright shade of orange, as the intensely bright stream of pure power, shot skywards and out into space once again.

"Recover!" Drax shouted out to his men.

The immense beam of energy shot passed the Flame of Celthris, briefly silhouetting the dark shape of the ship in its intense orange light, before hurtling onwards into the depths of space once again.

After several minutes of searching for Dracos structures built on Auriga III, the ships computer finally found something that matched. A layout of a giant energy installation known simply as the eye of the Dracos, Kaeleth was fascinated. Although Dracos technology had evolved over the three hundred years the base was abandoned, nothing they built today even approached the scale of the eye.

He contacted Drax, "I have the plans, transmitting now."

From inside Drax's helmet a tiny lens displayed the layout of the station over his left eye, he studied it intently, and after a few seconds of silently searching, smiled. The facility did indeed have another way in, after all.

"Follow me," Drax called out to his men.

Rachthausen turned towards Kalschacht and Gomez and asked, "when you saw the layout of the station, did you see any other means of access, an escape hatch, emergency exit or anything?"

"I'm not sure," they both replied in unison.

Rachthausen pressed them, "Think; this is important."

"I don't think so, not from what I remember." Gomez replied, his brow furrowed in thought.

"Are you absolutely sure."

Gomez nodded, his dreadlocks swaying gently as he did so.

"Okay," Rachthausen turned to address his other guards.

"Wait!" Kalschacht called out, "There is another exit."

Rachthausen froze, his worst fears had been confirmed, "shit." was all he could say.

"There is a small emergency escape corridor, it's on the far side of the facility."

Drax and his men forced their way onwards through the howling winds blowing across the surface, finally making it to the central focusing pylons of the facility, he loved the design of classic Dracos architecture, it looked so bold, so grand, like four giant claws reaching up from the ground ready to drag those down unwary enough to get caught in its clutches. Those grand old days were long lost to his people now, or so he had thought.

Once he has recaptured this base, it will re-energise his people, give them the boost they desperately need to once again become to scourge they were all those years ago. His people given the power of the old ones once again, the thought filled him with excitement and made him smile once again.

44

He peered down the gigantic aperture, which the focusing pylons ringed, and switched to his thermal view once again. He could just make out the huge spinning collider at the bottom. It still showed up white hot from the energy release earlier. No-one would know that, that collider was buried a kilometre into the planets crust, built over one of the largest geothermal vents on the entire planet.

There were many other vents on the surface, but none as big as this, it was all the vents and the geothermal activity that spewed out the methane and other gases, which created the methane clouds which swirl about this planet. Auriga III was a fascinating, yet deadly place for the unwary.

With a wave of his hand, he motioned for his men to continue towards the emergency evacuation hatch that had shown up on his A.R. uplink. It was tough going, even for the Kallan, the winds were making every step an effort and they could feel the biting cold through their carbon fibre environment suits, however, the thought of hunting down and hearing the screams of these interlopers, banished any negative thoughts any of them had. Once they got inside the fun could begin, and oh would they have such fun.

After about an hour of trudging through the windswept surface, they came upon a tiny hatch sunk into the ground and half covered with wild bushes and shrubs.

Drax and a few of his men began clearing back the vegetation in earnest, eager to get to those inside. They found the hatch was only big enough for one man at a time to enter, single file.

There was a small dirt encrusted panel next to the hatch, the Kallan trained their eviscerator rifles on the hatch doors, ready in case there was a guard stationed on the other side or some kind of booby trap.

Drax pressed a control on the panel, and with a faint hiss of escaping air, the hatch slid open. Gripping his pistol, the Dracos commander, cautiously ventured inside the escape tunnel.

It wasn't lit, however that posed no problem, as he switched his helmet onto infra-red mode, gradually the interior was revealed to him. It was a smooth cylindrical shaft which descended into the base at an angle of about forty degrees, it was steep, yet at the bottom of the shaft was a series of metal steps that ran down its length.

E.D.F Chronicles – Eye of the Dracos

Drax cautiously made his way down the metallic flight of steps and descended into the gloom, one by one, his men followed.

Rachthausen and Kalschacht studied the three dimensional display in the control room again, this time in closer detail. They studied each corridor, and panned around the entire facility, what they uncovered worried them immensely. They had found the escape hatch on the plan, and it led to a completely separate wing, or so they thought, as they continued to study the plan they realised that the 'dead ends' they had been coming to, were not dead ends at all.

They were enormous blast doors, designed to protect the base should the collider at its heart malfunction and explode. On the first and third floors, these were connected to giant semi-circular corridors that linked the other wing to this one.

Worst of all, they found that the control room they were standing in, was just an auxiliary. There was a far larger, main one on the other wing, which also looked suspiciously like a military wing, consisting of military store houses, mess rooms, barracks, and engineering workshops.

Great, Rachthausen thought, not only have they found an alternative way into the base, they now have the resources of a fully operational military complex with which to attack us from, this is going from bad to worse.

They did have one stroke of luck however, there was a maintenance room, probably used to make quick repairs to this side of the facility. It was also on this floor, whatever it took, they had to seal those blast doors. He hoped he could find something inside with which to either brace the doors, or even better, weld them shut.

The sergeant made his way back towards the assembled scientists and other soldiers to tell them the news.

"Here's what we are going to do," Rachthausen said as he studied their grim, worried faces. "I want two groups of three to guard the blast doors at the end of each corridor. They are not dead ends as we thought, if the enemy break through, they can very quickly overwhelm us."

Naturally his Sicarian guards were the first to volunteer, "Okay Johnson, Maxwell, Lindberg, you have the first floor. Anderson, Laveaux, Thorsson, you have this floor. Do whatever you need to do, but in no circumstances should they come through those blast doors, keep in contact at all times."

The six men saluted their sergeant, "yes, sir." Before getting their kit together, ready to take up position. Rachthausen reinforced the motto of the sixth ninth, "Fight hard, fight well!"

The men silently nodded, before heading out.

"Okay, Kalschacht, Gomez, Broadhurst, let's see if we can find something to shore up those blast doors."

The four men left the confines of the briefing hall and headed towards the maintenance store they had seen on the map, fortunately for them it was only a short walk away. The metal door slid open and quickly allowed them access; to what could only be described as a giant rabbit warren of shelves, spare parts and strange tools, all of which where alien in nature.

They searched dishevelled shelf upon dishevelled shelf, rack upon rack, until at last Broadhurst shouted over from a corner of the room, "Over here, I think I found something!"

He was holding a small handheld device, it bore a striking resemblance to an old earth plasma torch, it had a small yet sharp point at one end, and a trigger on the handle itself. They each inspected the device and found it had an intricate battery like power source in its handle, however the 'battery' had lost its charge over the centuries it had been left.

"See if you can find another power supply for that thing," Rachthausen said, the anticipation in his voice was palpable, they needed a bit of luck right now, and this just might be it.

Kalschacht was intrigued by a device affixed to one of the walls of the room, it possessed a small control panel, all in alien text. Its small lights blinked, lighting up the nearby shelving in an amber light. He had a hunch that this was some sort of charging station for the tools, he searched around for another of those 'batteries' to test, eventually coming across one, he cautiously slotted the end of it into one of the narrow groove like bays, half closing his eyes as he did so. It clicked into position, suddenly the amber light changed, into a solid green one, Dieter Kalschacht breathed a sigh of relief, within the space of a couple of minutes it had changed back to flashing amber again.

"Here, try this," he slotted the newly charged 'battery' into the handle and the device came to life, a series of buttons lit up on the side of the small device.

Broadhurst walked over to an empty patch of wall, tested it, and as he pressed the trigger a bright beam of laser energy shot out from its tip, and began to melt the metal, sending out a shower of sparks in the process.

"It's a laser welder!" He shouted elated.

"Let's get it to the blast doors, before the charge runs out," Rachthausen said.

Kathryn was sat on one of the dark chairs in the briefing room, a forlorn sense of sadness had come over her.

"Are you okay?" Mira asked.

"Not really," Kathryn replied flatly, brushing an errant strand of hair from her worn and tired face, "this was my mission, and look at the mess I've gotten us all into."

"It's not your fault," she placed a reassuring hand on her shoulder.

"Isn't it? If I hadn't requested a landing party to explore this place, we wouldn't have accidentally activated it. The Copernicus wouldn't be in a million pieces, and we wouldn't be down here fighting for our lives, and all for the cause of science."

"We'll get out of this, and when we do, you'll be credited with the most important discovery in the history of E.O.C.A."

Kathryn smiled a wanly at this, "or we'll all die, and all this will amount to is a forgotten chapter in history."

"We won't die, Rachthausen will see to that."

Rachthausen, Kathryn thought, that gentle giant of a sergeant, at first she had hardly known him. He was just another block head soldier from the troop division. However, he had a gentleness to him, a kindness that the had to admit was enticing. When he was showing her how to use her sidearm, she knew a spark had passed between them, was she attracted to the sergeant? Kathryn banished the thought as soon as it had emerged, she was a senior officer and had to set an example.

Rachthausen and the other scientists eventually made it to the blast door, Broadhurst began to weld the giant doors together with his small handheld device. He was unsure it would work given the size of the doors, but it might just buy the others some more time, so he kept at it anyway.

Drax had reached the bottom of the escape hatch and came upon a metal panel barring his way. With a forceful kick the offending panel slowly gave way, a second kick saw it collapse to the floor with a loud 'clang.' He and his men quickly filtered out, their weapons trained on anything that might surprise them.

He found the corridor was sufficiently lit, and so reverted back to normal vision. To his left lay an elevator tube, to his right the remainder of the corridor continued on into the distance.

The Dracos commander, split his men up into two groups, one would take the elevator to the floor below, while his own group would continue on through this floor. A silent nod saw the two group's part ways.

Drax's group continued on down the corridor, silently searching for any signs of traps or hidden explosives, there were none. He passed a sumptuous looking office with plush comfortable chairs and black granite desk. How his ancestors must have lived, he thought with pride. For him, it was like walking through history, he hoped his people could recreate those heady days when they were in their prime.

His men passed a giant mess area, an armoury, and a military barracks, he wondered what the Kallan must have been like three hundred years ago, how they had changed in that time.

Eventually he came upon a giant set of blast doors, he quickly reverted back to his thermal imaging mode in order to see if there was anyone waiting on the other side. To his chagrin, there wasn't.

He signalled to one of his men to open the door, the warrior keyed in a series of controls that unlocked the giant metal door. Another key press and it swung open slowly with a dull whine as heavy duty motors hummed into life, revealing a long curved tunnel illuminated by dull strip lights, positioned about a foot from the ceiling, situated in even spaces.

This was one of two main corridors to the other side of the facility, which skirted the 5 metre thick Toralinium wall of the central aperture. Toralinium was their own private wonder metal, only slightly heavier than titanium, yet stronger, and it had a special property that dissipated any known form of scan across its surface, meaning that enemy ships would know that a ship made of this substance was there, but not what it was comprised of, weapons, crew complement, power systems, shield generators, or any internal system. It acted as a kind of shroud, making it a very useful material to build ships and bases from.

Drax and his men continued on down this long curved corridor for well over half an hour, making thermal scans with their helmets as they went, still there was nothing. Then as they continued walking, the first colours of body heat began to show up, starting off as a faint, deep green in the shape of a bipedal alien like themselves. Then as they neared the colour started changing, cycling through to red, and then yellow highlights, there were three distinct shapes, roughly the same size as a typical Dracos except slightly bulkier in body, and shorter in the leg, the shapes weren't moving, it looked as if they were standing guard.

Drax ordered two of his men to cover either side of the door. He, using the magnetic qualities of his suit, crawled up along the side of the wall. A few others did likewise, more crawled up onto the ceiling. His men were eager, excited at the battle to come, at the blood they would shed.

Private Samuel Johnson, Johnathan Maxwell, and Lance Corporal Anthony Lindberg, gave their customary all clear report to sergeant Rachthausen on deck three. They were beginning to tire of this waiting around, were the enemy even going to attack? Spineless wannabes.

Then the blast doors opened of their own accord, someone had opened them, but it wasn't any of the men stood there. In the twilight gloom it looked as though the walls had come alive with shifting black forms, it took a split second to realise what they were seeing, which was all the time the Dracos needed.

Eviscerator rifles opened fire with razor sharp discs of metal, they emitted a high pitch whistling sound as they shot through the air, coated with incredibly powerful flouro-antimonic acid. These lethal projectiles whipped through the air as fast as any bullet, and sliced deep into Maxwell's legs and arm, he screamed in pain as the acid burned its way through his flesh, the Dracos were in ecstasy.

Drax himself fired his silencer, the tiny, yet deadly sharp metal spike, pierced Lindberg's neck, and jutted out the opposite side in a welter of blood, the vicious barbs contained within the bullet flicked out a split second later, embedding in the man's neck. Lindberg choked and coughed up a fountain of blood from his pierced trachea. Yet he still managed to open fire, his pulse rifle hit up the gloomy corridor and caught one of the Kallan in the chest. The shots slammed into the chest of the Dracos warrior, tearing apart the carbon fibre protection of the aliens environment suit and blasted several bloody ragged holes in the enemies body, it collapsed, convulsing on the floor of the corridor.

Lindberg staggered back also, just as Drax pressed a control to retract the barb lodged in the lance corporals throat, which the device duly did, at an incredibly fast rate. Ripping the small projectile back through the mans throat, the outstretched barbs tore the front of the man's neck open in the process, Lindberg collapsed onto the floor, suffocating on his own blood, and slowly, painfully, bleeding to death.

Samuel Johnson, the last man to survive tried to make a break for it, discs of razor sharp metal skittered off the ground all around him as he ran, he frantically pressed his wrist comm. "sergeant, they've broken thr......"

One of the Kallan crawling overhead had swung his wrist blades and decapitated the dark skinned American in one swift flowing sweep. His headless body collapsed onto the floor, the neatly severed head came rolling to a standstill a few feet away from his body.

Private Maxwell was trying to shuffle into a small store room containing scientific laboratory equipment, the slices in his leg from the lethally sharp metal discs, and the intense burning from their acidic coating was excruciating. The acid slowly burned into the flesh of his thigh, the cotton of his fatigues was slowly breaking down and searing into his leg.

One of the black suited horrors made to finish him off, and he wished he would. The warrior levelled his weapon, he stared down the horizontal slit of the barrel as he pressed it towards his face.

Another, took hold of the weapon, and thrust it aside, denying the warrior his kill. Maxwell was scrabbling around on the floor, the pain from his burning flesh was unbearable.

The alien gradually removed his helmet, revealing his pale, mottled complexion, and his dark almond shaped eyes. He regarded him with a kind of sickening amusement, as though the agony he was going through was a source of entertainment; sick bastard.

"I am Drax, I am the commander of these people, do you understand?"

Maxwell nodded a struggling yes, while trying hard not to grip his burning leg, he knew that if he did, he would simply end up burning his hand also.

"My people are called the Dracos, you are interlopers, why are you here?"

The private gasped, his mind a fog of agony, "I'm not telling you a goddamn thing." He spat in the Dracos commanders face.

Wiping the spittle from his cheek, the Dracos commander seemed to pace, as if he grew pensive. Then in a blur, he whirled around and slammed the end of the seized rifle into Maxwells sliced and badly burned thigh.

The young private screamed in absolute excruciating, intense pain, his mind reeled and he became woozy, threatening to pass out.

Drax leaned in, twisting the rifle barrel inside Maxwell's leg, blood poured from the wound. "Let me make this clear to you," he said as he twisted again, Maxwell gasped in intense agony, flailed trying to protect his injured limb, but to no avail. The other Dracos warriors laughed, and nodded appreciatively at the brutality their commander was showing.

"You will tell me who you are, and how many others are here."

The private, struggling to prevent himself lapsing into unconsciousness managed a weak, "Fuck you!"

"Unfortunate," Drax ripped the barrel from out of the private's leg, aimed it straight at Maxwell's face and fired. Blood and thick gobbets of brain matter exploded across the nearby walls and equipment.

Drax searched the bloodied body, finding a pair of dog tags. Stamped on the back were the words. Sixty-ninth Sicarian guards, E.D.F troop division, and the motto Fight hard, fight well underneath.

"Now at least we know whom we are fighting against," Drax said to his men, as he reattached his helmet.

Rachthausen sprinted towards the elevator with three of his men following rapidly behind. The contraption was still on this floor, good, he thought. If the aliens took the elevator and made it down here, they were done for. He could not let that happen.

Taking a small length of steel wire from his webbing, and some insulation tape, he attached a grenade, and, using a small pair of pliers, fastened the steel wire around the pin of the grenade, uncurling just enough wire to cover the door of the elevator. With some tape he attached one end of the wire to the elevator door, and carefully taped the grenade to the other.

When the doors opened, the pin would be pulled, and blow them all to hell in the process, that was he hoped anyway.

"This will give them something to think about," he smiled at the others, as they slowly stepped back from the elevator itself.

A light lit up, and the booby trapped contraption began its rapid ascent, quickly stopping on Drax's floor. Two of his best men awaited it, before the Dracos commander could even shout a warning, the doors opened, ripping the pin from the grenade. As the two men stood, looking at this strange alien device attached to the doors, oblivious to the danger it represented. The grenade detonated, blasting the elevator apart in a huge explosion explosion that hurled the two Kallan several feet back down the corridor. Their mangled bodies slamming heavily onto the floor, their environment suits ripped open by the razor sharp fragments that tore through the corridor. Two other Kallan suffered shrapnel injuries to their upper arms.

The corridor was quickly filling with smoke, and took on a new brighter amber glow from the flames of the wrecked elevator.

Debris rained down the elevator shaft, and slammed into the bottom, Rachthausen and his men had to dive backwards to avoid being showered with the flaming debris fragments.

Drax looked on at the carnage wrought amongst his men, and muttered a curse under pressed twisted lips, "Our enemy is a resourceful one."

In one fell swoop they had just taken out two of his best men, and prevented him from getting to the floors below, he would have to find another way.

He consulted the layout plan still being displayed by his A.R. uplink, searching the nearby rooms for any way to access the other floors, he motioned for his remaining men to do likewise.

The second squad of Kallan warriors had now approached the other set of blast doors, and was readying for their own attack, although this squad had a different strategy in mind. They hid as many men as they could around the lip of the blast door, it was a tight squeeze, yet had managed to hide six men around the semi-circular two foot wide lip. Others clung to walls and ceilings waiting for their moment to strike. Only one person stood upright on the actual corridor floor.

The three E.D.F guards posted to defend the blast doors on the third floor could hear nothing, though they remained cautious, nervous, they knew something was about to happen, it was just a matter of when. They had all heard the screams of the others over their comm. links, and certainly did not want to end up the same way.

Finally one of the Dracos bit the bullet and pressed the small keypad to open the giant blast doors, a familiar dull whine reverberated around the silent corridor as powerful motors strained to move the twenty tonne doors.

They parted, showing the faint black silhouettes of three Dracos warriors, the E.D.F troops, now much more alert to any danger, were quickest though, and they let loose the firepower of their pulse rifles. Before the alien warriors even had a chance to react Thorsson and Anderson had gunned two of their number down, their bodies fell from the ceiling, slamming into the hard floor with a resounding crunch.

The lone standing Dracos, returned fire with his own weapon, lethally sharp discs of metal whistled through the air, he was a poor shot as those he had fired missed their target. Except one that nicked Laveaux on his left shoulder, he ignored the wound.

The remaining Dracos warriors pressed their attack with a speed and grace unheard of by human standards. They charged along the walls and ceiling as though it has suddenly come along with alien bodies.

Thorsson and Anderson dived into the auxiliary control room near to the blast doors, in order to mount a better defence from there. Laveaux however, was temporarily distracted by the increasing burning sensation in his shoulder, suddenly he screamed as the acid from the disc that had nicked him began to bubble and dissolve his very flesh. The distraction was all that the Kallan needed, as two more discs tore into his chest and abdomen. He sank to his knees, blood spurted out from his wounds. Already the acid was taking its effect, burning its way into his exposed flesh.

In that brief instant however, he felt no pain, perhaps he was well beyond pain. He looked up at the black figures crawling their way along the corridor walls to either side and above him with a sense of incredulity, his mind could not comprehend what he was witnessing.

He could hear the faint shouts of his fellow guardsmen calling out to him in desperation, they were muted as though he had cotton wool in his ears. Then his head jerked sharply to the side as it was pierced by what felt like a bullet. The spike pierced straight through his neck and lodged through the other side, the wickedly sharp barbs pierced his skin. He tried to breath, but couldn't for some strange reason, he gasped and spluttered for breath, trying to look at who had done this to him. On the wall an alien warrior remained, the bright scarlet lights form the vision slits in his helmet regarded him, with what he could only describe as an evil delight. His arm was outstretched revealing the device. A tiny steel wire was attached to it, and extended out through Laveaux's neck.

Gurgling, coughing and spluttering for breath and bleeding profusely, the private nevertheless made one last vain attempt to bring his weapon to bear, to summon the strength to kill his adversary. The strength was gone, the pulse rifle clattered noisily to the ground.

The black alien, its knees and lower legs still attached to the wall made a single, silent gesture as he watched the slowly dying human. He put his finger to his lips and whispered a "shhh….." then retracted the silencer. The spike ripped back through Laveaux's throat with such speed and such force it ripped his ruined trachea clean away in a spray of crimson froth, the French private silently collapsed into a pool formed of his own blood.

Thorsson and Andersson were putting up an immense fight themselves, having taken cover either side of the auxiliary control door, they were outnumbered, outgunned, and couldn't get to Laveaux. Flashes of blue pulse rifle fire lit up the end of the corridor, another alien was blasted off the wall from the main corridor opposite them.

Sparks sprayed out as the Dracos returned fire, their lethally sharp discs lodging themselves in the door surround, already two dozen were jutting out from the small expanse of wall.

"Thorsson to Rachthausen, we are in deep shit here sarge, the aliens have breached the doors, we are pinned down, taking heavy fire, Laveaux is already dead, we need reinforcing right now!" She shouted into his comm. unit over the din of the battle raging ahead of him.

"Shit!" Rachthausen shouted as he heard the message, "We're on our way." He readied his weapon and sprinted towards the other end of the floor, at least there was some good fortune in this, his men had stayed alive this time. Though if they got to Kathryn and the scientists before he did, he would never forgive himself.

While his other unit were busily engaging the interlopers, Drax had found a new way to access the other floors. The lift shaft may have been destroyed, but the air circulation system wasn't. Studying the plans once again, he found that the air circulation system was an elaborate system to keep those underground breathing clean air, without the need to fill oxygen tanks from the surface.

It was remarkable how it worked, two giant vacuum pumps sucked in vast quantities of carbon dioxide from the planets atmosphere, and then chemically separated the carbon molecules from the oxygen ones, then pumped the oxygen into two gigantic storage vessels, located deep inside the facility. One provided oxygen for the science wing and the other provided it for the military wing. There was also a built in failsafe; that, in the event of one of the vacuum pumps failing for any reason, a series of valves could be opened along an emergency re-supply line, so that a single pump could supply oxygen to both tanks. The beauty of the system was that it was entirely computer controlled, it would have been revolutionary for its time, Drax thought.

However, if all else failed, if he could not eliminate the interlopers, he could simply shut down the air supply and let them all suffocate to death. He was not above this, as a last resort, even if it denied him his 'fun'.

He crawled along the walls and ceiling of the security check-in station for the floor, every floor had one. Security was tight here, no wonder, considering what the base produced, how important this place once was, and all the military resources contained within.

There was a notice etched into the wall, it informed the occupants that anyone arriving from the surface must first submit to a series of security checks. He shuddered to think what those 'security checks' might entail. The Dracos of three hundred years ago were a violent, angry race. Hunted throughout the galaxy and forced to live in underground cities like this one, hunted to damn near extinction. The ancestors built facilities like these on remote worlds, hoping to one empower the Dracos race once again. These became known as the Halo worlds, finding them was of the utmost importance to his people.

E.D.F Chronicles – Eye of the Dracos

It was a shame the ancestors never quite realised their grand plan, Drax thought, things would have been different. The Dracos were still a violent angry race, although now this violence and anger had been tempered into a love of torture, a delight in hearing the screams of any who dared to oppose us. We still lived in subterranean cities, and still longed for the glory days when we would burst forth into the galaxy once more, and dance to the screams of our enemies.

Drax had to admit though, that in reality the Dracos had become a tiny scared little people, so afraid of repeated the catastrophic events of the past, that they rarely even stepped out from the safety of their under-cities. The ships of the Dracos fleet, while few in number were mainly concentrated in a region of space known only as the veil, a giant nebula full of gas and dust, and strange cosmic interference that disrupts the strongest of navigational sensor systems so that ships crossing the veil were effectively flying blind. They were easy prey for the Dracos ships, although Dracos vessels themselves almost never left the veil, for fear they would be detected and attacked.

The only reason his own ship had left, was to investigate the Aurigan system for potential halo worlds and then head straight back to the safety of the veil again. However, upon encountering that energy release, realising it was Dracos in origin, and finding that strange alien vessel in orbit. His mission had suddenly changed, now here he was, hunting down these interlopers, these E.D.F whoever they were. He was confident that the planet would come under Dracos control once again. After all, this planet was now too important to ignore, the Dracos had used concealment as their weapon of choice, and become so good at it that the galaxy had forgotten about them. Perhaps it was time to remind the galaxy the Dracos do still exist.

With a warm smile he pushed the thoughts to the back of his mind, and motioned for his unit to follow him into the air duct situated in the centre of the security stations ceiling.

Rachthausen, and the E.D.F troops with him raced down the corridor, the lights suddenly went out, pitching them all into utter darkness once again. "Shit!" Rachthausen cursed again, before re-lighting his flashlight attached to the underside of the barrel of his pulse rifle. Then he realised the scientists might now have flashlights attached to their weapons. He knew Kathryn did, but he wasn't so sure about the others.

58

Ian J Smethurst

The four of them reached the raging firefight at the blast doors. It was obvious as Rachthausen cast his torch over the immediate area , the corridor walls were scorched with the impacts of pulse rifle fire.

The sergeant inadvertently kicked something, it squelched as his foot made contact with whatever it was. Casting his torch down to look at it, the sight made him sick to his stomach. It was the gore soaked, shredded body of private Silvain Laveaux, Laveaux was the youngest in his squad, barely eighteen years of age, he had been a private only three months after enlisting at a recruitment post on the colony world of Eidolon II, such a waste.

He heard movement close by, sweeping his weapon around to locate the source, he could see nothing, yet he could definitely hear something. A skittering noise, like rats made along the floor, but bigger, and heavier.

His heart rate began to quicken, it pounded in his chest, where the hell were they. He heard another sound, "psst!"

The whistle of something shooting past his ear alarmed him, and he swung his weapon around to get a closer look. Just as three metallic discs slammed home on one of his men, one jutted out of his chest, the other sliced open his upper leg, and the third and final shot tore open the front of the man's skull.

The trooper staggered back a pace, with the metal disc jutting out from his forehead, blood poured down his ruined face. His eyes glazed over. A reactionary impulse made the dead on his feet trooper depress the trigger on his weapon, which opened fire. Bright blue flashes of light, lit up their surroundings. Silhouetting the dark shapes that moved silently, unseen amongst them.

One of the Dracos warriors slumped to the floor with a dull thud, as the trooper miraculously managed to hit him, the flash of laser energy tore through his carbon fibre environment suit, and blasted open the aliens chest. The walking dead trooper also collapsed as his legs finally gave way from under him. He fell to the floor at the same time as the alien. His forehead and his deep lacerations hissing and bubbling as the powerful acid went to work.

"Bastards!" Rachthausen roared as he opened fire upon the dark moving shapes, the other two troopers did likewise, and suddenly the whole corridor was ablaze with the vivid flashes of weapons fire.

E.D.F Chronicles – Eye of the Dracos

Three of the Dracos warriors fell, their bodies crumpled to the ground.

"Over here!" Thorsson yelled over the whirling firefight going on just ahead of him, he levelled his weapon and blasted apart the head of a Dracos just about to pounce on the sergeant.

With a swiftness that belied his size, Rachthausen scooped up the weapon from the fallen Dracos in front of him and dived into the auxiliary control room.

The other troopers though were caught out in the open, both Thorsson and Anderson were giving covering fire, one of the exposed men managed to dive inside the room. Rachthausen was fighting like a man possessed, with his pulse rifle in one hand, and a Dracos eviscerator rifle in the other. He had no idea how the thing worked, he simply pointed it and kept on shooting. Two more of the brutal aliens fell to the withering hail of weapons fire.

Thorsson screamed out in agony, as one of the scalpel like discs, ripped into his knee, slicing apart the kneecap, and causing hi to topple over onto the hard floor.

The last two remaining Dracos slinked away out of sight, their scuttling slowly down away. Rachthausen and the other two troopers, risked a glance around the badly damaged doorway. The other trooper hadn't made it. His body lay convulsing on the floor, riddled with eviscerator rounds, before it stopped shaking and was still.

They had drove the Dracos back, but at a heavy price. Three of Rachtahusens men lay dead upon the ground, Thorsson was injured. Eight alien bodies lay in bloodied heaps, strewn across the corridor outside. The floor was almost slick with both human and alien blood; the only sound that remained was the faint hissing and bubbling of the slowly dissolving human corpses.

Thorsson screamed out in pain once more as the acid went to work on his already badly injured knee, snapping Rachthausen out of his post battle reverie, the stench from his burning flesh was horrible, and the sergeant had to refrain from the reflex to gag, as he tore off a strip of cloth from his fatigues.

"I need to do this quickly," he said examining his fellow troopers wound by torchlight.

He folded over the fabric, so as to give him a little more time, and, using it as a makeshift glove. Gripped the tiny metal disc, the fabric immediately began to sizzle and melt. Rachthausen pulled with all of his prodigious might, as Thorsson clenched his teeth so hard blood seeped out from his mouth. The sergeants arm yanked backwards, ripping the alien ammunition from Thorssons knee in the process.

The trooper screamed in absolute agony, and very nearly collapsed unconscious from the pain.

Rachthausen flung the ammunition back out into the corridor in distain, although Thorsson's knee was still coated in acid and was still burning badly. The stench of dissolving flesh, was almost more than those around him could bear, not just from Thorsson's knee, but from the slowly dissolving corpses outside too.

The sergeant pulled out a small canteen of water from his webbing, "It will help to dilute the acid."

Thorsson simply shook a weak affirmative, beads of perspiration trickled down the wounded soldiers face, in his immense fight to stay conscious and to ignore the searing agony he was in.

Gradually Rachthausen poured the contents of his water bottle over the soldiers ripped, blood soaked knee, Thorsson screamed out again in raw agony, it took the efforts of Anderson and another guard to restrain him, gradually the pain subsided to less agonising levels.

"I can't do anymore here, we need to get you to Kathryn, she'll be able to do more."

Thorsson nodded, the other guard helped him slowly to his feet, and leaning heavily on both Rachthausen and the other soldier for support, the Dane painfully limped his way back down to the briefing hall.

Anderson closed the blast doors once again, with his free hand Rachthausen passed him the laser welder, and the lone soldier took great pains to make sure those doors were thoroughly sealed. Before picking up a clutch of fallen alien weapons and heading back to the briefing hall himself.

Rachthausen carried the injured form of Thorsson into the hall, where Kathryn immediately came to tend to him.

Although the sergeant had succeeded in helping to dilute the acid, it was no where near enough and still continued to burn through the injured soldier's now almost half collapsed knee. Kathryn fumbled around in the dark for the medical supplies brought down from the shuttle.

Private Anderson entered the hall, the light from his flashlight played across the forms of those hunkered down in the briefing hall, some were desperately tired, and trying to sleep. Unaware of the danger still approaching, others like Kathryn were awake, and trying as best they could to keep going.

He dropped the small cache of weapons he was carrying, and made his way over to where Kathryn and Rachthausen were tending to the stricken Eric Thorsson.

Thorsson was a big Dane, he and Rachthausen had served together since just after the Krenaran war, although like the others in the sergeants squad, this was their first taste of action, and what a taste it had been so far, a baptism of fire. Thorsson was normally the heavy weapons specialist in the squad, and typically carried either an Armschlager forty four calibre heavy machine gun, or a steiger industries grenade launcher, which he lovingly referred to as 'the bucking Betty'. Though on this mission, no-one had expected to encounter serious resistance, so the whole squad was only lightly equipped with pulse rifles, a move that Rachthausen was now rueing.

All they had to do was to protect the scientists, while they did their bit, and checked over the structure. The planet was uninhabited, so there was no threat to themselves or the scientists. Funny how in the blink of an eye all that changes, Rachthausen thought.

"okay, I've managed to neutralise the acid with a saline based alkaline solution," Kathryn said, looking up at him, "But his knee is useless, the scapula has been completely melted away, the fluid sac within his knee joint has burst, and the ligaments are totally shredded, he will not be able to walk on that leg again. We're looking at an amputation."

With all the advances in medical science over the past decade, they were still unable to replace a knee joint, they could replace the entire leg easily, but not the joint itself.

Rachthausen looked down at Kathryn with a look of concern whispering, "things are beginning to get desperate, I've lost six of my men, two others are wounded unable to fight. That just leaves me and Andersson here left."

At this news, Kathryn could say nothing, except. "I am sorry, sorry I ever got us into this."

"I just hope that help comes soon, otherwise there won't be anyone left to rescue," Rachthausen said.

"The scientists are all armed, we can fight," Kathryn tried to reassure him. The sergeant looked around at the other scientists in the room, all huddled together in a group, talking amongst themselves with a torch in the centre.

"I hope, that it will not be the case, though I fear it will. These aliens are not like anything the E.D.F has encountered before Kathryn. They are vicious, brutal, but not like the Krenaran's were, they relied on brute strength. These guys attack from anywhere, from out of the shadows, they are damned near impossible to spot in the dark, and so far that appears to be their favourite method of attack, we are fighting on their terms at the moment." He showed Kathryn one of the captured alien weapons, "this is what caused Thorsson's injury, and the majority of the deaths out there. These aliens fight like they are a living weapon, their wrists have blades attached, they have other weapons that can rip men's throats to shreds in seconds, and they have these. They can crawl on walls and ceilings, they are some of the best nightfighters I have ever seen Kathryn. We are fully trained soldiers, and we are getting slaughtered by these guys, if they attack the scientists it will be a very short fight."

Kathryn looked into Rachthausens eyes, sensing his fear, but also sensing his stoic resolve to protect the scientists, and to protect her from harm at all costs, it felt comforting.

"I will protect you and the scientists Kathryn with my dying breath, that is my job."

"Thank you," she said earnestly and tenderly embraced the sergeant, she was scared and feeling those giant arms wrap around her, she felt protected, like nothing on earth could hurt her. They gently parted from the embrace, her eyes searched the sergeant's features, he smiled warmly.

"Wait a second," Kalschacht exclaimed, sitting bolt upright as though hit with a cattle prod.

"What is it?" Kathryn asked.

"I've got it!" he shouted in elation as he walked towards them, "they have blinded us right? By shutting off the lights."

"Yes," Rachthausen replied, wondering just what the physicist was getting at.

"So why don't we blind *them*."

"With what?" the sergeant replied, intrigued, but not quite understanding how it could be done.

"With the flares we brought down from the shuttle, we have a box of 6 here."

"Show me," Rachthausen said, now he knew the physicist was onto something.

"Even when the lights are on, they only ever give off a twilight glow, right?"

"Correct."

"So they must be sensitive to bright light, they have shut the lights off speicifcally because it benefits them. They can see us easily, but we struggle to see them. When we let off a flare, the reverse happens, suddenly we are much more tolerant to bright light than *they* are, it will be they who are blinded."

"Kalschacht, you are a genius."

He let out a loud chuckle, "just Newton's law in action, every action must have an equal and opposite re-action. "

Rachthausen took the box, quickly stuffing three of the flares into a pouch on his webbing. "Anderson, take these, if you hear the slightest hint of movement. Let one off." He passed the box to him.

"Gotcha."

The sergeant then turned to the small haul of weapons captured during the fighting, these thigns had been butchering his men, and he studied them closely, observing their shape, the short barrel ended in an almost slit like opening. It had a small magazine, which appeared to look like a pronounced bump on the top of the weapon about three quarters the way down. With an effort he managed to unclip the magazine by locating a securing hatch just below it.

The magazine itself stank of acid, he had to hold his nose away from the pungent fumes, the acid, despite being devastating to organic tissue, was not eating into the ammunition, or any part of the weapon.

He figured that the weapon itself must be constructed of some unknown acid resistant metal, he found that the weapon was actually very simple compared to the ubiquitous E.D.F pulse rifle. The magazine was a simple gravity feed, although the ammunition was barely thicker than a human hair, how it didn't just shatter upon hitting something, the sergeant had no idea.

The ammunition itself seemed to be dropped into a kind of guide rail within the firing chamber. A locating pin poked through a tiny hole in the centre of the lethally sharp, disc shaped projectile.

When Rachthausen pressed the trigger, he noticed that this pin spun incredibly fast, and then shot forward along a central groove in the chamber, the groove itself was deeper at the end that the beginning, allowing the locating pin, to disappear within it. The pin shot forward so fast, and spun so quickly, that Rachthausen barely even saw it once it fired.

He could only applaud the engineering of this thing, the guide rails were so smooth, and so slippery, it was as if they were Teflon coated, it offered no resistance to the to the ammunition travelling along it at all. The tolerances were so exact that it offered very little extraneous movement for the disc, so that it flew perfectly straight, and perfectly true, every time.

What's more, that little ammunition pod could carry hundreds of these metal slivers inside, due to their hair like width. The only sound it made was the gentle click of the trigger, followed by a slight hum of the pin spinning inside immediately after, and then the whistle of the disc as it cut through the air.

It truly was a marvel of engineering simplicity, there were very few moving parts to go wrong, used very little power, and could carry a massive amount of ammunition, and hardly ever jammed to boot. He had never known anything like it.

Fortunately for them, it could be used against their enemies just as easily, he immediately called for Anderson to use this weapon against their enemies, rather than their own.

Drax and his remaining men continued to scurry through the ventilation system, a gentle breeze flowed unceasingly through the cramped pipework, from the series of vacuum pumps above them through to the giant oxygen storage tanks located far below, and out through the rest of the complex.

A silent communication was coming through, audible only to him.

The A.R. uplink came to life again over his left eye, it was Raleon, one of the more inexperienced members of squad two.

"Commander," Raleon said nervously, "we are falling back, we have taken eighty percent casualties, and have encountered heavy resistance on the third floor."

"Calm yourself, Raleon, you men have no doubt fought bravely, worthy of the Kallan name."

"err…..yes, sir."

Drax had already lost three of his own men so far, but to lose eight like that was inexcusable, he made a mental note to have them both executed for gross incompetence , once the hunt was over.

"Join up with us, we are on the second floor, science wing."

"Yes, sir," Raleon said with renewed vigour.

With that the communication ceased, "young bloods," Drax murmured to himself with distain as he continued to creep forward through the narrow, pitch black tunnels, using his helmets infra-red vision mode to see.

He briefly switched to thermal view, there was nothing showing up within range, however they would have to search the floor anyway. These interlopers were cunning, as he had already found out.

Two more Dracos warcruisers had dropped out of plasma drive on the fringes of the Auriga system, they had picked up on the communications the Flame of Celthris had sent earlier. Their sleek, black, crescent shaped forms powered up as they inexorably ventured further into the system. Past the tiny, barren, frozen ice world of Auriga VII, the enormous gas giants of Auriga V and VI, Auriga VI being a grey-white in colour due to the vast amounts of dry ice that swirled amongst its kilometres thick gaseous soup.

Auriga IV was a runaway greenhouse world, its thick carbon dioxide atmosphere trapped heat given off by the Aurigan sun over millennia, down on the surface, where over millions of years, the planet gradually warmed, steadily increasing in temperature. Today it had a mean surface temperature of one thousand, five hundred degrees Fahrenheit, volcanoes are constantly active on its surface, throwing out great clouds of dust and debris, and the incredibly hot searing winds can reach up to three hundred kilometres per hour. The whole planet was a hot house, a death trap to life.

Eventually as they explored further into the system, they found the orbiting form of the Flame of Celthris.

"Two ships approaching, sir, they are Dracos, identified as the Blade of Rhovanion, and the Vengeance of Kelmarroth."

"Understood, Halloth," Kaelleth nodded toward his junior sensory officer, working at the sensory station in a recessed pulpit to his right.

So they brought the Blade of Rhovanion herself, this must be big news to attract the flagship of the Dracos fleet.

Another massive blast of bright orange energy shot past the two approaching warcruisers, bathing their dark, brooding forms in a gentle orange glow as they neared the Flame of Celthris. Their dark crescent shaped silhouettes and bladed fins along their rear flanks, almost made it look like some meeting between evil gods was taking place.

E.D.F Chronicles – Eye of the Dracos

"Incoming communication," Halloth announced.

"Let's hear it."

The features of a slightly aged Dracos filled the screen, his eyes black as jet, his skin pale, yet the figure possessed an aura of power, and a strict sternness that belied his withered appearance. It was Calvaris Senergid, the commander of the Blade of Rhovanion, and commander of the entire Dracos fleet.

Kaelleth visibly stiffened, it wasn't every day he got to speak to a Dracos Calvaris, the highest rank one could attain in the Dracos navy. Especially one as legendary as Senergid, he was one of the very few, who could still remember the great betrayal, three centuries ago. Travelling across the stars to a new future, and eventually settling on the Dracos homeworld, Corvandris.

"Where is Calvar Drax?" Senergid asked.

"He has travelled to the surface, with an assault team to clear out some interlopers that had infested the purity of the station, Calvaris." Kaeleth replied with considerable deference to the man that far outranked him.

"You are to be congratulated, the eye of the Dracos is one of the highest prized of all the halo worlds, it was this world that supplied the majority of the power needs for the fledgling Dracos empire, three hundred years ago."

"Thank you, sir." Kaeleth replied, nodding in deference once again, "If I may sir, why did our people abandon it?"

"At the time, we were reeling from the great betrayal, we were being hunted down and driven from planet-to-planet. The enemy were merciless, they would capture and destroy our fleets, and blast our planets from orbit. We teetered on the edge of being wiped from the face of the galaxy." Senergids face gave the expression that he relived those horrible times from when he was a child, whenever he spoke of the betrayal. "It was during one of these attacks when we were forced to abandon the planet, the facility was shut down, and the few remaining Dracos ships passed through the veil and found Corvandris. Wherever since, we have been quietly biding our time and rebuilding our strength." Senergid paused to inhale a raspy, wheezing breath. "Until now, myself, and the few Dracos still living who can remember back to those days had simply forgotten the planet, lost in the fog of everyday survival. Also we did not want to reclaim a new world so soon anyway, as we were a badly depleted people, and if we left the safety of the veil to reoccupy the planet, we might alert our enemies to our presence. It was deemed too great a risk, until it violently reactivated, two days ago."

"Do you think that we are strong enough to occupy the planet now?" Kaeleth asked.

"I believe that the time has come upon us to re-claim the halo worlds, yes."

That reply sent a shudder of excitement through Kaeleth.

E.D.F Chronicles – Eye of the Dracos
7. A call from afar.

Captain Michael Alexander was busily overseeing the final testing phase of the new graviton shielding system, only recently fitted to the Liberty, while the process was ongoing the former Krenaran stealth ship had been temporarily taken out of active service.

In truth, the graviton shielding system was an experiment, a collaboration between Solarian scientists and the E.D.F research division. It worked via a series of powerful gravitic generators placed at key points around the ships hull.

When these generators were all activated simultaneously, they produced a powerful gravitational field around the ship, thereby deflecting most types of weapons fire, well that was how it was explained to him anyway. Although to Michael it had looked like the Liberty had grown a few 'pimples'.

His crew were due back in the morning, they had all been given extended leave, while the upgrade work was being completed. Michael had come back a few days earlier as usual, to inspect his pride and joy.

He was sat in a small restaurant, overlooking the small dockyard where several ships were berthed. Today, he could only make out three E.D.F ships and two Solarian battlecruisers, the Solarians often used the dockyard as a re-supply point while patrolling the borders of their territory as the facility was close to Solarian space. He envied their clean, graceful, flowing design. Instead of the sharp, rectangular shaped hulls of so many E.D.F ships, in comparison the Solarian ships looked positively majestic, their silvery crescent shaped hulls and raised, sharp, beak-like command structure betrayed a love of technology far beyond the rugged utilitarian nature of E.D.F shipping, but also an aesthetic quality as well as the wildly advanced technology that he doubted the E.D.F would ever possess.

Despite being a predominantly peaceful people, the Solarians possessed some of the most advanced and powerful fighting ships he had ever seen. The irony of that was not lost on him.

"Admiring the view?" Commodore Solomon Valente asked as he motioned to sit with the Liberty captain, a motion that was readily accepted with a smile and a nod. Valente was the commander of this facility named Charlie Gamma base, a tiny experimental research post and sub-orbital dockyard orbiting the Malthus colony on Malthus IV. It had been re-built after the Krenarans devastated the colony during the war, and only completed barely three years ago.

"I was just thinking about those Solarian ships," Michael said as he turned from looking at the commodore to glancing over the vessels, one last time.

"I know, magnificent aren't they? Wondrous machines, and damned fast too."

Micheal smiled and nodded, he probably had more experience of their capabilities than the commodore had. Especially since the Liberty had fought alongside them practically throughout the Krenaran war.

"You know about the Valley forge project?" Valente asked enthusiastically.

"I know it's a design for a new type of experimental ship." Micheal replied, his brow furrowed slightly in thought. He hadn't really heard a great deal on the project, it was supposed to be top secret, senior admiralty only. It made him wonder how the commodore knew, but in all things, word eventually gets around in the navy.

"It's more than that, the Valley forge is going to be the future replacement for the Danitza class battleships."

Micheal remembered back to his time aboard the Ulysses, a Danitza class battleship itself. It was immense, glorious, packed with firepower and the latest advances in technology. Unfortunately, none of that did it any good, as the Krenarans blew it to smithereens at the start of the war. "The Danitza's are powerful ships, some of them are amongst the most powerful ships in the fleet, why replace them?"

"The Danitza is an old design now, it was conceived and built as a deterrent, back in twenty sixty when all we had to deal with was random pirate attacks. Now we have Krenarans, Solarians, and Christ knows what else out there. We need a new advanced ship of the line that can deal with these new threats the galaxy throws at us."

"The Solarians are not a threat to us, they are our allies."

"I know that, the Krenaran war proved just how vulnerable the Danitza is to the types of energy weapons used against us. Besides anyway, the Danitza is huge and costly to run."

Micheal smiled and suppressed a harrumph at this last point, it always came down to money in the end, now much were colonists lives worth nowadays anyway? Since when did the E.D.F go from protecting the people, to savings and cut-backs. He remained silent, not wishing to get into an argument with a superior officer about this.

"From what I gather, the Valley forge is going to utilise technology reverse engineered from the Liberty. If the new graviton shields work, they are going to be used on the Valley forge."

This did surprise Michael, he had not been made aware of any technology from the Liberty being used on any other ship in the fleet, mostly due to compatibility issues. He supposed it was just a matter of time until they got around it, although it would have been nice for command to let *him* know, especially since he was the ships captain and all.

"It's the E.D.F's attempt to merge the fighter carrying capacity of a carrier, with the firepower of a battleship. From what I hear, its primary weapons systems will be not one, but two high power fusion cannons. Each one considerably larger, and with a much larger bore than the one the Liberty carries. Designs have already been approved by E.D.F command, building has already started."

Michael had not even seen this new ship yet, and was already tiring of the commodores incessant repartee about it. He knew from experience that the fusion cannon was one heck of a power hungry weapon. The Liberties own fusion cannon was a Solarian designed one and is the most powerful anti-ship weapon currently available. If the Valley forge was to use two even larger ones, how the hell were they going to power them?

"How long until she is ready?" He asked, at least trying to make it look like he was still interested.

"It's going to take three years to build the prototype, then you have shakedown and fleet trials. It'll be a good five years or so until she is with us proper."

Jesus, Michael thought, it looks as though the age of the advanced battleship has come upon us, nothing would tempt him away from his beloved Liberty though.

A young fresh faced lieutenant rather hurriedly approached the two men interrupting their conversation, he was panting from his rush to get here.

"Sir, I am sorry to interrupt, but I have important news." The man breathed, a small bead of sweat trickled down his face.

"Do you know how rude it is to interrupt a senior officer's conversation!" Valente snapped at the impetuous lieutenant, "Straighten you uniform man! Stand up straight!"

Michael said nothing, yet chuckled inwardly at the inexperience of the lieutenant, being given a severe dressing down.

"Yes, sir." The lieutenant quickly flattened down his deep navy blue uniform, and stood briskly to attention, attracting a few chuckles from nearby personnel who happened to be passing by.

"Now that you have most rudely interrupted our conversation, what news do you have?" Valente glared at him, if this turned out to be something trivial, he would have the lieutenant on cleaning detail for a week.

"The E.D.F.S Eisenhower has just intercepted and picked up a sensor buoy, containing a distress signal from the Copernicus."

The Eisenhower was a Jefferson class heavy cruiser on routine patrol near the Solarian border. An unremarkable ship by many standards, she had nevertheless earned her battle honours at the battle for Gamma IV, during the closing stages of the Krenaran war.

The Copernicus, Michael remembered. Was the ship Kathryn Jacobs served aboard, after resigning her position as chief medical officer on the Liberty. He missed Kathryn, although he had understood why she had to leave. Eventually the trauma of treating so many wartime dead and dying had gotten to her, and affected her badly. It probably did all medical officers in the end, you see your friends and colleagues brought in, torn to pieces, on the operating table, and its your job to sew them back up, and send them right back out there again. It wasn't a job Michael particularly envied.

Kathryn went and spent some time in counselling and therapy, trying to exorcise some of those demons that she encountered on that operating table. Finally quitting the medical profession altogether and re-training as a planetary geologist, her other great love.

While his current medical officer and Kathryn's replacement, Lillian Goddard was the more experienced of the two, he missed Kathryn's gentle, warm smile and soothing touch. She had that rare quality to be able to put anyone at ease.

Lillian on the other hand, was harsher, colder. Michael had to admit she was good at her job, she definitely knew her stuff, yet lacked Kathryn's gentleness.

Commodore Valente looked grave, nobody launched a distress buoy for no reason, "have the Eisenhower transmit the contents of the buoy to us."

He gently rose from his seat, turning back to face Michael, "I'm sorry captain, but I must attend to this."

"By all means," Michael nodded in understanding.

With that Commodore Valente left the small restaurant, rushing to the nearest elevator with the Lieutenant hurrying to keep up.

Michael was left alone, quietly watching the berthed vessels once again. Wondering if Kathryn was alright. He hoped she was safe out there wherever she was. He drank the remainder of the lukewarm coffee in his cup, before returning to his quarters onboard the Liberty.

A few hours later he was quietly perusing the reports of the final test results that were completed on the Liberties new shielding system the previous day; his wrist comm. chirped.

"Captain, I know the hour is late, but a serious situation has arisen, I need to brief you immediately." It was the grave voice of commodore Valente.

Well, this is a turn up for the books, an emergency in a dockyard, Michael guessed it had something to do with the incident involving the Lieutenant and the Eisenhower earlier. "I'm on my way." He replied, as he hauled himself out of his enticingly comfortable bed, put down the data navigator containing the report, splashed his face with cool water to re-awaken himself, and straightened his tunic.

He made his way across the Liberties empty bridge, to an elevator which guided him to the deck where the main hatch was located on the port side of the ship. It was strange, he thought, with the Liberty berthed in the dockyard like this, instead of being out amongst the stars. Bereft of her crew, and only functioning on minimal power, it almost felt like the ship was sleeping. He had found that without a crew, six decks and one hundred and forty meters, was a very big place indeed. Though Michael had gotten used to it over the past three months while the ship received its latest batch of upgrades.

The elevator stopped on deck four, and opened out into a long corridor that ran the entire length of the deck, wiring and delicate circuitry for the myriad of the Liberties systems were all secreted away in overhead trunking, that, in some sections almost half covered the ceiling.

The floors were white, and the walls a very light grey, giving the corridor a clean almost hospitable like appearance. Fully customizable displays lined the walls in even intersections, where the corridor didn't branch off into separate sub-sections.

The displays were all powered down for now though, to conserve power. The corridor itself had a series of bulkheads every fifteen metres or so, that created a kind of octagonal archway. This proved to be a nuisance, because if one didn't mind their head, they could quickly be incapacitated by running into one of the armoured bulkhead surrounds, as several of his crew had already found out to their cost, Lillian had at least one concussion per week to treat. The idea was sound though, in the event of a fire or decompression, the entire area could be sealed off until repairs could be made.

Michael made his way halfway along this main corridor, eyeing the bulkhead arches with a kind of grim suspicion, he didn't feel like a trip to the stations sickbay tonight, thank you very much.

He then hung a right, turning into a much narrower corridor with only small displays and many more doors leading into several ships departments, crew quarters, maintenance access corridors, supply rooms, the ships main computer core was located on this deck although that was on the starboard side of the ship. Towards the aft of the deck lay the powerplant for the ships primary sub-light engines.

E.D.F Chronicles – Eye of the Dracos

The Solarian negative Ion propulsion drive, as they called it. He loved the engines on this ship, it was what turned the ship from an ordinary cruiser, into a hot rod. Able to fly at a speed, dive and jink to avoid attacks, that left other ships simply in its wake, and able to get out of danger quickly if the action became too hot.

This ship was unique, there was nothing else like it in the entire E.D.F, and Michael loved its uniqueness, which was why he was a little hurt when he heard of the E.D.F's plans to reverse engineer some of its technology. Suddenly, the Liberty was not so unique anymore, although he understood the decision, he didn't have to like it.

Nearing the hatch, which was attached to a small temporary berthing corridor, a relatively recent addition to the ship that allowed it to dock with stations and other ships, more easily, it led onto the main structure of the station. At last there was signs of human life, a few dozen E.D.F engineers were strolling back and forth, carrying equipment to, and performing routine repairs to a couple of freighters just recently arrived. They had already offloaded their cargo, and were just going through some minor repairs, before heading off out into space once again.

Michael made his way over to the nearest elevator and said, "command deck," into the speaker.

The elevator merrily chirped its response and sped him onto his destination, although Charlie Gamma base was only a small substation under the command of the E.D.F research division, it was still quite a sizeable installation in its own right. Made up of thirty six decks and over eight hundred E.D.F engineers and research personnel worked here, its small, but advanced dockyards could service anything from a single seat peregrine fighter all the way up to a Washington class heavy cruiser. Though not the Danitza class, or main carrier classes, as they were simply too large for the station to handle, they needed the services of either a major engineering facility like Echo base, or Delta base, the . naval headquarters, or perhaps Alpha base, as those were the only facilities large enough to accommodate those metal goliaths.

After a few seconds, the elevator stopped at the command deck of the station, and cheerily chirped again to let him know of the fact. Michael stepped out onto the command deck of Charlie Gamma base and was immediately shocked. For the size of the station, the command deck was tiny, the bridge of a Montgomery class carrier was bigger than this. Around twenty officers were sat manning stations, there was a central walkway that ran to the commodore's office. Either side of this walkway was a small flight of four steps that led to a pair of sunken semi-circular work areas, lined with complex displays, five men worked within each section.

To Michael's left and right, there was also a flight of ten steps that led up an overhead gantry, lined with yet more displays, here another ten men worked. He spied the commodore's office ahead and to the left of him. In the wall directly infront of him was giant viewer, partially obscured by the overhead gantry. It was currently showing the forms of the two Lincoln class supply ships which had docked earlier.

Michael could see the commodore waving from his office to enter, so he hurried along the central platform towards the sideroom, the etched glass doors opened automatically.

Valente had guessed Michael's surprise, "not what you were expecting?"

Michael had to admit, "not really, with a station the size of this, I was expecting something a little larger."

"That's what surprised me too, when I took command here three years ago, you would expect, for a station that essentially oversees all operations in the Malthus system and for several light years beyond, to have quite a sizeable command and control centre, but not Charlie Gamma base," Valente said, shaking his head. "Please take a seat."

Michael sat down next to the commodore's desk, as he did so a small monitor rose from the surface.

"As you are no doubt aware, the Jefferson class heavy cruiser, Eisenhower picked up a distress buoy from the Copernicus, which was conducting a survey of the Auriga system. From the logs and sensor data downloaded into the buoy we can confirm the Copernicus has been destroyed in orbit of the third planet in the system."

Michael looked ashen, shocked, he feared for the life of his former medical officer, his friend.

"However it is what destroyed the Copernicus, and the events leading up to it that has everyone talking."

Michael peered at the small video playing on the monitor, he watched the monumental release of energy that shot past, coating the ship in its intense orange glare in the process, and whispered, "What the hell?"

The video showed the enemy ship, Michael at first mistook it for a Solarian battlecruiser. Yet when he looked closer he picked up the subtle differences, the lower, sleeker, more severely angled command structure. The pronounced weapon arrays on the wingtips, together with the fact that this ship was black in colour and not silver. The dark leviathan began firing on the defenceless Copernicus; the image quickly went blank.

Michael had to ask the question, "Is that a Solarian ship?"

"No, the Solarian's have denied any involvement or even knowledge of the incident, but they are not saying who it is either. They are acting very stangely about the whole thing, and are absolutely adamant they won't get involved. So adamant in fact, that they have threatened to pull their ships out of the area."

"That's not like them, normally they are pretty co-operative with us, they never had a problem sharing information before, so why now?"

Valente simply shrugged, "beats me, E.D.F command has an inkling that the Solarians do know who is behind it. Or at least they have a very good idea, why they are being so reluctant, nobody knows. The planet isn't even an E.O.C.A colony world, there's no threat of invasion for now at least, so command has initiated a temporary alert level three on this, since it is an attack on E.O.C.A property, namely the Copernicus. This is our highest alert level since the Krenaran war."

Michael was still wondering just what all this had to do with him, but continued to listen to the commodore's briefing anyway.

"However, there are still a group of sixteen survivors from the Copernicus who were investigating some alien ruins on the surface, and we need to get them out of there fast. The Liberty is the only ship that can get there fast enough to save them, but you'll need help." Valente smiled, "fortunately for us, a group of twenty E.D.F commandoes have been training for just this kind of scenario at Bravo Delta base on the colony world of Gamma Aurigulon. It's a small military complex used for hostage retrieval training, Colonel Nikolai Vargev is currently commanding them. They have been scrambled, and are currently on route to the planet in a Stockholm class lander, your mission is to rendezvous with the lander, transfer the troops onboard, and land them on the surface so they can extract the survivors."

Michael understood the mission, however a few questions still lingered in the back of his mind, "If I may commodore?"

"By all means."

"Why doesn't the Liberty simply escort the lander in?"

"Command are worried that the lander may come under fire, as you know, the Stockholm class landers have no ship-to-ship weaponry, it is purely and simply a means of transporting troops to the battlefield. Out in space it highly vulnerable, that's why we usually have to clear the bad guys out first using the navy, before we can send the landers in. If those commandoes die on-route, the mission in scrubbed and the survivors die as well."

"Understood," Michael replied, it had seemed as though the E.D.F had learned its lesson from all those failed lander missions during the war, so many were simply torn to shreds by stealth ships before ever reaching the surface.

"The Liberty is still not in active service while we are field testing these new graviton shields, surely there is another ship closer, who can perform the mission just as well?" Michael pleaded, his crew were still not back, and he didn't want to be put in the position of having to take out the Liberty with a completely green, temporary crew, Especially if he was expecting to take her into a fight.

"The Eisenhower could, but you know as well as I do, the Liberty is more than twice as fast as her, far more heavily armed and much more survivable in an engagement. Yes, the Eisenhower is closer, but the Liberty is faster, in this type of mission it's a no-contest, we'll just have to test the new shielding system in combat," Valente said.

And hope to hell they work like they do in the simulations, Michael thought, the power supply to the ships previous reactive hull armour had been removed to stabilise the load on the ships main power core, if those shields failed, the Liberty would only be marginally more survivable than any other ship. "My crew have not yet arrive back from their shore leave, the Liberty can't leave immediately anyway."

"We have already contacted your crew and appraised them of the situation, most were on-route anyway, they have been given orders to scramble and should be here in the next couple of hours, no doubt you'll also brief them personally?"

"Of course."

"Look, Michael I don't like rushing the Liberty back into service like this anymore than you do, but we both know the best chance for the survival of those scientists is if the Liberty is involved."

Michael nodded, he couldn't argue the point, the Liberty was the fastest ship in the E.D.F anyway.

"The Eisenhower has been placed on standby should you need her, and a taskforce of four other E.D.F ships have been dispatched from Delta base, they won't arrive in system for another 2 days, and we are without Solarian help, it appears we are on our own on this one. Do us proud captain."

"I'll try my best, sir."

The two officers saluted one another, and commodore Valente gave him a disc for his data navigator containing the specifics of the mission.

"Good luck out there captain."

"Thank you, sir." Michael replied before the commodore dismissed him.

He wasn't happy with the circumstances, the Liberty wasn't really ready to be thrown into a combat environment just yet, and the Solarians acting weirdly was totally unlike them. He had a lead he could follow up on however, namely his own pilot, Eldathar, and failing that, ambassador Kerulithar on Solaria itself, the ambassador had helped them out once before when he accompanied them to Solaria to enlist the Solarian empires help in the Krenaran war, he was confident he would do so again.

He decided however, that the best course of action was to speak to Eldathar when he arrived back from his shore leave. With that, he left the confines of the command centre and headed back to the Liberty with more questions than answers.

Ian J Smethurst

He pored over the mission requirements as well as accessing the stations primary computer archives from the terminal in his quarters, he wanted to be absolutely sure of the circumstances surrounding the destruction of the Copernicus. He was also worried about Kathryn, he found that according to the ships logs she has leading a small science team to the planets surface to check out some alien structure.

So, she was on the surface after all, at least she might still be alive. This alleviated Michael's fears somewhat, although he knew he had to get her out of there, no doubt the ship that destroyed the Copernicus would quickly find the remains themselves. Things could get very ugly, very fast.

A couple of hours later, the first of the shuttles containing his crew had just arrived. Commander Quinn Kinraid, the tall, goatee bearded, long haired, red headed first officer of the Liberty stepped out onto the hangar bay and stretched his arms wide, it had been a long journey. Quickly followed by his shorter, dark haired, clean shaven companion Logan Jones, the Liberties chief engineer.

"Well this is all fine an' dandy now isn't it." Kinraid quipped in his customary deep celtic twang.

Logan simply nodded in agreement, the hangar bay they had been directed to was small and cramped, festooned with all manner of manned and un-manned repair vehicles, as well as a few smaller shuttles in various states of repair.

They had hitched a ride on the civilian deep space cruiser, *la Rochelle* transporting eager holidaymakers to the glorious sights of the crystal cities on the Solarian homeworld. Now that the war was over , and interstellar travel was relatively safe again, the crystal cities had become a popular holiday destination, much to the chagrin of Solarian officials trying to manage the constant morass of shipping going to and from the immensely busy world.

The two men gradually made their way through the corridors and confines of the station, passing a long corridor that offered views out to the dockyard and the ships contained within. There, nestled between two Solarian cruisers was the Liberty, their home away from home, looking as dark, as brooding and as menacing as ever. Both men noticed the newly acquired tiny 'bumps' that adorned the ships outer hull. Even though the old warhorse had changed slightly it was *still* the Liberty, still the most famous and instantly recognisable ship in the E.D.F fleet, and still like a friend to those who served aboard her.

Since the end of the Krenaran war, the E.D.F didn't have much use for a former captured Krenaran stealth ship, turned into one of the most advanced and deadly ships in the fleet, though they still retained her services.

During the early stages of the re-building of the devastated outer colonies shortly after the war, her immense speed and hitting power had made her an excellent anti-pirate patrol ship, although over the past couple of years the navy slowly recouped their massive losses and gradually reasserted control over E.O.C.A space. As a result, pirate activity died down once again to pre-war levels. This unfortunately left the Liberty virtually surplus to requirements amongst the more multi-role ships of the navy nowadays.

The two men made their way onboard the berthed ship, to stow their gear, as they had done a thousand times in the past.

"Smells just like home," Jones said as he walked onboard.

Kinraid nodded in agreement, "That it does, that it does."

Once the two officers headed to their separate quarters to change into their full naval uniforms, Logan headed to engineering to check if things were all right down there, while Kinraid headed to Michael's quarters to hear about this new emergency.

"Ah Quinn, welcome back, have a good time away?"

"Yeah thanks cap'n, although the crew are not appreciatin' having ta' hurry back like this, what's goin' on."

"We have new orders Quinn, the Copernicus has been destroyed."

"That's little Kathryn's ship!" Quinn said in alarm.

"I know."

"When's the briefin'"

"As soon as everyone is back onboard."

"Whatta' you think cap'n?"

Michael hesitated for a moment, contemplating his answer, "I think we owe it to Kathryn to go in, find out what happened, and get those still on the surface out of there."

"There 'r' people still on the surface?"

"Yes commander and they don't have much time, it will all be in the briefing."

"I understand," Kinraid nodded respectfully.

Michael rubbed his chin in thought, "my gut tells me this won't be easy Quinn."

"Is anythin' we ever do easy cap'n," Kinraid replied smiling.

"I guess not."

A few minutes later a small Lincoln class supply ship dropped off the remainder of the Liberties crew, they all hurried to get onboard to get their equipment stowed and begin to make the ship ready for departure. Eldathar, the tall Solarian pilot, returning from his stay on the Solarian homeworld itself was the last to arrive, Kinraid had informed the crew there was to be an immediate briefing as soon as everyone was aboard.

They all assembled on the ships bridge, it was a tight squeeze, but the crew of forty one just about managed to fit into the oval shaped room.

"First of all I'd like to apologise for making everyone rush back like this," Michael began, "however this is a unique situation, if there was any other way, we wouldn't have done it."

The crew all silently nodded their understanding.

"Those of you who were with us during the Krenaran war will remember our former medical officer, Kathryn Jacobs. The ship she currently serves aboard was destroyed by a new unidentified enemy, resulting in the deaths of over two hundred naval personell and scientists. The Copernicus itself is an unarmed survey vessel under the command of the research division, it was conducting a survey of the Auriga system. Although not everyone died, sixteen people are still trapped on the surface of Auriga III, including Kathryn, in an unknown alien structure. The vessel that destroyed the Copernicus is still out there, and is still a threat. Here is all the information we currently have on it."

Michael played a video feed containing the sensor data and the ships logs of the Copernicus through the shimmering holographic main viewer.

It showed the dark shape of the enemy ship closing with its prey, Michael studied the reactions of his crew as they watched. In particular Eldathar, the Solarian's eyes widened in shock and horror as he instantly recognised the alien vessel.

The crew witnessed the devastating impacts of the torpedoes, and the carnage wrought onboard, the smoke, fires, and lifeless broken bodies, and then the final coup de grace from those deadly laser lances, the video went black.

The crew stood in silence, not since the Krenaran war had they witnessed this kind of wanton destruction, and for many it brought back uncomfortable memories of that dark time.

"The E.D.F has initiated an alert level three, the highest alert level since the Krenaran war in response to this, so this is absolutely as real as it gets gentlemen. The Liberty is the only ship in the area fast enough to rescue the stranded science team. This is what we've trained for, what the Liberty is built for, we won't let her down, and we won't let those scientists down; for Kathryn!"

The whole crew echoed solemnly, "for Kathryn."

"Dismissed."

The crew all fell out and began to filter through to their familiar stations throughout the six decks of the one hundred and forty metre long ship.

All that is, except Eldathar, Michael needed to know what the Solarians knew about these new aliens.

"You know who that was, don't you?" He probed gently.

"It's a people long thought forgotten, and one I didn't expect to see again," he bowed his head low as though in shame, "They are called the Dracos, they were once Solarians; a breakaway radical group who placed the infliction of pain and torture above that of peace, culture and science." Eldathar took a long deep breath, as if trying to reopen a suppressed memory buried deep within his people's psyche, and never told to anyone. "They once tried to overthrow the Solarian government over three hundred years ago, causing a brief but bloody civil war, in the end they were defeated. Our people went mad, seized by a vengeance to right the wrongs they had done to us, we chased them throughout our space, the warfleet mercilessly harried them world from world, system-by-system, until they disappeared forever. We devastated their key facilities, infrastructure and bases from orbit, and thought we had destroyed all trace of the Dracos. In doing so we had destroyed a part of ourselves, though now three hundred years later they have returned." Eldathar sighed sadly as he recounted the tale.

"So they are like the Solarians smaller, evil little brother?"

"In a way, yes."

"So why don't the Solarians get involved, help us in eradicating this threat?"

"It is not a time we are proud of as a people, we derived no pleasure in turning weapons against our own kind, no matter how wayward they had become. They were still our brothers and sisters, this was a time of nothing but universal sadness for the Solarian people. Before this, no Solarian had killed another in anger, and to us it was just like killing our own family. Now three centuries on, we feel exactly the same, and that is why the Solarian empire cannot intervene."

Michael searched the Solarians features as he looked up at him, the sadness was plain to see, this news must be tearing him apart on the inside. "I understand, I will not force you to go on this mission Eldathar, if you wish to remain behind I will not hold it against you."

"I am a Solarian yes, though I am also a member of this crew, and I will continue to do my duty; Kathryn was my friend too captain."

Michael smiled knowingly, this was exactly the kind of response he had come to expect from his number one pilot, although he couldn't imagine how difficult this must be for him.

The Solarian quietly took his place in the Liberties pilot's chair, while Michael took up the centre seat.

"Kinraid, contact engineering, tell them to bring main power online."

There was a pause of a few seconds while commander Kinraid transmitted the command down to the Liberties engineering section from his console. "Engineering confirms, Solarian power core's charging up and is stable, we'll 'ave full power in two minutes for 'ya cap'n."

"Excellent, contact Charlie Gamma base control, and request permission to get under way."

Kinraid worked the controls again, after another brief pause the response came, "Clearance's been granted."

The holographic viewscreen shimmered into life once again, before becoming crystal clear, the face of Commodore Valente and the rest of the command team in the background became visible. "Good luck Liberty, and god speed." The viewscreen shimmered out of existence, leaving just the bare bridge wall.

Lights flickered into action and consoles came to life throughout the ship, the half-orb that housed the ships plasma drive system, laced with delicate conduits began to power up. Navigation lights fitted to the deepest part of the Liberties sloping, angular hull began to blink their respective green and red. The primary negative Ion propulsion drive lit up into its brilliant electric blue colour, as did the ships Ionic turning thrusters nestled within wide indents halfway along the ships hull.

Everywhere onboard people were glued to their stations, checking over the readouts of status displays flashing across a plethora of terminals.

The elongated barrel of the ships most deadly weapon, that Solarian designed fusion cannon lit up; being the most energy intensive system on the ship it was always last to fully power up, although the weapon itself wasn't active, that would only happen once the Liberty entered into a combat situation.

Finally, Michael gave the command, "Blow docking hatch, release all moorings, reverse thrust, one quarter power, manoeuvring thrusters at users discretion."

Keeping his eyes glued to the sensor readouts in front of his chair, Eldathar gently pulled on a small throttle control nestled within the palm of his hand just a fraction. The one hundred and forty metre long vessel gradually began to reverse. The confines of the small dockyard were tight, and the Solarian had to guide the ship skilfully around the hull of the Lincoln class supply ship that had docked earlier.

The Liberties port turning thruster flared a brilliant electric blue as power was shunted to it, lighting up a section of the transports hull as it gently glided around it, slowly edging its way out of the dockyard and into the star filled blackness of deep space. The only object to impose upon that universal blackness was the bright blue-green atmosphere of Malthus IV below them, the site of the Malthus colony, and the dull grey hull of Charlie Gamma base itself ahead. Festooned with its numerous shining port holes, and lit sections. From a distance the station resembled a giant oblong, with a tall cylindrical main structure at one end, it was in this cylindrical section where the stations crew lived and worked. The large oblong structure extending outwards from it was the dockyard itself, providing shelter for the ships huddled within, and wherefrom the Liberty had just emerged.

"Okay, now that we are clear, set a new course, bearing zero-six-seven degrees, elevation twenty one."

"Aye captain," Eldathar replied as he raised one arm of his pilots chair, while simultaneously lowering the other. The ship instantly responded to the pilot's movements and spun rapidly around to face this new direction. The fore section and fusion cannon was pointed away from the station, as the ship raised itself as though on a gentle incline to match the co-ordinates given for elevation.

Michael had to still hold onto his seat as the ship manoeuvred into position, unlike a big, bulky E.D.F ship that took a veritable age to turn, the Liberty was almost instant. At time Michael wondered whether the Ionic thrusters were too good. Though he rarely complained as they had proven to be such a boon when in battle.

"Full power to main engines, then initiate maximum plasma drive once we are clear."

"Understood captain," Eldathar replied, as he pushed sharply down on the same throttle control, the Liberty rapidly accelerated, soon leaving the colony world and its small orbital facility far behind.

After about ten minutes of sub-light cruising, the planet was little more than a tiny speck, barely visible in the surrounding vastness of space. In-fact the only thing that was visible was the bright yellow-orange of the Malthus sun.

The star of the Malthus system was a very old one, almost twice as old as the sun the Earth orbits, and had all but used up the hydrogen contained within its corona. As such, it was beginning its expansion, and slowly transforming from a yellow star into a red giant. Though scientists had predicted that unless no unusual phenomena interfered with the stars natural metamorphosis, the colony wouldn't need to be evacuated for at least the next five hundred years.

The Liberty reached a safe distance and then engaged its plasma drive, the half-orb beneath the warship glowed with barely contained power, as plasma energy filled the myriad conduits adorning the sphere. The plasma built up, and then shot forward along a wide slightly raised channel, running from the plasma drive itself along the length of the Liberties hull, to a sharp frontal emitter, where an intensely bright blue beam of raw plasma energy lanced out from the front of the ship. Exploding into the swirling multi-hewed plasma wake, fringed with its distinctive halo of bright white light. The Liberty itself, still hurtling along at full sub-light speed, dove headlong into the plasma wake and entered plasma drive proper.

Now travelling at plasma factor seven, seven times the speed of light, the small yet deadly warship shot through the swirling tunnel of light that was the plasma wake, racing towards its destination, just outside the Auriga system to pick up the commando assault team, before venturing into the system itself.

Michael prayed for the scientist's sake, that they would make it in time.

The Liberty continued to race through plasma drive, though the Auriga system was relatively nearby the Malthus system, it was still a journey of several hours.

Drax however, was enjoying hunting down the interlopers, he found them resourceful, worthy, but ultimately easily killed. Although his own men had taken severe casualties, his other team virtually wiped out, and his own team reduced to seven out of the original ten men. Now it was bolstered by the arrival of the two survivors from the second team. Even better news was on the cards however, as word had reached him of two more Dracos ships had come to join the fun, and would likely be despatching their own assault teams shortly.

He and his men had checked every room on the second floor, quietly creeping through ventilation ducts and service passages, never along the main corridor itself. Now they were heading down to the third and lowest floor, he knew they had to be here, there was nowhere else they could hide. The thought of the slaughter to come excited him greatly.

Further they crept, through the narrow square shaped metallic interior of the ventilation ducting. Following precisely the outline of the map displayed on the A.R. uplink over his left eye.

Then finally, when he switched his view onto thermal imaging mode, he was rewarded with what he was looking for, thermal signatures given off by his enemies body heat. Drax silently wave for his men to follow cautiously.

The Dracos Kallan warriors crept forward slowly, and with such skill that barely a sound was made, they were barely metres away from their prey now, some were sleeping while others kept watch, a few others were acting as sentries out in the corridor beyond the large room being watched by the arrayed Kallan.

Drax quietly ordered his team to split up, there wasn't much point in keeping all his men together, as had been proven by the ill-fated second team, he ordered two Kallan to drop into the next room, come around and eliminate the sentries, thereby creating a diversion, which would allow himself and the four other Kallan to swoop in a wreak havoc.

Drax and his guards silently waited as the two other Dracos peeled off down the narrow ducting.

The two scientists Matthew Broadhurst and Pablo Gomez were guarding the entrance to the briefing hall. They were tired, heck everyone was tired, though they didn't know just how long they had been down here. Everyone had lost complete track of time after the chaos of the initial attacks, and with the business of staying alive. For all they knew it could have been weeks, Broadhurst however doubted it was any more than a couple of days. The rations wouldn't have lasted that long anyway, food was already becoming scarce, if they didn't think of something soon, they would all starve to death down here.

Kathryn was still tending to the injured Thorsson as best she could under the circumstances, and as for poor Corporal Jankov, without his sight he was effectively a walking dead man. Still, Broadhurst and Gomez continued to scan the dark, wide corridor that extended into the gloom as far as they could see in either direction.

Broadhurst thought he could sense the faint shuffling of feet, a paralysing fear began to set in him, his skin ran cold and clammy, his nerves on edge. The gentle hairs on the back of his neck began to rise.

He swung his weapon in the direction of the sound, "What's that?" he whispered nervously.

"What's what?" Gomez whispered back.

"I thought I heard something, I'm going to check it out, stay here." Broadhurst crept through the darkness.

"Get back here," Gomez whispered after him, but it was no use.

Broadhurst ventured through the gloom alone, the flashlight from his pistol illuminating the various dark, foreboding panels, casting deep dark shadows, he nervously crept further and further away from the briefing hall doors, his weapon was shaking in his hands. He mentally tried to calm his jangling nerves. The shuffling sound was getting slowly louder, there was definitely something down here, and close. He risked a quick glance back over his shoulder, and could still see the faint glow given off from Gomez's flashlight; it reassured him somewhat.

Stopping at the entrance to the next room, the environmental systems monitoring room that had been damaged earlier in the fighting. He tentatively shined his torch inside the room, almost afraid of what he might see, there was nothing. He breathed a sigh of relief, perhaps he had just imagined it? after all, tiredness and extreme stress can do strange things to a man.

Wait a second, there it was again, a faint, almost imperceptible shuffling, now he knew he was not imagining it, his nerves set on edge once again, the cold fear reasserted itself with a vengeance, slowly he peered closer, his breathing quick and shallow, straining to hear the strange noise again. He drew level with the door itself, looking around at the interior of the room, there was nothing but smashed consoles, a few were working their lights shining brightly in the surrounding darkness, coating the nearby panels in flickering red, green, blue and yellow colours. The shuffling had stopped, and so did Broadhurst, standing absolutely still, barely daring to breathe in order to pick up the faintest of sounds. Cold sweat began to trickle down his temples to the side of his neck, his hands felt clammy as he clutched at his weapon, eyes constantly flickering around the room, alert to the slightest hint of movement.

There was a whoosh of displaced air, as a black arm whipped around and slammed into his throat, Broadhurst felt a searing agonising pain across his throat, coughing and spluttering he realised he couldn't breathe. He stumbled backwards, coughing and spluttering, his neck felt warm and wet, the arm retreated back behind the other side of the wall, festooned with a series of razor sharp blood soaked blades like a row of sharks fins. Broadhurst dropped the weapon and clutched at his throat, his vision began to get spotty, cloudy, he was weakening, slumping to his knees he coughed and gurgled on his own blood, before slowly collapsing onto the floor. The slash of the Dracos wrist blades had torn his throat wide open. The last thing Matthew Broadhurst saw was the forms of the two Dracos warriors rushing past him in the reflected torchlight, the bright scarlet of their helmet lenses permanently etched onto his slowly dying mind. He lay still in a slowly growing pool of his own blood.

E.D.F Chronicles – Eye of the Dracos

The two Kallan sprinted into the corridor, zig-zagging and crossing paths wildly so as not to afford Gomez a clear shot. He heard the footfalls racing toward him and instantly levelled his weapon, the flashlight illuminated the on-rushing black figures. He pressed the trigger and opened fire, the muzzle flashed brightly in the dark and the shot echoed loudly. He managed to clip one of them in the upper arm as he charged, sending it stumbling off balance into the wall of the corridor, before quickly leaping to its feet again.

The second came on relentlessly though, the dark suited alien launched itself through the air, its wrist blades outstretched. The lethally sharp blades sliced right through the exposed neck of Gomez. His body seemed to freeze for a split second, and, just as the Kallan warrior executed a neat forward roll upon landing. The scientists head, slowly, wetly separated from its body, before both collapsed into a bloodied heap.

The gunfire just outside instantly alerted those sheltering in the briefing hall, they rushed to grab their weapons. There was shouting, screaming, and widespread panic at the horror they had witnessed at Gomez's decapitation.

The two Kallan who had just slaughtered Gomez and Broadhurst, now took up positions either side of the doorway, effectively laying siege to the room, they released their eviscerator rifles, magnetically attached to their backs.

Rachthausen hefted his own captured Dracos eviscerator in response, and quickly took cover amongst a small row of chairs.

The other scientists were all trading fire with the two Dracos looming either side of the doorway. Though not as highly trained as an E.D.F soldier, they were poor shots, many simply blasting away in their fright. The energy blasts slammed into the walls surrounding the door, and the far side of the corridor beyond. Sparks showered from the small impact craters, the wall was quickly becoming pock marked with these small impacts as the untrained scientists blasted away.

Coporal Jankov, unable to see due to the intensely bright energy release from the facility that had scorched his eyes, attempted to shout over the din, "What's happening!"

Anderson was also busily blasting away at the two attackers who had them pinned inside the room, completely oblivious to the small air circulation vent opening behind him, one of the Dracos warriors slowly emerged out of his hiding place and crept along the ceiling.

"Shit!" Thorsson shouted at the top of his voice, although he couldn't move due to his ravaged knee, he could see perfectly well what was happening. He quickly gripped his pulse rifle next to where he was propped, levelled it and opened fire. Several laser energy pulses blasted open the chest armour of the Dracos's environment suit, while the last one tore away half of its helmet, the warrior fell from the ceiling with a dull, sickeningly wet crack next to Anderson, who spun around to be confronted with yet more Dracos emerging from their hiding place within the ducting. Just as he brought his weapon up to bear, an eviscerator disc sliced deep into the back of his head with a spray of blood and bone matter; fired from those still at the doors. He began frothing at the mouth, his grip slowly relaxed, and he dropped his weapon, before slumping face first onto the smooth, deep grey floor.

"Bastards!" Thorsson screamed out at the top of his voice at the loss of his friend, opening fire again and managing to dislodge another of the black suited monstrosities from the ceiling, the laser pulses had blasted its head apart in a great gout of blood, brain and black helmet fragments, it toppled lazily to the floor, gore oozing out from the headless alien.

Two lethally sharp eviscerator discs sliced into the abdomen, and upper chest of the immobile Thorsson, his entire body shuddered under the impacts of the two simultaneous strikes, he laid still, a thin dribble of blood emerging from his mouth, and small crimson patches began to form through his ragged and torn fatigues. Cold sightless eyes looking upon the dark form of two Dracos warriors dropping from the ceiling onto their prey.

Drax and the other Dracos warrior were amongst them now, and the whirlwind of bloodshed began in earnest, with acrobatic leaps and bounds wrist blades whipped and slashed out, eviscerator discs sliced through flesh and bone. The Kallan whooped and revelled in the gore fest, this was what they had looked forward to.

"We have to get out of here!" Rachthausen shouted to a terrified Kathryn, caught up in the bloodletting.

"I can't just leave them to die!"

E.D.F Chronicles – Eye of the Dracos

There was no time to argue, the burly sergeant leapt over the chairs, barely missing a swipe from a passing Dracos wrist blade. Hefted Kathryn over his shoulder, and with his free arm lit one of the flares, bathing the room in an intensely bright red light.

Drax and the other Kallan in the room flinched and recoiled under the onslaught of the light burning at his sensitive eyes, he dived into a shadow provided by a bank of chairs further up the incline.

Holding the flare aloft Rachthausen sprinted through the room, over the torn and shredded bodies of scientists, soldiers and Dracos alike. The two at the doorway shuddered and retreated away from the intense light as the sergeant forced his way through, carrying Kathryn. His stolen eviscerator rifle swinging across his back. One of the Dracos behind him took a swipe, the blade bit deep into the flesh of his upper arm, he winced crying out, and almost dropped Kathryn. Whirling around, he held the flare aloft, blinding the alien warrior. Rachthausen fled down the corridor with the still protesting Kathryn, the red light illuminating his path as he went.

The briefing room had been turned into a scene from hell, a gore streaked bloodbath, bodies of dead and dying scientists lay scattered across the floor, their groans, like a sweet symphony to the Dracos commander, who stood in the centre proudly.

Severed limbs and body parts lay like bloody, grisly trophies around the smooth floor, their inferior blood tainted this place Drax thought as one of the scientists was giving a spirited effort in trying to crawl away to safety. The primitive environment suit that he was wearing was sopping wet with blood seeping out through a long, deep slice to his back, he whimpered pitifully with each and every movement due to the excruciating pain his wound was causing him.

The Dracos decided to have a little fun, and with a wide grin, deftly made his way over the fallen corpses to where this strange creature crawled in a desperate bid to escape the slaughterhouse.

He nonchalantly kicked the scientist in the ribs, unimpressed. The body sprawled across the floor, a loud whimper made the Dracos smile, now this was entertainment, he thought. He allowed the creature to continue on its hopeless bid for safety, before viciously kicking it a second time, a weak but nevertheless audible gasp of pain, emerged from its lips, Drax laughed in delight.

"Such pitiful creatures, they are squidgy, and die easily."

He picked up the struggling scientist by the wounds slashed across its back, causing him to scream out in intense pain, and almost losing consciousness altogether. This sent waves of delight through the Dracos commander. Before he placed the barrel of his eviscerator pistol against the scientists dark haired head, and pressed the trigger. A resounding crack echoed through the now silent room, as the disc sliced through Dieter Kalschacht's skull, before he flung the blood soaked body aside indifferently.

"See, easily killed."

The other remaining Kallan warriors stood and watched appreciatively at a master at work, before drax turned his weapon on them, and gunned all three of them down in cold blood, their bodies slunk to the floor just ahead of him.

Two of the prey creatures had escaped, and he was going to be the one to finish this hunt personally.

Sergeant Rachthausen and Kathryn fled toward the blast doors, once there though, they had realised their mistake. In their hurry to escape the butchery, they had forgotten that private Anderson had earlier welded the doors shut, if they could not find a way though, those alien warriors would catch them for sure.

"Shit! we're trapped down here." The built up desperation and frustration plainly evident in his voice.

"There has to be something we can do?" Kathryn panted as she tried to regain her breath, she risked a look back, and was reassured that nothing was following them, at least nothing she could see anyway.

There was one last thing Rachthausen could try, he pulled out the final grenade from his webbing and with some insulation tape attached it to the blast door itself, right over the scorch marks of the weld that Anderson had done.

The blast of the grenade might just be enough to crack the weld and get the doors to open, it was a long shot, but the only one he had.

"Get ready to run." He said as he pulled the pin from the affixed grenade.

"Run!" he shouted as he sprinted away from the door, Kathryn ran with him, they had just four seconds before the grenade went off. There was an almighty explosion as the grenade detonated. The explosion echoed down the entire length of the dark corridor, Drax heard the faint explosion even from where he was stood. "come out, come out, wherever you are." He whispered maniacally, as he clambered back inside the air ducting, he was smarter than to risk the wide open corridor.

Sergeant Rachthausen checked over the weld line in the light given off by the flare, luckily for them Anderson was a far better soldier than a welder, and it had cracked under the immense pressure of the exploding grenade.

Kathryn desperately pressed at the door control, just wanting to get out of there, get out of this nightmare, although she felt guilty about leaving the others behind. She had understood Rachthausen's descision in the end, if they stayed they would have wound up dead too. Finally, the door opened, and the two of them made their way through, pressing the control to close the giant doors behind them. They were free from Drax's clutches for now.

Michael was studying a computer enhanced representation of the ship that attacked the Copernicus, it definitely bore more than a passing resemblance to a Solarian ship, although the Solarian ship's looked sleeker, modern, and ultra-sophisticated. This too looked sleek and sophisticated, but not quite as modern, almost as if it was a throwback to an outdated design, a precursor to what the Solarians now have. He supposed that being constantly attacked, always on the move, then effectively disappearing for three hundred years. The Dracos no longer had the resources or the access to technology that the Solarians enjoy. He also wondered whether just plain jealousy was a part of the enmity the Dracos showed toward the Solarians. He also wondered just how old the Dracos ships really were, and how they had managed to survive for so long, alone, isolated from the rest of the galaxy.

Saying that, humanity was the same up until five years ago, blissful in ignorance, not knowing who or what surrounded us, the Krenaran war had changed all that. Changed humanities view of themselves, instead of being this one race carving out a small part of the galaxy to call their own, master of all they surveyed, they learned that they were, in fact, just one of many doing the exact same thing, a small backwater people just trying to get along. This more than anything finally broke through mankind's arrogance, and as a people, we had come to appreciate just how humble we really are.

"One weird lookin' ship eh cap'n." Commander Quinn Kinraid said as he stood over him.

"Not really, it has some design similarities with conventional Solarian shipping, but that's about it."

"you've bin' staring at'tat picture fur' five minutes, is everythin' alright, cap'n?" Kinraid asked with a hint of concern to his voice.

"Everything is fine, commander, I've just been thinking, that's all."

"Well don't you go givin' yerself a hernia now Michael." the Irishman said with a mischievous smile.

"I wonder Quinn, if E.O.C.A ever had a civil, and the E.D.F was forced to fight itself, would we be able to survive it, like the Solarians did?"

"Pray it'll never happen, sir."

"I hope so Quinn."

"Asteroid field coming up ahead, captain," Eldathar announced from his position.

Michael returned to his chair, "okay, drop us out of plasma drive, slow to sub-light speed."

"Slow to sub-light, aye." The Solarian pilot confirmed.

A gigantic bright white flash opened up, heralding the Liberties exit from plasma drive, the ship slowly glided at sub-light velocity.

"We're approaching the outer dust clouds," Kinraid announced.

"Slow to one half sub-light speed, and put it up on the viewer."

E.D.F Chronicles – Eye of the Dracos

The viewscreen shimmered into life, displaying the wide asteroid field. It was some three light years across and two wide, one of the biggest in the sector.

"This is the Van Aiken asteroid belt," Michael knew without even looking, the Krenaran's famously used it as a hidden staging post, before going on the devastate the Malthus colony during the war.

"Can't we go around it?" Logan Jones asked.

"If we do, we'll have to detour another seven light years to skirt it, the scientists may not have that long," Michael replied.

They had no choice but to go through it, the thing is, Michael thought. There were rumours that the Krenarans had mined the asteroid fields.

"Cut all power, except for minimal power to the thrusters and engine, activate the graviton shields, take us in, slowly."

Eldathar gently leaned forward on the throttle arm, as console went black, all except the emergency running lights winked out, the fusion cannon was powered down, even the ships main engine died down to a shadow of its normal brightness.

Michael prayed that the old re-programmed Krenaran IFF codes, the Solarians changed when they upgraded the Liberty might be enough to fool the mines into thinking she was on the same side. Although all the extra upgrades she was carrying might not, it would be touch and go.

The ship slowly crept forward through the thin veil of dust clouds, it was like a thin fog, made up of all the tiny chips and slivers of rock broken free from the larger asteroids colliding with one another, constantly pummelled over millions of years into a fine dust, gravity held the cloud in place, so that it formed a kind of long meandering fringe around the edge of the field. The Liberty gradually emerged through this thin dust cloud, blocking the view of the larger and infinitely more dangerous obstacles beyond.

Gigantic asteroids were floating haphazardly with smaller ones, making it difficult for Eldathar to plot a steady course through; still the Solarian persevered.

He deftly guided the ship around a particularly large, crater strewn space rock, it was large enough to be classified as a planetoid. Michael witnessed several scorch marks, and what resembled metallic hull fragments clustered around a small area, he guessed the pirates who tried to gain a foothold after the Krenaran war ended, didn't figure on the mines strewn amongst the asteroids.

The Liberty glided deeper inside the field, flying in-between two other space rocks, it was an incredibly tight squeeze, and the audio warning of the collision detector blared from Eldathars console in alarm. The Solarian ignored the klaxon wailing at him, knowing the exact dimensions of the ship he was flying to the millimetre. He knew better than anyone which places the Liberty could go, and which ones it couldn't. The experience he had accumulated over the past five years of flying the vessel, and several hundred years of flying other craft, had told him the ship would get through.

What he hadn't counted on however, was the two mines, heading straight for them.

The Liberty had been lucky so far, it had already glided past half a dozen mines, no doubt fooled by the old Krenaran IFF signature, however these two were not so easily shaken off. The mines had detected the Liberty and were now picking up speed.

"Incoming mines, we 'ave two of the buggers coming in fast, impact in twenny seconds!" Kinraid shouted out in alarm.

"Ready a salvo of torpedoes, lock onto the mines and fire!" Michael gnashed his teeth, it would be close, Lieutenant Jones mashed the button on his gunnery console.

"Torpedoes away."

A bright flash erupted from the Liberties twin upper launchers, heralding the launch of the two high energy torpedoes straight towards the incoming mines, their sophisticated targeting systems quickly locked on to the targets, and they raced headlong toward it.

"Impact in three, two, one!"

E.D.F Chronicles – Eye of the Dracos

A gigantic, intensely bright fireball lit up an entire section of the asteroid field, before slowly dying down into blackness again.

Michael figured that the mines sensory nodes had probably malfunctioned, most likely due to lack of maintenance. It had been five years since the last Krenaran ship even thought about passing this way; things can happen in that time.

The Liberty cautiously advanced through the remainder of the field, flying under yet another large asteroid and around two more before the command crew got their first glimpses of starlight that lay beyond.

Then disaster struck.

Another mine raced toward the aft engine of the ship, zeroing in on the energy emitted by the powerful Solarian drive systems, the Liberty, defenceless from a rear attack, could do nothing. Eldathar strained at the controls, trying desperately to shake it off their tail within the limited confines of the field itself. However the mine was not to be shaken off this time, it hurtled towards the ship, skipped off its graviton shields in a clear wavy ripple effect, not dissimilar to looking through textured glass, then detonated in an almighty explosion.

Those onboard were thrown hard to the ground under the force of the impact, a flurry of sparks burst forth from overloaded circuits, Michael desperately held on to prevent being thrown from his seat. The red alert siren immediately sounded, to warn the crew they were under attack.

The whole ship had lurched diagonally forward under the immense force of the explosion, Eldathar fought hard to keep the wayward vessel under control, he knew if he lost control in this kind of environment they were all done for, as the Liberty would simply crash onto one of those asteroids out there. He barely managed to retain control of the ship, after it came within metres of slamming side on, to a large floating asteroid, the Solarian breathed a sigh of relief.

Michael resettled himself in his chair, "well, at least we know the new graviton shields work." He knew full well that if that was the Liberty of five years ago, they would all be playing harps right about now, "damage report!"

Kinraid took a moment to understand the data flashing across his console, "Both th' aft graviton generators 'r' down, th' force o' th' explosion overloaded both, it'll take anot'r minute or so to vent off th' excess energy from th' blast.

Luckily th' hull escaped major damage though, some minor 'lectrikel damage from overloaded circuits, but 'tat's about it, and no injuries."

"Good, have engineering teams repair any damage, and Eldathar, get us the heck out of here!" He shouted over the din of the wailing siren, his face was covered in a dark ruddy hue from the red alert lights.

"Aye, sir."

The Liberty flew under, around and above the few space rocks remaining, and out through the thin veil of dust the other side, finally the full inky, starry blackness was revealed to them once again.

"Resume course to rendezvous with the lander, maximum plasma drive."

"Aye, sir." Eldathar replied as he punched in the controls to activate the Liberties plasma drive systems again.

The small ship accelerated to full sub-light speed, before firing a burst of bright plasma energy, opening up the plasma wake in an intense burst of energy, before racing through, and disappearing inside it. The wake closed as easily as it had opened.

Kathryn and the injured Rachthausen continued to hurry down the long semi-circular corridor, which skirted alongside the main aperture, again the deep rumbling began to reverberate throughout the facility as the collider geared up for yet another release of energy.

Kathryn wanted to tend to the sergeants badly bleeding arm, sustained from a slash from one of those evil dark warriors. They both knew they could not stop yet, the enemy commander was right on their tail, and would make mincemeat out them if they did.

They continued running down the dark corridor, trying to put as much distance between them and their pursuer as possible, Rachthausens flare was beginning to die down, and so he flung it to the side, and replaced it with the torch from Kathryn's weapon.

Finally, they came upon the second set of blast doors separating the military wing from the science wing.

Not knowing whether there would be an army of Dracos on the other side, Kathryn nervously, hesitantly pressed the control. The great metal doors in front of them slid open, revealing empty corridor once again. With a gentle sigh of relief, she and Rachthausen stepped through into this new unexplored area of the facility. The lights were still down, and it was still pitch black inside, they were travelling solely by torchlight. The low, deep rumbling of the collider, sounded ominous in the darkness.

They searched for somewhere, anywhere to hide, to give Kathryn tide to tend to his wound, finally they came to a vast control room, full of complicated looking consoles, displays and systems, far larger than the one they had previously discovered. Setting Rachthausen down gently, she closed the door behind them, although she had no way of locking it, and no time now to find out how.

Kathryn took a small amount of what water they had left and bathed the wound with it, the laceration was deep, almost to the bone, Rachthausen flinched as the water ran over the cut. She tore off a strip of plain white cloth from the arm of her coat and slowly, gently began to wrap the strip of cloth around Kinraid's blood soaked upper arm with a practiced skill. The sergeant looked up at her as she continued to tend to him, she had a sweet vulnerability about her, such a kind person, often going without herself in her effort to care for others. Rachthausen knew he had feelings towards her, and also knew that those feelings had grown the more time he had spent with her. She was far more than just a fellow officer to be protected now, that both scared him and enamoured him in equal measure.

Finally, he could stand it no longer, for too long had he put what he wanted to say off, and he might not get another chance. "If we are to die here, will you grant me one last request, So that I may die without regret?"

"What's that?" She asked while she finished tying the makeshift bandage tightly around his arm, making him wince and gasp in pain once again.

"Kiss me."

Kathryn was shocked, taken aback, yet not overtly so, she was more surprised that Rachthausen had developed the same feelings for her, that she had been suppressing all this time.

"If you do not want to, I understand," he said a little sheepishly.

Ian J Smethurst

Kathryn could suppress her urges no longer, she was attracted to him, wanted him, from the first time they landed on the planet and were stuck in this predicament together. Desire burned within her as though he had just poured petrol on the spark she was carrying for him. She quietly, slowly leaned down beside him; the lights from a dozen consoles gave the room a kind of hypnotic kaleidoscope effect. She searched his features; saw his longing for her in his eyes. She leaned in closer, fixated on those gorgeous blue orbs of his, their lips touched and she kissed him deeply, longingly and passionately. A gentle warm wave of pleasure filled her body, and at the same time a weight had been lifted, the weight of her own suppressed emotions, she could hide it no longer, she felt in love with him.

She was now torn, a battle was raging inside her as well as outside, her head was telling her that she was a Lieutenant commander and should not be fraternised with junior ranks, even one as comely as this. Her heart however, was telling her that she wanted him so badly that it hurt.

Gently he released her form their tender embrace, "Now, I can have no regrets."

Outside the base, the rumbling reached a critical peak once again as the base shot forth its fury in the form of another gigantic stream of intensely bright energy out through the planets atmosphere and through the darkness of deep space, illuminating the three black Dracos ships orbiting nearby, as though three dark spiders come to consume the planet.

The two other craft sent down a pair of assault landers each, four small black craft arced down through the planets upper atmosphere trailing fire from the heat of entry. They had cleared the majority of interlopers from their ancient facility, now it was time to claim the planet the structure was built on, in the name of the Dracos.

The sleek, advanced looking assault landers cut through the thick layer of methane cloud, the diffused sunlight from the Aurigan sun glinted off their bullet shaped fuselage, sickle wings, and upper engine pods, as they gently touched down on the surface, throwing up an immense cloud of dust as they did so.

Dracos Kallan warriors quickly emerged, charging down the access ramps of the craft and surrounding the immediate area, within seconds forty more elite Kallan warriors dominated the area around the landed craft. The time for the ultimate Dracos victory was at hand, their squad leaders barked out orders for those under their command to fan out along the ground near to the base. While another squad enters to find out what Drax has been doing inside.

"Landers from the Blade of Rhovanion, and the Vengeance of Kelmarroth have successfully landed on the surface." A junior Dracos officer announced.

Kaelleth held his head in hands, not believing how badly this was all going, twenty of his finest men were sent down there, to clear out a few pitiful interlopers, now just one Dracos remained. One so utterly devoted to finishing the hunt, that he had turned mad, and may very well end up dead too. Yes the facility was all but secure, but it had cost the Dracos dearly in blood to do so.

He looked up from the centre seat of the Flame of Celthris, "understood," he managed after a short pause, "keep me informed." He really just wanted to put this whole sorry mess behind him now, and return to his home within the warm subterranean depths of Corvandris once again.

The Liberty was closing in on the small Stockholm class lander that carried Colonel Nikolai Vargev and his elite team of E.D.F commandoes. Michael could now see the olive green coloured square looking craft in the Liberties viewer. He had seen this type of craft a hundred times before, used extensively in the Krenaran war, but he never got over just how ugly the thing looked.

They resembled little more than a flying brick, in fact that was their nickname amongst the soldiers of the troop division and the navy alike. It was wide, yet short and stubby; from its central crew compartment, which took up the majority of the tiny vessel. Two winglets jutted out, on the edge of each was a powerful gravitic engine, rotatable through ninety degrees. At the back of the main crew compartment were two large stabilisation fins, which served as the crafts tail when in a planetary atmosphere. There was a very small reinforced command bubble located at the front of the thing, about three quarters the way from the bottom, looking like the top of a small cut diamond jutting out from the front of the craft, yet devoid of any kind of sparkle or lustre. It did however, provide the pilot an unparalleled view of the terrain when flying within a planetary atmosphere.

"Open a channel to the lander," Michael said.

"Channel open," Kinraid replied.

"E.D.F lander, this is Liberty, we are alongside you, request permission to soft dock to allow crew transfer."

The Liberty, being one hundred and forty metres long, utterly dwarfed the tiny twenty metre long lander. One of the few things the Liberty did dwarf, Michael thought with a smile.

Colonel Vargev's voice came over the speakers, a voice Michael recognised, but one in which he hadn't heard from in five long years. "This is lander alpha-two-niner, glad to hear your voice Liberty, we are ready for soft docking procedure."

Michael was surprised to find that the lander could only communicate via speakers, although he quickly remembered that the Stockholm class, only had one long range radio transceiver. He guessed the troop division didn't really go for complex electronics that could go wrong, they preferred their equipment rugged, simple and survivable.

"Err, cap'n." Kinraid spoke, "ya' do realise, 'tat the Liberty has never performed a soft dockin' manoeuvre before don't 'ya, we really don't know how this is gonna' go."

"We'll be fine," Michael replied confidently as he turned toward his pilot, "Eldathar, we need to stay alongside that lander, and our docking hatches need to come within five metres exactly of one another, think you can do it?"

The Solarian nodded, then set to concentrating on making the tiniest of movements in the pilot's chair. Banking the Liberty very gently, so that the two ships hull's came closer and closer together, the proximity alert went off once again, as slowly they continued to drift closer until it seemed as though their hulls would touch. Eldathar frowned in concentration, his blue Solarian features flushing a deep purple as he concentrated ever harder on the smallest of movements he was making with his arms. Eventually he stopped all movement and proclaimed proudly, "Five metres, captain."

"Excellent work," Michael replied.

Docking with a Stockholm class lander was proving to be an exceptionally tricky affair, part of the landers wing was now holding steady, just a few feet above the Liberties sloped hull. If either ship deviated from their manoeuvre, even by the tiniest of amounts, it could mean disaster for both.

"Okay, now extend the port docking extension, and connect to the hatch on the lander."

"Aye, sir." Eldathar replied as he keyed in a few controls on the monitor in front of him.

A tiny extension corridor snaked out from the port side of the Liberty, it was not solid like the rest of the ship, but flexible, instead made from a lightweight, but extremely strong carbon cloth. The temporary corridor un-coiled toward the lander, growing a little longer each time it did so, very similar to the old folding fabric rooves of twentieth century automobiles. The corridor continued to extend telescopically until it reached its maximum length of five metres, now within touching distance of the landers own hatch.

"Magnetise the hatch, and pressurise the corridor once connected." Michael whispered as he anxiously oversaw the complicated operation.

Eldathar silently worked at the controls again, and the flimsy temporary corridor suddenly latched on hard to the landers own hatch with a resounding 'clunk'.

The corridor stiffened noticeably as air was pumped into it, to pressurise it, making it safe for those on the lander to cross. Although it lacked the sophisticated artificial gravity systems that the Liberty and the lander enjoyed, it would serve its purpose.

"Pressurisation complete captain, we can now begin transferring the troops onboard." The solarian said with barely contained relief.

"Fantastic work, Eldathar," being a pilot himself, he knew just how tricky that manoeuvre was to accomplish. "open the port hatch, and let them through," Michael turned toward Kinraid, "send them the all clear, commander."

106

"Aye cap'n." Kinraid replied, "message sent; and received."

Michael smiled down at Eldathar manning the pilots chair quietly, still concentrating hard on maintaining the equidistance and speed vital to a successful crew transfer. If the lander accidentally increased its speed by even a fraction, it could tear the delicate temporary corridor right off the hull of the Liberty, causing a devastating explosive decompression across the entire deck. If the lander slowed or the Liberty accelerated, the Liberties hull could collide with the landers, destroying it and potentially crippling the Liberty as well.

One by one, the commandoes all carrying their gear and full breathing apparatus for the mission ahead, began to float weightlessly across this small, cramped, cold corridor. Michael watched from the viewscreen as their tiny bodies floated across to the Liberty. With their camouflaged combat fatigues, helmets, black boots, their packs and heavy weaponry, they looked oddly conspicuous amongst the royal blue naval uniforms and Solarian uniforms the crew of the Liberty wore. It was like they didn't really belong in space, these were E.D.F commandoes, the most highly trained fighting force humanity possessed, armed to the teeth. They had but one purpose, to fight and to win, on whichever planet they were assigned.

E.D.F Chronicles – Eye of the Dracos
9. The landing

Once all the commandoes were safely aboard, the link separated from the lander and retracted back inside the Liberties own hull, where it resealed itself, an armoured hull panel gently slid over it, in order to hide the weak point and maintain the warship's stealth abilities.

The tiny lander banked slowly away from the Liberty, as the dark, angular, wedge shaped craft powered up its main engines and glided gently away from the small craft.

"Set course for the Auriga system, bearing zero-one-seven degrees, elevation twelve."

"Understood, captain." Eldathar replied as he worked the control again to manoeuvre the Liberty into position, the ship banked left slightly, the intense electric blue of its main engines and thrusters flared brightly in the blackness of space, as the ship swung quickly around.

"Maximum plasma drive."

The Liberties main engine flashed brightly as the ship rapidly accelerated to maximum sub-light speed before activating its plasma drive engine, shooting forth an incandescent blue beam of plasma, which collided in an intense flash of bright white energy, slowly coalescing into the swirling plasma wake. The Liberty leapt through it at full speed, and onwards to its final destination.

Michael prayed they were not too late.

Nikolai Vargev strode onto the familiar looking bridge of the Liberty, a place he had not visited for five years. It had changed little in that time, the last he set foot here, he was involved in the mission to prevent an assassination plot at the hands of the rogue Krenaran agent, Lathiel. That all seemed like a long time ago now. While Michael was forty years old, Nikolai was almost ten years his senior, a forty nine year old commando; despite his advancing years, the big Russian could still mix it with the best of them, he strode over to an old friend still sat in the centre seat.

"Hello comrade, pleased to see me?"

Ian J Smethurst

Michael swivelled in his seat, unaware of the approach of the commando colonel, "Nikolai Vargev!" Michael announced with a broad grin, his old friend was with him again.

"How are ya' buddy?" He said as he almost leapt out of his seat to give the big Russian a tight hug.

"Not too bad, yourself?"

"Oh you know how it is, come we have much to discuss." Michael said, beckoning for the colonel to follow him to his personal quarters, just off the bridge itself, "Kinraid you have the bridge."

"Understood, Cap'n," Kinraid replied from his station.

The two men made their way across the busy bridge of the Liberty, and through a set of sliding doors that led into Michael's personal quarters.

He sat at his glass-topped desk, strewn with the usual maintenance reports that always seemed to filter through to his quarters; Nikolai sat opposite.

"Coffee?"

"Yes, I would like one thanks."

Michael walked over to a small personal drinks synthesiser, and keyed in a command for two latte's.

"I guess this mission must have come as quite a shock?" Michael asked as the machine did its work.

"Kind of, we have been training in simulated hostage rescue missions for the last three months on Gamma Aurigulon, but we didn't expect to go into a real one. They only told me the gist of what has happened, but nothing more."

"That's because, to be honest, they don't know. All E.D.F command really knows is that the Copernicus; a small survey ship, doing a routine survey in the Auriga system had found some unusual alien structures on the third planet of the system. A team was sent down to investigate, the station somehow re-activated itself. Then, within a couple of hours, boom! The Copernicus was blasted into space dust by some unknown alien ship, which bears more than a passing resemblance to a Solarian battlecruiser."

"So the science team are still on the surface?"

"As far as we know, yes."

"How many?"

"Sixteen, although when I looked at the timestamp on the logs, it showed the information to be three days old now."

"So, we could go in there to them already dead," Nikolai stroked his dark moustache in thought.

"Quite possibly, Kathryn Jacobs was the one leading the science team on the surface."

Nikolai remembered Kathryn fondly as a flicker of a smile came to his lips, he first encountered her at Delta base during the Krenaran war, rescuing her from the besieged and battered station, she was out of her mind with fear. They crossed paths again when he and Michael fought the Krenaran commander Alax together. It was Kathryn who had patched him up after that. Both men knew that they would never stand idly by, and let Kathryn die on that forlorn alien world, no matter what problems she had in the past, they knew they had to get her and the others out of there.

"These aliens, any other info?"

"I spoke with Eldathar about that, it turns out these aliens call themselves, the Dracos."

"Huh, nice name." Nikolai grunted sceptically.

"It gets better, these Dracos were once a part of the Solarians, in fact they are Solarians, they were a radical sect promoting violence, extreme pain, and torture. The Solarians, kicked them off their homeworld, and systematically hunted them down like dogs, throughout their space."

"A little harsh for the Solarians," Nikolai interjected, "they must have really pissed them off."

"From what I have been able to gather, three hundred years ago they attempted a coup of the Solarian government, when it was defeated, they chased them away."

"Well, that'll do it alright." Nikolai shrugged.

"These Dracos have been living in isolation ever since, slowly re-building themselves, strengthening their own military. They only showed up to destroy the Copernicus after the base activated, this facility has been shooting massively powerful streams of energy out into space, and I'm pretty sure that's what attracted them. It seems very convenient that within the space of a couple of hours they show up, despite being unheard of for three hundred years."

"Like a giant, come get me sign?"

"Exactly."

"The thing is though, where that one ship has come, there might be more of them out there."

Michael passed Nikolai his cup, "thanks," he said as he took a sip. "It looks to me, like the odds of finding anyone alive down there are slim to none, and these Dracos like inflicting pain and torturing those they come across."

"Its more than that, Eldathar says that to them, they treat it as an artform, they revel in it."

"So, we are dealing with an isolationist, probably paranoid fledgling empire, who just love to maim and torture, and possibly using some form of old Solarian technology."

"That about sums it up."

"I would say the odds of finding anyone alive after three days of being up against that, would be along the lines of, slim, to you've got to be fucking kidding me. Do you even know just how screwed we are?"

"I know, but we have to try anyway." Michael sighed deeply.

Vargev studied him for a moment, "There's more isn't there?"

Michael paced the room, peering out through the oversized window into the translucent swirling multi-hued mass, that was the plasma wake. "Things have changed Nikolai." He stared out from the viewport, "since peace broke out, it seems that there is less and less need for a dedicated warship like the Liberty anymore, apart from the occasional escort run or anti-pirate sweep. We've just been upgraded with these new graviton shields, great, I thought. Until I realised it was just as a test bed for a new secret project. It's as though the Liberty has become little more than an afterthought, a glorified lab rat, so that its technology can be disseminated through the fleet"

Nikolai studied Michael, feeling his frustration, "The Liberty is *still*, the most advanced and one of the most powerful ships in the entire navy. This ship is absolutely unique because it was not built by human hands, we don't have the skill or the technology to make more Liberties. But that is not to say the fleet cannot benefit from her; this ship became a legend through the Krenaran war, its crew heroes. The memory of this ship and its crew will never fade in the minds of the people. Peace is never a good time for a soldier, especially ones who are forged in the fires of the battlefield. When the time comes, the E.D.F will need good, strong troops once again, and the navy will need the Liberty."

Vargevs lucid response got Michael thinking, his features softened as he turned back to face the colonel, "You know what, you're right," he said with a gentle smile, "Thank you."

The two men headed out onto the bridge, Michael re-took his seat from Kinraid.

"I see you *still* haven't got a haircut," Vargev teased as he eyed Kinraid's neatly pony tailed ginger curls.

"Get away wi' ya', ya' cheeky old bugger ye'" Kinraid replied, smiling back at the colonel.

"Oh, I almost forgot to mention, we have set up temporary quarters for my men in the main cargo hold. We've also brought aboard a couple of crates of heavy weapons and ammunition for the mission."

"No problem." Michael replied.

Vargev left the bridge and headed to the cargo hold himself, to brief his men on the new intelligence, he had just gleaned from Michael.

"Come on, we'd better keep on moving." Kathryn said as she got back to her feet.

Rachthausen hefted his weapon and began to make a move with her, the doors slowly opened to reveal the dark form of Drax stood before them, the scarlet light from the lenses on his helmet seemed to glow with a crazed light now. "Going somewhere?"

Both Kathryn and Rachthausen froze in terror, as their pursuer made ready to level his eviscerator pistol. Kathryn dropped to her knees and shone her torch directly at the Dracos commander. The beam of light was enough to temporarily blind the delicate eyesight of the Dracos, although he had managed to fire off a single shot, the small eviscerator disc whipped through the air, although his aim was off, it embedded harmlessly into a computer console barely inches away from Rachthausen's head.

Kathryn fired her own pistol in response, but Drax had already dived into the cover of darkness on the other side of the wall. The energy pulse thumped into the wall of the corridor, causing a small spray of sparks.

"Come on!" Rachthausen shouted, as the two of them sprinted out of the control room, and down the long corridor to safety. Drax was nowhere to be seen.

As they ran, Kathryn managed to ask between breaths, "How did you know he wouldn't attack us?"

"You blinded him, at least temporarily, he'll hide now until his vision clears again, which could take a while if he is sensitive to bright light, like Kalschacht said he was. He can't attack what he cannot see."

Unbeknowst to the two escaping survivors, that was exactly what Drax was doing, he had taken cover amongst a small recess, near to the second set of blast doors, while he waited for his sight to clear.

His eyes burned, and fluid streamed from them, he cursed under his lips in a maddened rage. He knew he had to remove his helmet, albeit briefly, to allow the cool air circulating around the base to cool his streaming eyes. He pressed a small catch just under the chin, and the fully enclosing black helmet separated down the centre via a pair of tiny hinges, hidden beneath small armour plates above his crown. Grasping the front of the helmet with one hand, and the rear with another, he slowly pulled the helmet out wide enough in order to release his pale skinned head.

113

E.D.F Chronicles – Eye of the Dracos

The cool air was welcoming, though he cursed his luck that he had not been able to end the hunt right there, if that pitiful female hadn't blinded him, her would have already been on his way back to the lander, having eradicated the taint of the interlopers.

He wiped at his irritated eyes with his gloved hand, managing to wipe away some of the tear fluid, he blinked as his vision slowly began to return to normal, he could just begin to make out the delicate panelling of the corridor wall opposite him. Snapping back into action, he clipped his battlehelm back on, running a cursory systems check on the display attached to right arm. He was glad he did, he had just over one percent of power remaining from the power cells contained in his suit, they were designed to last for seventy two hours, without the need to recharge. That gave him around one hour before his suit shuts down completely, and would need to be recharged from a Dracos docking station either on the lander or on his ship.

If the suit did shutdown, he would lose all the functions of his helmet, together with the silencer attached to his wrist, and the magnetic charge that allowed to cling to the walls and ceiling. Rendering him suddenly very vulnerable. He would have to finish this hunt quickly, he no longer had time for games. His vision had now cleared sufficiently so that he could see properly, so he immediately set after his quarry once more.

Kathryn and Sergeant Rachthausen made it to the end of the corridor where they came across a second elevator.

"Maybe it will take us to the surface?" Kathryn asked.

"I doubt it, underground facilities like this usually only have one way in, and one way out, its easier to defend that way. There must be an emergency escape hatch though, to be used in the event of a fire or some other disaster."

"It's worth a try."

"We have to get off this floor anyway," Rachthausen looked nervously over his shoulder, he could see nothing in the pitch blackness.

The elevator automatically stopped in front of them, exactly like the first one did, the two of them stepped inside.

Drax however, had taken a different route, throwing caution to the wind he raced up the facilities air circulation ducts, and, using the magnetics within his suit, was climbing swiftly up an air shaft that supplied oxygen to the floor above. The gentle breeze buffeting his suit produced by powerful pumps within the oxygen storage tank over a hundred metres below him, was soothing as he climbed. He knew where his prey was heading, and was determined to cut them off.

The elevator stopped on the floor above, Kathryn and Rachthausen exited and looked around this new unexplored floor. It had basically the same layout as the others, one long wide corridor, with a plethora of rooms tailing off it, for various purposes.

"If I remember the plans correctly," Rachthausen said, thinking aloud, "I'm sure there was an emergency escape hatch located on this floor somewhere, it was how those Dracos, managed to get in, try looking for a panel or a large hatch." The sergeant suggested.

The two of them searched frantically for the panel covering the hatch that would guide them to safety on the surface, though in the darkness they could find nothing. Eventually while searching, they found their way into an elaborate, plush office with a thick black granite table.

Two black armoured boots slammed heavily into the sergeants chest, sending him sprawling to the ground. Kathryn tried to bolt for the door, however a tiny metal spike like projectile attached to a thin wire wrapped itself around her arm.

Drax retracted the silencer as he jumped and clung back onto the ceiling, Rachthausen was still dazed from the blow he received to his chest, the wire shot back with such a force it threatened to tear Kathryn's arm from its socket, she screamed aloud in pain as she was forcibly hurled to the floor, landing heavily.

Drax hissed his anger at the pair who had eluded him, the device uncurled from Kathryn's arm and fixed itself back in his silencer.

Rachthausen got to his feet, and drew his combat knife, he knew he was hopelessly outmatched by Drax. Nevertheless, it might buy just enough time for Kathryn to escape.

"Kathryn, get out of here!" He shouted more forcefully than he intended.

She got back to her feet again, hobbling from a bruised thigh suffered from the fall, "What about you?"

"Don't worry about me, just run!"

Kathryn turned to leave, watching the sergeant square up to the vicious black suited alien ahead of him, the red eyes shone menacingly in the darkness.

"Kathryn I will always love you," Rachthausen said softly.

Sorrow welled up from deep within her, a tear ran down her gentle cheek as she realised that Rachthausen was sacrificing himself so that she may live. She was torn asunder as the two combatants stabbed and sliced at one another. Her love, the one person she really, truly loved was destined to die for her, at that point, that very second, she wanted to die too.

"Get out of here!" Rachthausen repeated as he grappled with Drax.

Kathryn could say nothing, but whisper a faint, almost imperceptible, "I'll always love you," before running headlong down the corridor, away from her nightmare.

Rachthausen was the stronger of the two, yet significantly less agile than Drax, the sergeant managed to hurl the Dracos commander to the floor, landing with a heavy 'thunk' Rachthausen followed up by trying to stab the Dracos warrior. Drax however was far quicker and deftly swept the sergeants legs from under him. The heavy, burly sergeant toppled backwards over the granite desk itself.

Drax hissed again, pure hate in his voice as he advanced, slowly, purposefully toward the sergeant, who struggled to get back to his feet. The maddened Dracos lunged with his wristblades at him with such speed they could scarcely be seen, though Rachthausen managed to parry the frenzied attack with his own blade. The sheer force of the clash of blades sent them both staggering backwards.

Drax swiped his blades at him again, hacking and slashing in a whirlwind of deadly blade strikes, he launched himself acrobatically into the air, latching onto walls and ceilings to launch yet more blows. Rachthausen was putting up a brave defence, he had managed to parry the worst of the onslaught, though Drax was fighting like a madman, a rabid wolf, launching attack after attack, ultimately however a few slashes had made it through the sergeants desperate guard, he was bleeding from several nicks to his chest and arms, and was slowly weakening.

The Dracos aimed a vicious swinging kick, catching the sergeant square in the chest again, and sent him tumbling to the ground, his fatigues now stained and torn in several places from the cuts he had sustained.

"This is too easy," the Dracos commander jeered, "this is no sport."

Rachthausen panting heavily, staggered back to his feet. Through the haze of pain filling his mind he just hoped he had bought enough time for Kathryn.

Drax kicked him hard in the ribs, sending him sprawling across the ground once again, tumbling over and over, another kick landed, then another, and another a deadly torrent of blows rained down on the badly weakened sergeant, and Drax threatened to kick him to death. Blood streaked down Rachthausen's face from a nasty cut on his forehead, his ribs felt like they were on fire, he feared that several were broken. Yet fixed the Dracos commander beating him to a bloody pulp, with a defiant stare, the longer he was taking to finish him, the more time he was buying for Kathryn.

Drax kicked him hard again, and the sergeant let out a small whimper of pain, a sound that delighted the Dracos warrior, "this is starting to be amusing after all."

He kicked him one last time, causing the sergeant to gasp aloud in pain, dropping his guard for just a second, drax took full advantage and slammed his fist into the sergeants injured arm, Rachthausen screamed in agony.

Drax was delighted in hearing the screams of his enemies torment and anguish, this was his time, the thing he loved about being a Dracos commander, it made him feel alive to hear his enemies screams, just as it did his ancestors.

Finally, the kicks and torture stopped, Rachthausen was a bloody mess lying in a foetal position on the floor, his combat fatigues sodden with blood, the floor slippery. Drax gripped the sergeants matted hair, pulled his head back exposing his neck, and whispered, "playtimes over." Before slicing open the sergeants throat with his lethally sharp wristblades, and shoving the body to the ground.

He left the office with a maniacal laugh, as Rachthausen's corpse slowly bled to death across the office floor.

"We are entering the Auriga system," Eldathar pointed out, after studying the real-time data from the starmap laid out in the console in front of him.

"Understood, prepare to drop out of plasma drive on my mark, we need to get as close as possible, before we re-enter normal space."

The Solarian pilot silently nodded his understanding, a tense few seconds passed as Michael waited to give the order.

"Now!"

A blindingly bright flash of energy heralded the re-emergence of the Liberty into normal space once again. The deep beige coloured sphere that was Auriga III was clearly visible ahead of them, together with its twin moons.

"Excellent work," Michael showed his praise for the crew, at least now he hoped they wouldn't be blasted into space dust before they even reached the planet.

"I've got some bad news for ya' cap'n!" Kinraid said as he studied his sensory console, "we 'ave 'tree unknown alien ships orbiting the planet, so we 'ave. Not just the one; and they all match the one 'tat destroyed the Copernicus."

So Nikolai was right, there were more of them out there, "any chance they have detected us?"

"Two of them are breakin' orbit, heading straight for us, the other is maintaining its orbit."

Damn, it looks like they can see through the stealth abilities of the hull, "looks like we are going to have to fight our way through this one."

"I would advise caution," Eldathar replied from the pilot's chair, "Even though those ship are based on old Solarian technology. They are still powerful, and it looks like they have been doing a few upgrades of their own over the years."

"Enemy ships 'ave now broken orbit, and 'r' now changing course 't' intercept."

"Full alert status, full power to main engines and thrusters, charge main fusion cannon, and activate the high energy launchers. Initiate graviton shielding system."

"Aye sir," Logan Jones replied as he frantically worked at the tactical console, the bridge darkened noticeably and red alert lights reflected off the darkened consoles, bathing the entire command centre in a deep ruddy glow.

"Fusion cannon is powering up, torpedoes are standing by, main engines and thrusters are at full power, graviton shields are charging." Logan informed Michael, who watched the dark shapes of the enemy craft approach intently. Their command sections swept forward sharp and angular, like a serpent poised to strike.

Michael gnashed his teeth in defiance, "If they want a fight, then by god they are going to get one!"

The Dracos ships, *blade of Rhovanion* and *vengeance of Kelmarroth* advanced upon the tiny E.D.F cruiser, at over four times its size each, the Dracos commanders on both ships figured this was going to be a short battle indeed.

"Ready all weapons and defensive systems, order our escort to do the same." Senergid, Calvaris of the *Blade of Rhovanion* ordered, the flagship of the entire Dracos fleet was not about to be embarrassed by this little upstart pipsqueak.

"Dracos ships continue to close, they'll be in weapons range in ten seconds," Logan informed.

"Eldathar, send the ship in a spinning barrel roll on my mark."

"Sir?"

"I know what I'm doing."

"Err…aye, sir."

The dark predatory hulls of the alien craft continued to loom ever larger in the display, then suddenly, a burst of bright flashes erupted from their torpedo batteries.

"We have incoming!" Logan announced in alarm.

"Eldathar, now!" Michael shouted as he clung onto his seat.

The Liberty corkscrewed toward the alien craft in a whirling blur of black hull and blue light, the crew onboard fought to hang on as artificial gravity systems struggled to keep up with the frenetic rate at which the ship was spinning.

"Multiple torpedoes, fire!" Michael shouted, as he clung onto his seat.

Half a dozen high energy torpedoes shot forth from the spinning Liberties own launchers, in a cacophony of bright light as the warheads streaked to their targets.

Some collided with the approaching Dracos torpedoes, resulting in gigantic, bright explosions that lit up large areas of space in flame as the Liberty spun past towards its attackers. The other warheads, raced toward the Dracos ships themselves, streaking toward their targets and smashing home with incredible force, a bright green energy haze formed around the dark crescent shaped hulls of the alien craft.

The Liberty itself raced between the two giant alien vessels, aboard the *Blade of Rhovanion,* Dracos warriors and crew alike were flung to the ground, as Senergid clung to his seat for dear life, showers of sparks burst forth from damaged and overloaded circuitry. He couldn't believe it, whatever that thing was, it was no ordinary ship, it hit with the force of a Dracos prowler beast.

"Damage report."

"Shields at sixty percent, minor damage to port thrusters."

The tiny Liberty had shot past both ships, and was now heading toward the planet itself, "Follow that thing!" Senergid shouted to his men.

120

The Liberty continued onward to the planet, "okay, you can level us out, now." Michael said.

Eldathar did so, much to the relief of the crew, who had been clinging for all they were worth to their stations and chairs, many of which now had a healthy dose of motion sickness.

"Enemy ship status?" Michael asked.

Kinraid studied his display, "both 'ave suffered minor damage, they're coming around to intercept. 'Ya sure gave them a right sucker punch their eh!"

"Let's just hope they don't give us one in return." Michael replied, his lips pressed into a thin whisper as he thought. He was outnumbered, and outgunned, the only advantage he had was the Liberties speed and manoeuvrability, on top of all that, he had to get Nikolai's troops onto the surface in one piece.

"Head for the planet, maximum possible speed," he said, "Shot down the forward graviton emitters, and shunt the remaining power to the rear." That should help, he thought. Though he had no idea how long the graviton shields would stand up to a pounding from those two ships, he figured he would find out soon enough.

The two Dracos ships finished coming about and resumed their chase of the Liberty. "If he thinks he has escaped us, he is sorely mistaken," Senergid said, almost to himself, "Ready laser lances, and dark matter torpedoes, destroy that thing!"

The two craft opened fire on the Liberty now out-pacing them, Eldathar did his best to evade the withering fusillade of fire, torpedoes streaked out towards them, multiple violet flashes from laser lances lit up the space the tiny ship was flying through. Though even with the Solarian's skilful flying, the weight of fire was just too great; several torpedo and lance hits slammed into the Liberty, causing it to shudder violently under the impacts, several crewmembers were launched from their consoles.

"Graviton shields are taking a hammering!" Logan shouted over the din of explosions and weapons fire.

Another hit slammed into the ship, sending more crewmen flying from their seats.

"Hold your course, Eldathar!" Michael shouted.

The Solarian strained to keep the bucking ship steady under the intense barrage.

"Shield status!" Michael shouted as another impact threatened to hurl him from his seat.

"Graviton shields at forty percent and weakening, they won't be able to last much longer before they have to shut down to vent off excess energy," Logan replied.

Another barrage hammered into the Liberty, sending sparks flying out from a ruptured console, smoke billowed out from the fried circuitry.

"Twen'y seconds until we hit the atmosphere!" Kinraid announced

Just a little bit longer, Micheal willed his ship on through clenched teeth, "ready two torpedoes, set them to timed detonation, five seconds each."

"What for?" Kinraid asked.

"Mines," Michael replied, "Fire!"

Logan pressed the fire control on his tactical console, "torpedoes away."

Two dumbfire torpedoes were launched lazily from the Liberties launchers, their engines did not ignite, and the ship hurtled straight past them, leaving them directly in the path of the pursuing Dracos ships.

Michael silently counted, three, two, one.

Both torpedoes detonated in a massive explosion, throwing up the familiar green haze around the Dark enemy cruisers, and rocking the Liberty itself in its violence.

"Both ships have taken damage to their forward shields, they are backing away, though still pursuing."

That should give us some breathing space, at least, Michael thought as he watched the deep beige of the planet fill the viewer.

"Atmospheric entry in five, four, three, two," Kinraid counted down as he watched the fast approaching atmosphere on the viewer.

The Liberties hull began to rapidly heat up as the ship entered the upper atmosphere of the planet, it was a familiar sight to Michael. He felt almost like he was reliving the giant battle of Gamma IV during the Krenaran war, where his ship crash landed on the planet surface. Enemy ships had chased them then too.

A violet energy flash shot past the Liberty and snapped him immediately out of his reverie, the shot coated the ship in a bright purple light it was so close. It hit a pocket of methane gas in the planet's atmosphere, the heat of the laser instantly detonated the dangerously flammable gas in an almighty explosion that ripped through the upper atmosphere, temporarily blinding the bridge crew in the process, a gigantic shockwave raced outwards toward the Liberty.

Michael strained to see in the brightness, watching in horror as the massive shockwave surged towards them, unable to do anything except shout, "brace for impact!"

The massive shockwave slammed hard into the ship, with all the force of a tidal wave crashing headlong into a beachhead.

Crewmen were thrown completely clear of their stations, landing hard onto the unforgiving deckplating, conduits ruptured in the intense impact, sparks and glass showered the crew, and fires broke out in a number of areas.

Smoke filled the bridge as Michael slowly, gradually picked himself back up amidst the debris of collapsed supports, broken girders and crackling power conduits. A combination of sweat and soot lined his features, as he coughed a hacking, dry cough.

The Liberty itself was spinning out of control; it had been thrown into a vertical spin as it careered through the atmosphere pulled along by the planet's own gravity.

Kinraid gradually took his seat, and studied his own flickering, partially working console, "Hull temperature exceedin' maximum tolerances, if we don't get the ship under control quickly, we'll burn up."

Eldathar strained for all he was worth against the controls, trying desperately to regain attitude control, "come on!" he shouted as he clenched his teeth.

The ship's wild careering through the atmosphere began to slowly stabilise, as the Solarian fought against the controls.

"Looks like we're through the worst of it, hull temperature's returning to normal," Kinraid announced.

Thank god for that, Michael thought letting loose a relieved sigh, as did the entire bridge crew. "Great work, Eldathar."

The Solarian risked a quick glance back at his captain, and smiled.

"Status report?" Michael asked.

Kinraid studied his instruments, "Graviton shields 'r' down, we 'ave some minor hull fractures, there 'r' some injuries amongst the crew. If it wasn't for those new fangled graviton shields, we'd all be toast; beggin' ya' pardon cap'n."

"I know, those graviton shields, have definitely proved their worth, what about those Dracos ships?" Michael asked as he wiped his brow with the sleeve of his uniform, leaving a dark smear across his forehead.

"They've both backed off, resumed orbit. Guess they didn't wanna' be on te' receivin' end 'o' that explosion."

"Guess so," Michael replied as he shook off his debris littered uniform, and brushed down his seat with his hand. The environmental control systems had kicked in and removed the smoke, small jets of carbon dioxide extinguished the remaining fires. Things slowly returned to normal as he surveyed the extent of the damage to his bridge.

Several consoles had completely exploded, leaving blackened twisted remains along the bridge perimeter, dark scorch marks lined the walls. Others, like Kinraid's were barely functioning, their flickering and buzzing a constant distraction. The snap and hiss of flailing damaged circuits from the roof hung limply, adding to the scene of desolation.

"There is nothing stopping them simply bombarding our position from orbit, should we ever land," Michael said.

"Not if we land close enough to the facility, I doubt they would risk firing on their own base," Eldathar suggested.

"Good idea," Michael smiled, "head for the base."

The Liberty flew over a windswept jagged mountain range, through a forest of strange alien looking trees, like enormous hyacinths their petals instead were leaves.

"With a carbon dioxide atmosphere like this, I guess photosynthesis must work backwards here," Kinraid said as he perused the viewscreen from his position, "instead of producing oxygen as a by-product, these plants must produce carbon dioxide instead."

The dark warship glided over a flat land, with what appeared to be a river meandering its way through it, the silvery sheen of the water reflecting the sunlight at them as they glided past.

"well now I know why the Dracos chose this planet, ample water supply."

"Yea' but for all we know, tat could be the only river for a t'ousand miles," Kinraid replied.

The sharp inwardly curving pylons of the Dracos structure became clearly visible on the horizon as the Liberty gently glided towards it.

"My god, the thing is gigantic, those pylons must be a good thousand metres tall," Michael gasped, indeed they were, and were visible for miles around, an enormous set of four focusing pylons, gently curving towards one another, exactly like a giant set of claws had sprouted out from the ground and was reaching up to pull the sky down. The sun was slowly setting on the horizon, bathing these mighty monoliths in stark shadow.

Michael touched a communications terminal on the arm of his chair, "Michael to Nikolai; have your men ready, we'll be touching down in around one minute."

"Understood," Nikolai said as he spoke into his helmet mic.

Colonel Vargev spoke to his arrayed commandoes one last time before the fighting commenced, "okay, as per the briefing, we'll be splitting up into two teams of ten men each, I'll be leading alpha team who will go in and storm the complex, bravo team will be providing close fire support. Razor, your in command of Bravo team."

"Sir, yes sir," the powerfully built Robert Jansen, A.K.A Razor replied.

"This is what we've trained for people, remember, don't let the enemy get too close. Intel says they have a lot of bladed weapons, and love to slice and dice, don't give them the opportunity. We all have motion scanners, and we have night vision attached to our breathing gear, so we should be able to see them just as well as they see us. They are very fast and highly acrobatic in combat, so watch yourselves."

"Yes colonel," they all shouted in unison.

"Let's show these bastards, who they are really messing with." Vargev grinned.

"ooragh!" came the loud reply.

Nikolai had armed his men heavily, and they all carried the high power, ubiquitous fourty four calibre armschlager heavy machine gun, which had proved to be so devastating to Krenaran troops during the war. In addition to this however, he had ordered his men to wear the new apex body armour, consisting of ultra tough carbon fibre plates hidden under their traditional camouflaged flak jacket. Each man had half a dozen grenades, a pulse pistol sidearm, and two men of bravo team also carried the slingshot, a rocket launcher equipped with deadly new dead aim missiles, a missile who's guidance system was so accurate, so finely tuned, it could lock onto and track a target, purely from its body heat. To save them being blown to pieces by their own missile, all commandoes wore a tiny microchip concealed deep within their chest armour, which allowed the missile to identify between friend and foe, the missile was not to be used where civilians would be present, as it could just as easily kill them. But on an open battlefield, was a formidable weapon.

"Commandoes, form up by the port access hatch."

"Yes, colonel!" The troops all shouted in unison, and as one the body of twenty men all marched their way through the confines of the ship, passed blown out, smashed consoles and damaged circuitry. The glass littering the deck plates crunched under their heavy military boots.

The Liberty swooped in fast, Michael saw the six Dracos assault landers all arrayed near to the structure, it was one headache he could do without. "Logan, target those landed ships, fire at will."

"Aye,sir."

The Liberty dived low and opened fire with its devastating fusion cannon, the raw power of the beam slammed into the first of the landers, tearing it to pieces in a fountain of twisted blackened debris, the bright incandescent blue beam raked the area tearing into the other craft just as easily as the first. Bright plumes of flame and explosions lit up the dusk sunset as onboard power cells and munitions ruptured, before the carbon dioxide rich atmosphere quickly quelled the blazing inferno of the wrecked craft. The wreckage however, still smouldered and sent out plumes of thick smoke into the darkening sky.

Michael could just about, faintly see the tiny black specks of Dracos warriors scurrying about on the surface below them.

A powerful blast rocked the Liberty, Eldathar fought to keep the ship stable, "The Dracos ships in orbit, are resuming their bloody firin' on us!" Kinraid shouted, stating the obvious.

"Quickly Eldathar, set us down near the landers, get us as close as possible to the structure." Michael said, he had a plan, he was going to use the smoke billowing out from the destroyed craft as cover for the landing.

"Lowering landing legs, gravitic engines to maximum, main engine thrust at five percent," Eldathar exclaimed.

The Liberty slowed to a virtual hover, its powerful gravitic engines kicking up great plumes of dirt and dust.

"Open the port hatch."

Kinraid pressed the port hatch release control on his console. The hatch depressurised, and then gradually opened.

"Go! Go! Go!" Nikolai shouted to his men, all of which had donned their breathing apparatus now.

E.D.F Chronicles – Eye of the Dracos

The twenty commandoes surged out from the Liberty, sprinting across the narrow stretch of open ground towards the smouldering wreckage.

The ground near to the Liberty erupted with a deafening explosion as a torpedo fired from orbit, ripped into it.

"Close the hatch, and get us airborne again, quickly!" Michael shouted his urgency, if they stayed too long on the ground they were a sitting duck for those shooting from orbit, and he didn't feel like dying today.

The Liberty quickly picked up speed as it took off once again kicking up a hale of dirt, dead foliage and various detritus, and raced through the atmosphere, as weapons fire from the three ships orbiting above poured down towards it. Eldathar continually jinked the ship in a zig-zag fashion to avoid the fusillade of laser lance fire and torpedoes streaking down towards the tiny ship.

"Eldathar, give it everything you've got!" Michael shouted as the viewscreen became littered with the violet slashes of weapons fire, and the occasional blinding flash of a torpedo explosion.

"Logan, how are the shields?"

"Just about finished recharging after venting off the excess energy of that last pounding we took."

"Shunt everything you can get your hands on to the shields, take it from non-essential systems, even environmental support if you have to!"

"Gotcha, captain." Logan worked furiously at his console, as he tried to divert every last scrap of energy he could muster into the shields.

The Liberty continued on its race through the atmosphere, charging towards its assailants, who were still busily pouring fire towards the small, but nimble warship.

"Is the main fusion cannon charged?"

"We'll have full power back in fifteen seconds, captain," Logan replied as he studied the power readout for the weapon from his console

That should give us just enough time to get a single shot away, before we emerge from the atmosphere, Michael thought, the Dracos were about to get a very nasty surprise, the thought made his lips curl into a wide grin.

Several laser lance shots slammed into the Liberty, the rippling transparent graviton field deflected the worst of the energy, still the impacts themselves violently rocked the ship, it felt like the ship was being pitched about amidst stormy seas. Michael held on as the vessel shook under the withering barrage of fire from the three Dracos ships slowly beginning to come into view ahead of it.

"Fusion cannon ready." Logan announced.

"Target the closest ship, fire!"

The fusion cannon roared its fury, an incandescent bright blue beam of utter destruction shot through what remained of the upper atmosphere and tore into the Dracos ship beyond with such force, that it spun the ship almost ninety degrees. Its shields flared violently under the sheer power of the impact, however it could not withstand the awesome fury of the Liberties fusion cannon for long. The shields withered and died, as the beam ripped straight through the *Vengeance of Kelmarroth's* command section, blasting it completely clear of its main hull. The ship listed almost inverted, as though a boxer just hit with a powerful uppercut, explosions ripped through its outer hull, as the vessel was dragged awkwardly down toward the planet. Caught helplessly within the gravitational pull of Auriga III, a few escape pods were visible jettisoning from the ship as its hull began to heat up in a bright fiery glow, before the entire vessel burst apart in a gigantic fireball within the planets upper atmosphere.

Senergid watched the destruction of the vengeance of Kelmarroth in stunned silence, as the tiny Liberty shot past once again.

"Head for one of the moons," Michael said.

"They'll only chase us again, so t'ey will." Kinraid replied.

"This time, I'm counting on it," Michael replied with a wide smile.

"Slingshot manoeuvre?"

"Exactly."

E.D.F Chronicles – Eye of the Dracos
10. The storming of the eye.

The chattering sounds of the commandoes weapons fire rang out in the darkening dusk sky. Bravo team were taking cover around the wreckage of the destroyed Dracos shuttles.

"Keep your fire trained on them!" Razor shouted over the comm. link to his men as he took aim and opened fire again with his armschlager, the heavy machine gun bucked and swayed in his hands as the rounds peppered the onrushing Dracos Kallan warriors, their reputation for being nimble fighters was well deserved, in fact, it was hard enough just to get a bead on them.

Nikolai's team was pinned down by the Dracos positions firing flurries of eviscerator discs at them.

"Tomahawk, Rapier, use you slingshots, see if you can get some fire on those Dracos pinning down alpha team."

"You got it sarge!" came the response.

The rest of the team covered them, as the two heavy weapons specialists lined up their shots, tracer fire lit up the area, as the two men fired their slingshot missile launchers almost simultaneously, the rockets roared through the air far faster than the eye could see, all that was visible was the briefest of faint white contrails from the dead aim missiles, as they shot past the closest fighting Dracos warriors and detonated in two loud, powerful explosions that for an instant lit up the entire battlefield. A plume of smoke and earth was thrown up, and three Kallan were blasted high into the air, landing heavily in bloodied heaps nearby. Sensibly the other Dracos kept their heads down.

"That's the signal! Move it!" Vargev shouted as he, and the rest of alpha team broke cover and sprinted headlong toward the giant blade-like pylons of the facility itself.

Three eviscerator rounds sliced into Santiago, sending him toppling to the ground. Though not dead, his screams as the acid tipped discs began to dissolve his flesh was horrifying to hear.

"Keep moving!" the colonel shouted to his men, there was no time to go back for him, and risk more men ending the same way.

A Dracos warrior leapt from behind a small boulder as the commandoes sprinted past, performed an overhead somersault in mid-air, and brought his wrist blades hard down, slicing straight through the neck of one of the sprinting commandoes, who flopped motionless to the ground. Nikolai returned the favour as he gunned down the Kallan warrior with a burst from his armschlager, the muzzle flash lit up the Russians breathing mask in a fiery glow.

"Jesus Christ! They're quick!" another commando said to Nikolai.

"Yeah, and we're all dead unless we get into cover, and fast, so keep moving!"

The battle was proving to be a tightly contested affair, between the most highly trained troops the E.D.F possessed, and the lethal Dracos elite guard. The bright red glow emanating from the eye lenses of the Dracos battlehelms, was unnerving to the E.D.F troops, as all they could see was red eyes looking at them in the darkness.

The sun had all but set over the horizon, and nightfall was fast approaching, the E.D.F troops grew nervous, as they knew from the intelligence they had received, that these Dracos were exceptional fighters at night, and night on impossible to spot.

Razor's bravo team was taking heavy fire ensconced in the smouldering ruins of the alien shuttles, two of his men were already dead, riddled with the strange incredibly sharp disc like ammunition, the stench of the acid consuming their flesh was nauseating, even through the filters of his breathing gear.

Another missile smashed into the Dracos positions, briefly lighting up the kill zone once again, a cloud of white smoke from Tomahawk's position betrayed the firer. While Razor himself, and his men continued to pour fire into the Dracos, spent casings clattered to the ground from their armschlagers, as multiple muzzle flashes lit up in an almost strobe like effect, though with their forms barely visible in the darkness, the commandoes were having a hard time finding actual targets.

E.D.F Chronicles – Eye of the Dracos

Razor knelt beside a bent and twisted, blackened panel, several eviscerator rounds carved tiny furrows into it as they skittered off of it, he dug deep inside a pouch on his webbing as the rest of the squad all continued to rake the Dracos with heavy calibre slugs.

He pulled out a flare gun, popped a flare canister into it, and pointed the device skywards, and pulled the trigger, just as an eviscerator round whistled through the air and sliced his hand off at the wrist. His severed hand simply plummeted gently to the floor, still grasping the flare gun.

Razor, in shock simply stared at the bloody stump that had been his right hand, blood fountained down his arm, and then screamed out in acute agony as the acid set to its work, burning its way through his flesh.

The flare had cast the Dracos into shadow, making them much easier to see, and causing immense pain to their delicate eyesight. E.D.F troops from both teams pressed their attack, a cacophony of machine gun fire, rang out even louder than before, as dozens of the dark Kallan warriors were scythed down by the merciless gunfire, missed with the occasional grenade that blasted apart great plumes of earth and smoke.

The Dracos themselves, now taking heavy losses, abandoned their defence of the facility and fell back towards the safety of the pylons themselves, straight into the gun sights of Nikolai's team, who tore through them ruthlessly, the high calibre rounds punching great holes into the Dracos's black armour and hurling them to the floor, where they lay convulsing for a short time, before lying still.

Although the Dracos defenders were now being cut to shreds by the commandoes rapid, unceasing gun fire, they were still making a good fist of trying to fight back, despite the pain the bright light of the flare was inflicting upon them, casualties amongst the outnumbered commandoes was mounting too. Particularly amongst Nikolai's exposed team, six of which now lay in bloodied heaps upon the ground their bodies torn and shredded by the lethally sharp eviscerator discs, alongside dozen's of Dracos corpses, riddled with fist sized bullet holes.

Nikolai and his few remaining men had finally made it to the safety of the giant pylons and took cover amongst them. If I'd known it was going to this fierce, I'd have brought more men, the Russian thought as another eviscerator disc rattled off the pylon he was taking cover behind.

The gunfire had gradually lessened, the remaining Dracos finally surrendered, only four remained out of forty, they had fought almost to the death to protect this place, their comrades torn, bullet ridden bodies littered the entire area. Smoke hung like a pall in the cool night air from the blast craters caused by the missile impacts, as well as the still smouldering wreckage of the Dracos landers.

The battle had lasted just forty minutes, a short yet bloody affair, nine of the twenty E.D.F commandoes were either wounded or killed, almost fifty percent casualties. The Dracos Kallan warriors had indeed earned their fearsome reputation in the eyes of their enemies who had fought against them that day.

"Bravo team form up on me," Nikolai said into the mic. attachment on his breathing gear, as he and the depleted troops of alpha team, searched the top of the gigantic installation.

Eventually they found the main entry hatch, and studied it for a moment, Vargev managed to uncover, a small dirt encrusted access panel. He pressed what looked like the hatch release control, to no avail, the colonel harrumphed as he squatted near to the hatch.

"Looks like it's sealed," One of his subordinates spoke up.

"Thank you for pointing out the perfectly fucking obvious!"

"Sorry, sir."

Nikolai rummaged through one of the larger pouches on his webbing, near to his hip, and eventually produced a small, cigarette box sized bar of sem-tex. He unwrapped the plastic explosive, before pulling off a thumb sized amount, rolled it between his fingers into a sausage shape, and pressed it against the centre of the stubborn hatch. He took out a small pen-like radio blasting cap from inside the packet and stuffed it deep inside the explosive, and then held the thumb trigger detonator in his hand.

"Back up a few feet!" he said as took a few steps backward, mindful not to pull the cap out of the explosive itself.

The rest of his squad complied and slowly backed away a short distance, just as the remainder of bravo team, with their injured squad leader, Razor joined them. Nikolai pressed the trigger, and almost instantly, a deafening explosion tore the hatch completely open in a cloud of billowing white smoke

Drax heard the almighty explosion from the far side of the facility as a faint 'thud,' still he could not let things distract him from his final, ultimate kill. He would take his time with this one, have a little fun with it, before killing it slowly. He switched his battlehelm to thermal imaging mode, it picked up the bright colours of his quarries body heat thirty metres away. It was time to end the hunt, he would be, at last, victorious.

The outline of her body showed her to be female, lacking the physical strength that the males of this strange species possessed; it would make for a poor finale to the hunt. Perhaps he had already experienced the great climax in combat with that tall male earlier, he was strong and had proven to be a stern test, yet in the end, as in all things, he had overcome him easily.

Drax silently, carefully pursued his prey through the dark passageways of the facility, she had stopped to rest in an old barrack room, a room in which his ancestors had once slept and trained, now she had defiled it with her presence. It would make a fitting place for the final kill.

Knowing full well that his enemy was still armed, Drax used the magnetics within his suit to climb up through the ventilation shaft once more. Slowly, silently he stalked his prey, giving away almost no noise whatsoever as he crept forward. The sense of that final moment, the final kill, was almost upon him, the moment he had waited for, a sense of nervous excitement filled him.

Kathryn had stopped to catch her breath, desperately tired and weak after having barely slept for three days of this hellish nightmare. She knew though, that it was not over yet, that crazed psychotic alien madman was still out there, the maniac who had killed the one person she had truly cared about besides Michael, the one person she could have loved. She allowed herself the time to softly cry, to release the pent up emotion she was feeling, the tears fell down her cheeks and stung her eyes.

Unbeknownst to Kathryn as she sat in-between two abandoned beds, a small vent was slowly, silently opening in the ceiling to her right. The dark figure of the Dracos commander crept silently through, inching towards his prey.

Kathryn wiped her eyes with a sleeve blotched with the dried blood of Thorsson, whom she had worked to help heal his ravaged knee. None of that mattered now, as him and all the rest were dead, she was the only one left alive.

She gradually willed herself to get back to her feet, and take a look around the room, fiddling with her torch which was beginning to flicker, the power cells were almost drained, she played the faulty light over the arrayed beds and empty storage lockers, there was no movement, she breathed a sigh of relief.

She jumped, her heart leapt, there was a figure in front of her cast in shadow by the light emanating from the torch. Her pulse pounded in her chest as she brought up her weapon to shoot it. The figure didn't move, there were no evil red eyes in the dark. Kathryn peered closer, seeking some kind of confirmation that whatever this was, it wasn't going to hurt her. Her nerves settled after finding that it was only a training dummy, though full of nicks and scratches. No doubt the Dracos who used to live here used it to practice their horrific propensity to stab and slash at their foes.

Kathryn forced herself to calm down again, in a vain effort to steady her already frayed nerves, she realised that she was sweating, a nervous, scared sweat.

She made to leave the barracks, and that was when Drax pounced, he fell upon her with such speed that the gun flew out of her hand, skittering across the smooth floor. She screamed out in abject terror and utter desperation as she kicked, thrashed and bit to get her assailant off of her, she managed to just about scrabble free.

She felt the sharp pain of something just nick the outside of her calf as she ran, Drax's silencer had wrapped itself around her right leg, and he quickly pressed the retraction control. The device whipped the steel monofilament line back with such speed and such force that when it tightened, it cut deeply into her shin and calf, upending her and hurling her to the floor, she landed heavily screaming out in wild agony. A scream that was like a symphony to Drax, blood ran down her leg and pooled at her foot, she could feel the horrid warm, wetness of it.

She clawed and scrabbled in desperation along the smooth floor in a last ditch attempt to reach her weapon, the silencer still tethered to her leg retracted a little more, tightening even further the grip on her leg, the tiny monofilament wire bit deeper into her now blood sodden leg, pulling her away from the weapon with a whimper of pain and defeat.

In her desperation she lashed out again, trying to kick the Dracos warrior away from her, Drax though, easily swatted aside the clumsy kick.

"Now my dear, we are going to have a little fun!" Drax hissed menacingly.

"Fuck you!" Kathryn spat back, with all the hate, all the malice, all the pain that this evil being had brought out from her.

Drax nonchalantly backhanded her, sending Kathryn sprawling to the floor in a whimper, a thin smear of blood trickled down her lip.

The Dracos commander smiled at her hopeless predicament, "You couldn't leave well enough alone, could you; you had to go interfering, you had to re-activate this place. A facility that does not even belong to you, this is our station, built upon our world, now your interfering has cost you dearly hasn't it."

Kathryn silently nodded, the agonising pain in her leg was driving her to distraction, she needed some time to come up with some sort of plan to free herself, to get the hell away from this maniac.

"It's cost your little band their very lives, and it is just what they deserved for tainting our facility, your very presence here disgusts me, GET UP!" He snapped.

Without a word, Kathryn did as she was told, the wire from the device was still biting into her foot, she felt faint from blood loss, shock, and exhaustion. The blood was still flowing profusely from the wound, although now her adrenaline had effectively taken the pain away.

"You are a pitiful species, weak, easily killed. Not a single one of you can hold a candle to the raw prowess of the Kallan."

"Hey asshole!" A deep, rasping Russian sounding voice from behind him spoke.

136

Ian J Smethurst

Drax had made one critical error. In focusing so intently on finishing the hunt, in his manic devotion to perform the final kill, capture the final glory. He had not noticed Colonel Nikolai Vargev step through the door behind him.

The Dracos commander whirled around to face the commando colonel, who grinned widely before pressing the trigger of the armschlager pointed directly at Drax's chest at point blank range. High power rounds tore through the Dracos's body, three slugs ripped through his chest and stomach, throwing him through the air, before slamming him down onto the hard smooth floor.

An accompanying commando stepped forward and produced a pair of wire cutters, and quickly managed to extricate Kathryn's badly injured leg from the device.

"Are you okay?" Nikolai asked.

"I am now." She almost fainted, as a wave of exhaustion washed over her.

"We'll get that leg seen to straight away, any other survivors?"

"Err…no, only me."

"Jesus, out of sixteen, you were the only one to make it?"

Kathryn hobbled over and gently hugged Nikolai, the big Russian towered over her, as he looked down and regarded her badly weakened form with concern.

"Thank you Nikolai." She whispered softly, a mixture of relief and profound sadness welled up inside her. Her ordeal was finally over, the nightmare was now gone.

She had lost so many colleagues, friends, people she had come to admire, and in particular the loss of Sergeant Rachthausen, the person she wanted so desperately to love.

Tears flowed onto Nikolai's camouflaged combat fatigues, a slight damp patch formed just below his thick barrel like chest.

"Let's get you out of here."

The Liberty had shot passed the Dracos craft that had been attacking it, and continued on toward one of the moons of Auriga III, the two remaining Dracos ships, the flagship *Blade of Rhovanion* and the Dracos warcruiser *flame of Celthris* slowly began to break orbit, power up their engines and give chase.

Senergid, a hero of the Dracos people himself, and commander of the entire Dracos fleet was still amazed that this little ship had withstood attacks from three of his best ships, and even gone on to destroy the *vengeance of Kelmarroth*, sure their foe was quick and nimble, but it was nowhere near the size and power of the warcruisers. The destruction of the *vengeance of Kelmarroth* should never have happened.

The fight to reclaim the lost halo world was proving to be a costly one, if they could not recapture the planet, Senergid was going to abandon it, there was no way he was going to risk an empire to capture a planet, no matter how important the Eye of the Dracos was to his people.

The small enemy ship had gained quite a headstart, as his larger warcruisers were much slower to turn, though now they had successfully broken orbit and were chasing after this annoying little ship.

"Reinforce the aft shields, take the forward graviton general offline, and shunt the extra power to the rear ones, just as before." Michael said as he turned from addressing Logan to the viewscreen ahead, the moon was become larger as they neared, its cratered surface more detailed.

The destruction of the Dracos ship had buoyed the crew up immensely, their weapons could in fact hurt these Dracos ships, and they could be destroyed. Although they are not out of the woods yet, not by a long shot. There were still two more of them out there, and coming in from behind where the Liberty was weaponless.

However if Michael's plan was to succeed, they would need to take a little pain for a lot of gain.

"Incoming!" Logan shouted.

Torpedoes raced towards the small warship, as Eldathar swung the ship from port to starboard to evade the worst, two of the warheads flashed past the Liberty overshooting their target, the contrails clearly visible on the viewer as they sailed by.

Two others however slammed hard into the Liberties reinforced aft shields, pitching several of its crew, including Michael forward. The Liberty captain braced his fall by landing on his outstretched palms, the deck plating thrummed gently to the touch, as the Solarian derived Ionic engine worked at full capacity, catapulting the ship forward in an effort to get some distance between the Liberty and those chasing Dracos ships, the plates were also cool, which felt reassuring as Michael scrabbled back to his seat.

"Shields at eighty three percent."

The Liberty continued to hurtle headlong through space towards the safety of the moon, the tiny ships flight path was criss-crossed with deep violet laser lance blasts from the Dracos ships, several other hammered into the Liberties aft shields, weakening them further.

"Shields are down to fifty one percent, we won't be able to withstand this kind of pounding for much longer!" Jones replied.

The ship rocked violently under the onslaught; a console shorted out and exploded in a shower of sparks and shattered glass, flying headlong across the bridge.

"Hold your course Eldathar!" Michael shouted over the din of explosions and violent shaking.

The Solarian pilot nodded an affirmative as he concentrated on trying to dodge the withering hail of weapons fire directed at them. He had managed to dodge the majority of the fusillade of laser lance fire, but in doing so had flown straight into the path of three torpedoes, heading straight for them.

"Brace for impact!" the Solarian shouted in alarm.

All three warheads slammed headlong into the Liberty, crewmen were thrown through the air from the sheer force of the impacts. Conduits exploded

139

all over the ship, power flickered in sections, smoke and the debris of collapsed supports filled the bridge, virtually all the command staff were thrown to the floor.

Kinraid lay unconscious on the floor near to his ruined sensory console, the display had shattered, leaving nothing more than a blackened charred wreck, filled with sparking and damaged circuits.

Michael groggily got to his feet, his head throbbed, he rubbed his temples to clear the fog from his mind. Clearing away the debris from the grey leather of his command chair, and slumped slowly back into it.

"Status," he asked weakly.

Logan managed to make his way to an auxiliary sensory console to the left of where he fell, picking his way through the detritus littering the floor. "If I'm reading this right, we've lost the aft port graviton generator, and the other one is about to shut down to vent off excess energy. Main engines are still intact, though we have several stress fractures along the aft hull."

"So we are defenceless?"

"It looks that way."

"Injuries, casualties?"

"Yet to come in, so far we have two casualties reported."

"How long until we reach the moon itself?"

"Another three minutes sir," Eldathar replied studying the display in front of him, one of the few that remained undamaged on the bridge.

"This is it, we have no more room for error, if we even take a single hit, we are done for."

Eldathar gravely nodded his understanding, just as a laser lance shot smashed into the undefended rear of the Liberty, blasting straight through the hull, and almost pitching the ship into a spin.

The Solarian wrestled against the controls with every ounce of his strength, in an effort to keep the ship stable, if he lost control again they were all doomed. Alarms signalling damage to the ship, blared out loudly, throughout the vessel.

"We've got a hull breach, deck three, aft section, casualties reported," Logan said.

Michael slammed his fist down into the arm of the chair, he was getting a little sick of being shot to pieces, "main engines?"

"They missed them, by a matter of just two metres."

The Liberty captain let out a relieved sigh, at least he still had the engines intact.

"Structural integrity is at sixty three percent," Logan reported.

Eldathar managed to jink the ship to avoid another barrage of fire, just as a voice came across the speakers.

"You have fought bravely, your ship and crew should be commended, however you cannot win this battle. You are out-gunned and outmatched in almost every regard, it is over. If you surrender now you have my personal word that no harm will come to your men."

Michael considered this for a moment, but didn't believe a word of what he was hearing, "To whom am I speaking?"

"My name is Senergid, commander of the *blade of Rhovanion.*"

Michael carefully picked his way through his debris strewn bridge to Eldathar's position, before whispering, "are we still on course for the moon?"

"Yes, captain."

"Good, don't deviate for a second."

"Understood."

"I am giving you one last chance to leave here with your ship and crew intact, I await your reply." Senergid said once again.

Michael calmly sat down into his chair, eyeing both Logan Jones still manning the tactical station, and Eldathar in the pilot's chair.

"It's a fine offer, Senergid, a noble one. But one thing you do not know about us; is that the Liberty or its crew, never surrenders to anyone. So in the words of my people, screw you!"

"How dare you spea……" Michael nodded to Logan to cut the transmission, which he did with a smile.

Kinraid slowly regained consciousness, and staggered his way over to the auxiliary sensory console that Logan was using, his face was burned and bore a nasty cut down one side, which had bore the brunt of the console exploding. The pain in movements was evident to see.

"Glad to have you back commander."

"Wouldn't miss it for te' world cap'n." Kinraid smiled weakly.

"You cannot hide, you cannot run, we will hunt you down and destroy you, I am offering you a way out." Senergid's voice came across the speakers once more, his voice still betraying the anger at being unceremoniously cut off.

"Is he still speaking?" Michael asked with a smile.

Kinraid whispered, "Approachin' the moons gravity well in t'irty seconds."

"Can you get a transmission to the Eisenhower?"

"Once we're on te' other side of the moon, yes. T'ey won't be able to jam our transmissions then."

"Good, do it, we'll need their help." Michael smiled, he had the plan, now all he had to do was carry it out.

"You cannot possibly think you can mount an effective defence any longer, surrender……" Michael motioned for the transmission to be killed with a silent wave of his hand.

"Approachin' gravity well in five, four, tree, two."

"Hold on to your hats," Michael smiled.

142

Eldathar poured every last drop of power remaining into the engines at the exact instant the Liberty hit the moon's gravity well, the ships own speed, in addition to the gravitational pull of the planetoid, meant that the Liberty surged forward, far outpacing the Dracos ships in pursuit.

The small ship shuddered and rocked as Eldathar fought against the gravitational pull of the moon that threatened to pull the vessel toward it.

"Speed is at twenty percent over maximum, we are approaching eighty percent of light speed."

"Keep it coming!" Michael shouted over the din of violent shaking and rocking, the occasional snap of a torn power cable, and general rattle and crash of fallen debris.

The Liberty raced forward, inverted to the cratered lunar landscape below them, giant boulders, impact craters from asteroid strikes, peaks and troughs shot past them in a blur as the ship continued to ride the crest of the moons gravity well.

The Dracos ships attempted to maintain some kind of a pursuit, but their hesitation had cost them dearly, the Liberty was now far ahead of them. Senergid ordered the ships to a stop while they awaited for the Liberty to come around the far side of the moon.

"Transmissions 'r' free cap'n, 'te moon itself is blocking their jammin' systems."

"Send out an alert one message to the Eisenhower, tell them we require urgent assistance, that should get their attention."

"Aye, sir. Transmittin' now." Kinraid said, as he worked the controls as his console.

After a brief pause, the commander spoke up again, "Message received, 'tey are inbound, an' 'tey are not alone."

Michael looked at Quinn questioningly, the commander simply winked back at him.

"The E.D.F have been busy," Michael smiled as he settled back down into his seat, things were about to get interesting.

The Liberty shot forth as it continued to circle the moon, increasing speed all the time. The shuddering increased in its intensity, an occasional panel blew out, resulting in a loud explosion and almost blinding shower of sparks, they had to hold on, had to stay the course.

"Approaching ninety five percent of light speed!" Eldathar announced.

The craters, boulders, and mountainous terrain of the lunar surface shot by even faster as the Liberty continued to build up speed, it shot headlong around the moon, and as the ship came around to face their attackers, who were in the process of coming about to bring their own weapons to bear. The Liberty with all its accumulated momentum behind it, was far faster, the Solarian gently glided the ship on its apogee from the moon, and used the last remnant of the force emitted from the gravity well itself to slingshot the ship towards the Dracos cruisers, the Liberty rocketed toward them with incredible speed, the Dracos ships simply had no chance to react.

"FIRE!" Michael shouted, fist clenched.

The Liberty fired torpedo after torpedo, a flurry of five warheads all shot towards the Dracos ships as the E.D.F warship continued to close with terrific speed.

The torpedoes slammed home with such force that it caused one of the Dracos cruisers to lurch wildly, its shields flared brightly as they desperately tried to absorb the explosive force of the high energy warheads. The third impact caused the shields to ripple and fade, the remaining two torpedoes smashed directly into the ships hull with tremendous force. Devastating one of the ships wing-tip mounted laser lances in an intensely bright explosion that lit up the entire port side of the vessel.

The second tore its way deep into the ship's main hull, a gigantic explosion carved out a deep, black crater. Torn and blasted decks were visible and flames streamed out of the hull breach, which gave the appearance of an open wound, smaller nearby explosions continued to burst out through the ships dark outer hull in miniature fireballs. The ship slowly listed, as the fires inside gradually began to consume the entire vessel, escape pods could be seen jettisoning in a desperate attempt to flee the growing maelstrom.

The intensely bright incandescent blue beam of the Liberties fusion cannon, tore the stricken enemy ship apart in an almighty explosion, sending out a powerful shockwave and debris in all directions.

Senergid was dumbfounded as he witnessed the fiery destruction of the *Flame of celthris*, the small enemy ship which should have been destroyed a long time ago, now slowed to a stop dead ahead of his ship.

Towards the rear of *the blade of Rhovanion*, four bright flashes heralded the arrival of the *Eisenhower*, two Ghandhi class destroyers, and the Washington class heavy cruiser *Arizona*.

Caught between the guns of the Liberty ahead, and the firepower of the E.D.F flotilla closing in from behind, Senergid knew it was over.

"Contact that alien ship," Michael asked, staring intently at its dark crescent shape filling the viewer.

"Channel open."

"Senergid, your position is hopeless, now it is you who is outgunned and outmatched, we demand you unconditional and immediate surrender."

The Dracos fleet commander looked up from his chair at the face of his enemy, filling his own viewscreen, straightening his black robes in a last ditch attempt to retain what was left of his shattered pride.

"Well played captain, well played. However this is not over, your people have made a powerful enemy here this day, you cannot protect this system forever. We will return one day, and we will reclaim that which is rightfully ours."

"And we will be ready," Michael replied calmly, though in truth the force behind the enemy commanders statement send shivers running through him.

The communication ceased, and the mighty Dracos flagship slowly banked, and made to leave the area. It moved slowly, and solemnly, as though a dark monster who knew it had been defeated and was slinking back into the darkness of its home. Its giant engines lit up in a bright orange colour, as it accelerated away from Auriga III.

"Eisenhower is requesting if we should pursue?" Kinraid asked.

"Negative, there has been enough bloodshed for one day, let them go."

In a way, Michael realised, he felt sorry for the Dracos. Though once Solarians, they had let their hate consume them. Their hate of the Solarians who they blame for almost destroying their people all their years ago, their newly found hate of the E.D.F for keeping a planet that they think is theirs away from them, and their hate of the galaxy as a whole. And in their hate, they had become insular, isolationist, and fiercely paranoid; in a people that held the kind of power the Dracos did, that was a dangerous cocktail.

It's a shame, Michael thought, if they learned to co-exist peacefully with those around them, they wouldn't need to resort to their isolationist ways.

"Set course for the veil, it is time to return to Corvandris, the galaxy is not yet ready for us to emerge just yet." Senergid said with a mournful sigh, a lot of Dracos had died to reclaim a world that was theirs by right.

One day he knew they would have to emerge from their self-imposed isolation, although he also knew of the problems plaguing his people. In their isolation, the galaxy had forgotten about them, history had moved on, new races had come to the fore and overshadowed them. Like this E.D.F. a great sadness came over the Dracos commander as his ship returned to the all concealing darkness of the veil, the electromagnetic interference overcame his ships sensory systems, rendering them useless, and he piloted his ship by memory alone. Just as every other Dracos ship had done within this all consuming nebula.

The Liberty, now too badly damaged to risk atmospheric entry, docked with the comparatively giant *Eisenhower*, the four hundred and thirty man heavy cruiser dwarfed the Liberty at over five hundred metres long, it was fully four times its size.

Michael said to Kinraid, "You're in charge until I return."

"Where 'r' you goin'?"

"To say hello to an old friend."

With that Michael left the battered, debris strewn bridge of the Liberty and headed down toward the ships main docking hatch, passing various member of his crew attempting to affect temporary repairs, restoring broken power conduits. The crew seemed in good spirits, despite the utter pounding they had taken, he wondered just how much of those spirits were down to the fact the fighting had stopped. Many crewmen saluted him as he passed, smiling at him warmly.

The elevator he had taken was not its usual self, a little stop-start instead of its smooth three hundred mile per hour transition of the ship, still it was to be expected.

He passed sickbay on his way to the hatch, partly to get cleaned up a little, he was bearing a number of scrapes and bumps himself, covered in the soot and grime of battle, and partly to see how Lillian was coping with the casualties the ship had taken. He did not want to bother her, as he could see the ship's tiny sickbay was simply swamped with crewmember bearing various forms of injuries. The scene made him feel guilty, Michael, being the experienced ship captain he was, knew he had to keep his own form of professional detachment from his crew, just like Lillian had to when she declared a crewmember deceased, or at least he tried to.

Truth be told though, the Liberty had come through so much, it had fought through the entire Krenaran war, fought against pirates in numerous engagements, and now this, that the crew had become so close, it wasn't like they were a typical crew on a typical ship anymore. It was as though they were brothers and sisters, they felt each others loss, and grieved accordingly; that was a hard thing to keep a professional detachment from.

There were just three beds in the Liberties sickbay, all were full, and Lillian was frantically working from bed to bed, stabilising one, and then moving on quickly to the next, Michael had to admire her skill.

Her two medical interns wheeled away a body zipped up in a black bodybag, with the occupants name and serial number written onto it in white pen. One of the interns looked at him with eyes filled with sadness. "Sorry sir, we lost another one."

He hated these moments, a lump began to form in throat, which he fought to keep down, "Who?"

"crewman Lonaz, sir."

That made it all the more difficult to bear, crewman Lonaz, a mexican, was one of the youngest to serve on the Liberty, just sixteen years old, on a placement from the E.D.F academy he was training as a propulsion technician, so would have been near to where that Dracos barrage breached the hull. He was a good man, had a bright future ahead of him, Logameier often spoke of him.

"How many so far?" He asked the interns.

"That's the fifth, sir." They said before they wheeled the body away down the corridor to the ships morgue. It was times like these when he would give anything just to be a simple lieutenant again, spared of the responsibility of having to fill in killed in action reports, and informing next of kin that their wife, or so, or husband had been killed. It was an awful reality of command, and one he did not relish performing.

Michael continued towards the hatch itself, and pressed his wrist comm. "Kinraid, decompress and open the hatch."

"Aye, sir."

After a pause of a few seconds while Kinraid worked at his console on the bridge, a green panel alighted above the circular hatchway doors themselves, indicating it was safe to enter. Michael took two deep breaths and pressed the hatch release.

A blast of air rushed past him to fill up the small temporary inter-locking corridor between the Liberty and the Eisenhower, almost blowing him off his feet in the process. He gently pushed off the edge of the hatch, where the artificial gravity generated by the Liberties environmental systems ended, and weightlessness began. He floated slowly, silently along the delicate little corridor the connected the two ships, the sudden blast of cold made him shiver, even though it took only a matter of a few second to traverse the distance.

Once at the other side, a second hatch opened and allowed him egress onto the Eisenhower itself. Slowly rather clumsily Michael stepped onto the floor of the hatch, and artificial gravity resumed again.

Ian J Smethurst

It had been a long time since Michael had stepped within the confines of another E.D.F ship, the difference to what he was used to on the Liberty was startling, and he needed a few seconds to adjust to his new surroundings.

Instead of the Liberties ultra-modern, highly advanced Solarian derived systems, the Eisenhower was a relic in comparison. Clumsy, utilitarian and heavy, instead of the customisable touch screen displays the Liberty possessed, the Eisenhower had keypads and clunky monitors that jutted out from the walls at odd angles. This was all very strange to Michael, almost as though he was stepping into the past.

A female officer approached him, escorted by two other junior officers, judging by the rank insignia's on their epaulettes, he quickly found that one held the rank of lieutenant, the other a more senior lieutenant commander. The woman leading them was slim, in her early thirties, and had a gorgeous mane of auburn hair, tied neatly in a bun, she was not altogether unattractive, and bore the rank of commander. They all saluted Michael appropriately.

"Welcome aboard the Eisenhower, captain. I am Commander Erica Fontain, commanding officer of this vessel," she motioned with her hand introduce her accompanying officers, "This is Lieutenant Commander Ben Maddox, my executive officer, and this is Liu Chung my senior sensory officer. Both ourselves and the Arizona, have made shuttles ready for dispatch to get everyone off the surface quickly should the Dracos return in greater numbers. I trust you wish to begin the evacuation immediately?"

"Of course," Michael replied simply. He was a little surprised to find merely a commander in charge of such a ship. Nevertheless, he had found in his experience, it was not always prudent to question the orders of the admiralty."

"If you would like to follow me, I'll escort you to our hangar bay."

Michael fell into step behind the entourage, which led him down a long, slightly cramped corridor, festooned with all manner of pipes and conduits overhead. The interior of the Eisenhower was painted in the traditional military olive green. This instantly signified to Michael that this was, in fact, an old ship. The engineering services stopped painting these ships that colour fifteen years ago, in favour of the more familiar battleship grey of today.

As they walked, commander Fontain spoke up, "It has been a great honour and a privilege for us, it's not every day we get to walk with such a living icon

149

as yourself. The Liberty, its crew, and your exploits throughout the Krenaran war are legendary to us."

Michael was growing a little uncomfortable with the hero worship, "just doing what we had to do," he replied meekly, sometimes he hated being the most decorated captain in the navy.

"I wish I could have been there with you, and experienced what you had experienced, the Eisenhower was mostly assigned to the defence of Charlie base at sigma XI, far away from the fighting."

Michael lost his cool a little at this, "do you know what we experienced; do you? It was brutal at times, bloody, ships being torn apart and people dying all around us. Whenever I go to sleep it haunts my dreams, I get no rest, no solitude from it; ever. Nobody should have to experience what we experienced."

Fontaine stared at Michael in shock, "forgive me, I meant no offence."

"None taken," Michael replied calming himself once again, "but these heroes, this larger than life captain you depict. We are not those people, we did what we had to do to survive, nothing more."

"I understand."

Eventually they came upon the wide hangar bay, it was home to a dozen short range shuttles in two rows of six, one side facing the other. Their elongated bullet shaped fuselage, and downward curved cockpit, made the place look like the interior of some gigantic rifle magazine.

The ceiling of the hangar bay was high, a good fifty or sixty feet above them.

"Two shuttles are launching from here, and another two from the Arizona," Fontaine informed him.

"Good, then let's get moving shall we," Michael did not want to waste any time in getting the survivors and Nikolai's men out of that hellhole."

"Understood, lieutenant commander Maddox, and lieutenant Chung will be piloting the second shuttle, I will be overseeing things from up here."

"Thank you commander," the two officers saluted the commander.

Michael silently nodded his understanding. Fontaine was in command after all, and while he had no doubt she would have loved to accompany him, her first duty was to her ship. If he was in her position he would of most likely done exactly the same thing, so he would most likely be piloting the first shuttle, alone.

Commander Fontaine curtly turned on her heel, left the hangar bay, and the men to begin their flight.

Michael and the other crew members all pressed the door release at almost the same exact time, and the small hatches at the rear of the craft both opened outwards in unison. They all climbed onboard the shuttle and the hatch door slowly closed back down automatically, re-sealing itself.

He began the start up sequence of the shuttle, it had been a while since he had taken a ride in one of these, he thought, as he worked he could feel the old techniques coming back, the rust coming away. Controls flickered on and panels lit up across the pilot's instrumentation, attitude sensors came online, short and long range communication systems came to life, and main power began to build up to full charge.

Michael pressed a few controls on the console in-front of him, opening up a communications channel with the Arizona, "Arizona this is Michael Alexander in shuttle Eisenhower alpha-six, preparing to get underway."

"Confirmed; Arizona shuttles are clear, and have left hangar bay, awaiting rendezvous."

Damn they're quick, Michael thought, "understood Arizona, getting underway now."

He keyed in the gravitic engine start up sequence, and powered up the main boosters. The boosters themselves roared into life as the solid fuel ignited, slowly filling the giant hangar bay with steam and exhaust gases, keeping the thrust for the boosters at a lowly ten percent, and instead using the gravitic engines to manoeuvre steadily within the hangar bay.

The small shuttle gently inched forward, slowly picking up speed as it began to taxi out into the wide launch bay, he saw his shuttle slowly pass the other in his peripheral vision.

The hangar bay doors opened with a blast of escaping oxygen, and the rush of exhaust gases venting out into space.

"Well, here goes." Michael said to himself as he increased thrust to the main boosters, the nozzles on the twin directed thrust booster engines opened fully as Michael eased the throttle to maximum. The roar of the engines echoed loudly throughout the entire hangar bay as the shuttle rapidly accelerated, shooting past the hangar bay doors and out into the blackness of deep space.

The stars shone brightly through the cockpit glass; he could just make out the swirling emerald green clouds of a distant nebula, and the bright glow of the second moon of Auriga III, as the light from the Aurigan sun reflected of its rocky, cratered surface.

Michael had always loved the serene quietness of space, it was one of the reasons why he had joined up to serve in the E.D.F as a naval officer in the first place, it was calm, and contemplative, immense yet also giving a sense of freedom to those who travelled through that vastness. There was no better view than up close through the simple cockpit glass of a shuttle, sure the Liberty with all its technological wizardry could depict a one hundred and eighty degree, high definition depiction of surrounding space on its viewscreen. It still could not match actually being here, witnessing the spectacle for yourself.

He sighed contentedly as he looked down at his sensors, which were telling him that the other two shuttles were holding position between the Eisenhower and the Arizona, he keyed in a few controls to release a short burst of thrust from his port thruster to bring the tiny craft around, using the forward momentum the shuttle deftly flew around the relatively huge primary inter-system boosters of the Eisenhower, each one over three times the length of the shuttle itself. They still gently glowed with the intense heat produced when they manoeuvred the ship into orbit after cornering the last Dracos cruiser.

The Eisenhower and the Arizona, at five hundred and seventy four, and five hundred and fourteen metres respectively, dominated everything around them. The Arizona in particular, being a Jefferson class heavy destroyer, a class which had garnered the nick-name of 'the mini-monty,' due to the classes resemblance to the much larger Montgomery class carrier.

As the shuttle flew past the raised crew blocks, the dozens of port holes shone out towards him. The Jefferson was designed as a heavier, more survivable alternative to the ubiquitous Gandhi class destroyer, one of which was holding position to the other side of the Arizona out of sight of Michael in the shuttle. The Jefferson was almost twice the size of the Gandhi, and possessed twice the firepower too, in addition it sported a tough reinforced ablative armour hull, designed during the height of the Krenaran war, to make it that bit more survivable when in combat against Krenaran forces. It had mixed success however, many had still bought the farm, despite this improvement.

Michael could see the tiny shapes of the awaiting shuttles, silhouetted against the deep beige backdrop of the planet itself. The shuttle flew past the various gently raised panels of the Arizona's reinforced hull, passed its command structure with its tall whip-like communications and sensor antennae, and past the four turreted high power laser batteries adorning the ships gently sloping wedge shaped hull, that were its main armament.

He gently manoeuvred the shuttle into position, and joined up with the small formation waiting for him, within a few seconds the other shuttle from the Eisenhower which had been tailing him, had also joined them.

"Glad you could join us; stopping by for a little sight seeing on the way were we, captain?"

Michael recognised that voice, it was one he hadn't heard for over twenty years, "Ruiz, is that you?"

"In the flesh."

James Ruiz was one of the cadets who studied in the same pilot training school as Dylan Marcos and himself. Though for several years Ruiz and Michael were rival, not only as pilot's but love rivals also.

"She's one heck of a ship isn't she? But not a patch on the Liberty, you lucky old swine."

Michael was about to tell him that luck had nothing to do with it, but decided to let the matter drop instead. "She sure is, and upgraded too I see."

"Yeah, she got virtually a complete refit after the fall of Sigma XI, where she was badly damaged by Krenaran attacks, we were lucky to get out of their in one piece. She didn't re-enter the war for another six months after that."

Michael remembered that incident well, the fall of foxtrot base, it was one of the opening battles of the war. The Krenarans had taken out our primary intelligence hub, almost one hundred and forty two thousand people, died in an instant. It was one of the worst atrocities of the war. The massive complex had largely been rebuilt now, though there is now a giant black memorial monolith, built just outside of the new foxtrot base, commemorating all those who had died.

"Shall we?" Michael said over the comm.

After you, flight lead."

The small squadron of four shuttles accelerated ahead of the comparatively giant ship of the E.D.F flotilla orbiting high above the planet, keeping in formation for the entire time.

"Okay keep close, but not too close, we still don't know what we'll find down there."

"Right with ya, flight lead."

The shuttles all hit the atmosphere of the planet simultaneously, their hulls heating up rapidly until they trailed fire ad super heated plasma, the small craft shuddered violently under the forces exerted upon them as they sped through the upper atmosphere like four bullets shot from a giant gun.

Michael fought hard to keep control of the small craft through the violence of atmospheric entry, eventually the craft punched through the atmosphere, and descended through the thick swirl of the methane clouds.

"Ready atmospheric flight systems, deploy wings and stabiliser fins."

"Copy that, flight systems engaged."

Ian J Smethurst
The shuttle's large Delta shaped wings slid out from underneath its fuselage, its twin tails swung out from recesses within the crafts two powerful boosters. The small winglets, essential to help stabilise the small craft when in flight slid out from small panels either side of the shuttle's cockpit, as the four craft gracefully emerged through the thick cloud cover towards the giant structure, dubbed the eye of the Dracos.

"Ready landing gear, descend to one hundred feet, then engage gravitic engines for touchdown."

The commandoes on the surface gave out a great muted cheer, as their breathing apparatus prevented the full sound from travelling, as they saw the silhouettes of the four shuttles emerge through the cloud cover towards them, the four captured Dracos simply groaned.

The shuttles came into land, their powerful gravitic engines kicked up a giant plume of dust, blowing over small shrubs and plants in their force, as they seemed to hover for an instant before finally touching down on the surface itself. Their forward landing lights lit up the whole area as the scarlet light from the flare fired earlier had, by now faded. The landing legs themselves had sunk almost a full foot into the soft ground, as the weight of the craft bore down on the ground around it. A loud hiss of released gas from the shuttles landing legs equalised the pressure placed upon the landing gear themselves.

The occupants also donned breathing gear, before emerging from the landed craft, now gently powering down.

There were a small group of commandoes guarding the Dracos prisoners, one of which peeled off to approach Michael as he made his way towards them.

"I am so glad you guys are here for the extraction."

"Any casualties?" Michael asked the rather young looking sergeant, his hand noticeably a mass of bandages, a deep crimson smear beginning to show through. "Nine, sir. It was one helluva fight, those Dracos over there can really fight, sir."

"I'm sure they can sergeant, are they prisoners?" He asked eyeing the bound and sitting Dracos warriors suspiciously.

"Yes, sir. They surrendered during the battle."

As they were speaking Nikolai emerged with a wounded Kathryn, she hobbled over on her injured leg, now tightly wrapped in bandages also, towards her former captain, whom she hadn't seen in almost four long years. Michael strolled over towards her, and they embraced each other closely, tears began to run down Kathryn's cheeks onto his uniform. She was finally free of the nightmare she had endured, she sobbed, her body trembling with emotion.

"It's all right Kathryn, your safe now."

"Just get me out of here Michael, get me off this horrible world," then she seemed to stop in mid-sentence, "no, I have one last task to accomplish, I have to bury a true hero, one who has fought and died to save me. I owe him that at least."

"We can return as soon as the medics have taken a look at you," Michael quickly realised she was traumatised by what she had witnessed down in the dark corridors of that strange structure.

Michael turned to Nikolai, "any survivors down there?"

"None comrade," my men are bringing the bodies up now, he shook his head solemnly, "it's like a slaughterhouse down there."

Michael managed to carry the badly injured Kathryn into his shuttle, despite her objections, "Michael we can't just leave them down there?"

"We are not going to, we are transferring the bodies to our ships in orbit, so they can have a proper burial."

She noticeably calmed after hearing this, and slumped exhausted into the co-pilot's chair, resting her leg gingerly. Michael studied her for a moment, she looked tired, drawn, he guessed after three days of going through what she had just gone through, he guessed anybody would.

He wanted to ask her, if she would consider re-joining the Liberty crew; but decided against it. Right now Kathryn wasn't exactly in the best state of mind, instead he would silently watch over her, but at the same time giver her the space she needed to get over these recent events.

The remainder of the commandoes were to be transported on another shuttle, save two, who would travel with the Dracos prisoners as an escort, while they were being transported to the Eisenhower's brig, until Michael could contact E.D.F command who could advise on what to do with them.

That left the last remaining shuttle to transfer the bodies to the E.D.F ships waiting in orbit, of the sixteen scientists and guards that were stranded on that god forsaken planet. Only Kathryn had survived, not to mention another nine commandoes who died in the rescue attempt, twenty six lives lost, plus whatever casualties the Liberty had sustained; it had proven to be a dark day for the E.D.F.

The gravitic engines thrummed into life, kicking up a great whirl of dust once again, just as Michael's wrist comm. chirped, it was commander Ruiz. "Once we've got all this straightened out, I'll see you back at the ship."

"yah, no problem, it will be a little while before the Liberty is space worthy again, the old girl has taken quite a beating."

"Fantastic, I'll see you soon. I look forward to catching up on the old times."

"Me too commander," Michael said before ending the transmission with a press of a red stop key on his wrist communicator.

The shuttle gently lifted off, as Michael increased thrust to the boosters, with a loud roar the craft raced skywards.

Nikolai and the surviving commandoes all filed into the second craft, piloted by Maddox, he decided that he would hang back slightly from the prisoner shuttle, keeping his forward mounted gatling laser trained upon it. If the prisoners did make any attempt to gain control of it, he would blast it out the sky.

Fortunately, the return trip wasn't as eventful as Ben thought it would be, they returned to the awaiting Eisenhower and Arizona, without incident.

The Dracos prisoners were quickly assorted, under armed guard to the Eisenhower's brig, they were strangely quiet and subdued, they didn't make a single move to struggle.

Kathryn benefited from the Eisenhower's larger, moderately more advanced, and well stocked med-lab, a female officer perused the injured leg. The razor sharp wire from the Dracos silencer had sawn its way through her flesh, sliced her calf muscle virtually in half, severed her Achilles tendon, and even scored a deep gouge into the bone itself.

Ian J Smethurst

The young medical officer stepped quietly out of the med-bay and made her way towards a waiting Michael, who was watching over her from a waiting room.

"She'll need surgery, the damage is extensive, if we don't operate she may never be able to walk on that foot again."

"Do what you must," Michael replied gravely, he cared about her, remembered back to the time when he rescued her from Delta base during the Krenaran war, just a young nineteen year old ensign, barely out of medical school and out of her mind with fear. He watched as she had to endure the personal torture of operating on wounded and sometimes dead friends during that war, a part of him felt responsible in that too.

The medical officer nodded gently, and as quietly as she left, re-entered the sterile room, a team of six other surgeons gradually surrounded Kathryn, he watched as they administered an anaesthetic, she slowly fell into unconsciousness.

Michael felt himself wince as a tiny laser cutter made the first incision, the fold of skin around her blood soaked wound, folded back in two halves, just like the skin of an over-ripened fruit, and exposing the delicate, damaged muscle tissue underneath. A suction pipe was used to clear away the excess blood, precious minutes ticked by as Michael watched the operation being performed, occasionally he would look away, the pain almost too much to bear.

He remembered Kathryn having to perform harder, more complex operations than this throughout the war, often on her friends, and people she really cared about, for the first time he truly experienced what she must have felt. No wonder why she quit the medical profession in the end, Michael doubted that he would be able to stomach it either.

A small injection of protonase was injected directly into the back of her shin bone to promote bone growth and slowly re-grow the damaged parts of bone. One of the surgeons held a small sonic oscillator over the muscle tissue. It gave off a gentle thrumming noise as the tiny waves of sound worked to relax the damaged muscle tissue. Small, microscopic implants were then placed around this severed tissue and worked to repair the damage, and to also emit minute, controlled bursts of electricity into the surrounding muscle, it would feel very much like the sensation of pins and needles. These would cause muscle spasms, the constant contracting and relaxing of the calf muscle would help to speed up

159

its regrowth. It was a technique only recently come into practice within the medical profession, called micro-static therapy.

Michael continued to watch the surgeons at work, both in awe, and wincing as he imagined the pain Kathryn must be going through.

The severed Achilles tendon was an altogether different prospect, if the surgeons could not fix that, Kathryn would never be able to walk with that foot again. This would require a previously experimental technique in medical science, known as servo-assistance. It involved placing a pair of tiny servo's, no bigger than a pin head, and attaching them to the tendon via degradable sutures. The servo would assist the severed tendon to move the foot, though the servo would pull ever so slightly harder on the tendon each time, in order to aid in its natural re-growth.

Michael watched as the surgeons performed the most delicate and complex of all the operations, one that had never been attempted before. The concentration and dedication lining each and every one of their faces was plain to see. In a way, he wished he was in there with them, yet he was a ship captain, medical techniques were not his forté. He could fly a ship halfway around the galaxy, yet this tiny operation was beyond him, he felt the whole experience humbling.

Nikolai eventually found his way inside the viewing booth to join him, "How is she doing comrade?"

"The operation is almost over, the techniques used, the way they work, it's incredible to watch."

"I know, one of ours; Razor, is having a cybernetic hand attached on the Arizona."

"I'm sorry about the losses you took Nikolai, I know the men in your unit are close to you."

"It goes with the territory, every single commando knows the risk when he enlists. They have no regrets."

"So what will happen now?"

Ian J Smethurst

"Well," Nikolai gave off a gentle sigh, "Once we are all finished here, it will off to Alpha-centauri for de-briefing." The Russian gave off a deep growl of a yawn, "But, I'll tell you something comrade. I never want to have to come up against those Dracos again. They give me the creeps, they can come out of absolutely anywhere, and they are so well trained, so fast and acrobatic. You could be patrolling happily one second, and you've just lost a squad member the next. As night fighters, I don't think I've ever seen better."

"Let's just hope we don't have to fight them again."

The surgeons had finished their work on Kathryn's leg, and wheeled her bed around to a small side ward for her to recuperate.

"Kathryn belongs with you comrade, with the Liberty, where you can keep watch over her, and take care of her when she falls down. She needs you, and you need her."

Michael knew within himself that Nikolai was right, for five long years, ever since his wife and son had died, the caring side of him, the tender side, had died along with them. People had suffered because of that, people like Kathryn. "I know Nikolai, in the time she has been gone, I've come to realise that." Michael looked out across the med-bay to the small side ward in which she was sleeping, "the question is; has she?"

"Give her time, she's been through a heck of an ordeal."

"I intend to."

The group of six surgeons all entered the booth, and faced the two men. One of them, a middle aged man, still wearing his surgical scrubs said. "The operation has been a success, she will have to be very careful over the next few weeks; if she aggravates the wound, she could tear out the sutures tying the servo to her tendon, and would need a further operation to re-attach them."

"When can we expect her to be back at full health doctor?" Michael asked.

"I would say with this type of injury, not for another six weeks. Then she would have to come for a check up before she regains active duty."

"Thanks."

"She's currently sleeping off the effects of the anaesthetic, and should be awake again in a couple of hours. She'll be a little sore, and the twinges from the micro-static implants will take some getting used to; but she should make a full recovery."

"Thanks for all you have done, doctor."

"Just doing our job captain," the doctor replied, before he and his entourage of surgeons left the men alone again.

"Now to find out just what to do with our captured Dracos friends," Michael said with a smile, as he turned to leave the booth.

"You have a plan, don't you?"

"I always have a plan, Nikolai."

"That's what worries me."

Michael made his way through the thirty four decks of the Eisenhower, to the tiny hatch that connected it to the Liberty which floated alongside.

After a few minutes of walking through his old ship again, he stepped out onto the battered command deck of the Liberty once more.

"Hello there stranger, just where the bloody hell 'ave you been, I thought I would 'ave to promote me'self as new cap'n while you were gone, so I was." Kinraid said with a mocking wink.

"You know where I've been Quinn," Michael smiled at his first officer. "If you need me, I'll be in my quarters, I have some important business I must attend to."

"Understood, sir. Logameier's been making temporary repairs, he thinks we should be able to make the jump into plasma drive soon without fallin' to bits."

"Good work, we may need to."

He stepped through the doors and into his quarters, it was a mess from various objects fallen from tables and shelves during the battle, now lying broken on the floor. Luckily the food synthesiser was still intact, he keyed in the control for a latté, double sugar, with a sigh. Taking the cup after it gradually appeared he slumped down at his desk. The deep beige colour of Auriga III was visible through his window, god it even looked ugly from space, he thought, and hoped he would not have to set eyes on this fateful planet again.

He needed to contact Admiral Montrose at alpha base and inform him of what had happened here, that the E.D.F had encountered a new hostile alien force in the Dracos, though first he had other ideas.

Punching in a few controls on his personal terminal, he attempted to contact Solaria, he eventually got through to an official acting for the Solarian government.

"I'd like to speak to ambassador Kerulithar please, it's a matter of some urgency."

"I'm afraid no ambassador by that name exists?" The softly spoken echoic voiced Solarian replied.

Michael's brow furrowed in thought, that's odd. "He must do, five years ago, he was instrumental in the Solarian involvement in the Krenaran war, I've personally worked with him."

"You must mean governor Kerulithar of Celtris III, I'll transfer you to his office."

Huh, governor now, Michael thought, raising an eyebrow in the process, the plucky ambassador has done well for himself over the years."

Gradually the familiar face of Kerulithar appeared on the screen, "Michael Alexander, my old friend. This is a surprise, how are you doing, and how is Nikolai and the Liberty?"

"We are good actually, the Liberty has had a few more upgrades, since last we spoke, you have done well for yourself, a governor now I hear."

"After the events surrounding the Solarian entry into the Krenaran war, and our subsequent victory over them, they made me a governor of my homeworld

163

of Celtris III, no more hopping around the galaxy for me, I have a family now."

"That's fantastic news!" Michael said with a genuine smile, he was delighted things were going so well for his old friend, "but hold the phone with that galaxy hopping thing, would you?"

Kerulithar suddenly took on a far more serious tone, "what's on your mind?"

"Know anything about the Dracos?" Michael rubbed his chin as he asked the question.

"Sure; all Solarians know the story of the Dracos, how their evil and murderous ways threatened to almost overthrown our people, and how in response we chased them through our space, it was a terrible time, very sad."

"Okay, have you heard about their return?"

"I heard rumours of their name being bandied about again in the senate, rumours of trouble in the distant Auriga system, our government has taken a strict non-interference policy on this, if I'm correct. Our people do not want to get involved, the gulf of differing philosophies, ideologies, everything about the Dracos runs contrary to our own beliefs. They are a people who actively condone violence and torture as a way of life, where we advocate peace, harmony and advancement through art and the sciences. The Dracos turned from that path a long time ago, and in so doing, stopped being Solarians, they are regarded as their own people now."

Michael was stunned at hearing this, shocked at how two races, who had once been one, could turn out to hate each other so vehemently, where was the higher sensibilities of the Solarians now? "There is an old Earth adage Kerulithar, that time heals all wounds."

"What do you mean, my friend?"

"I have four Dracos warriors, all taken prisoner while we rescued what was left of our science team."

"So it is true, it is not just hearsay and conjecture, the Dracos do still exist!" Kerulithar gasped.

164

"Oh yes, they have just killed a good two hundred and fifty E.O.C.A citizens, however this presents us with a unique chance."

"For what, exactly?"

"Re-unification, to right a three hundred year wrong."

"Too much time has elapsed my friend, there is too much hatred on both sides now," Kerulithar sighed, shaking his head.

"I'm asking you to be that plucky little ambassador I once knew five years ago Kerulithar, one last time, for your own, and for your peoples benefit."

The Solarian stared through the monitor at him, and it seemed as though long seconds passed between them, "if this goes wrong, it could mean my political career."

"Or it could be the making of it, all I'm asking is for you to trust me once again, as once did old friend."

"I worked with you once before, and that turned out to be the greatest case of my ambassadorial career. I will work with you again, but I make no promises."

Michael was buoyed that he managed to get Kerulithar on-board with this, "I will arrange for the talks to be heard at a neutral site."

"Excellent, once the location has been transmitted, I will be there."

"Thank you, Kerulithar."

"Don't thank me yet, I am only doing this because I trust you Michael Alexander," Kerulithar smiled, "Kerulithar out."

The screen went blank, and Michael slumped back down into his chair, he felt elated, but also exhausted. He rubbed at his temples, and let loose a long sigh, it had been hard work. But the first step toward a peace process and re-unification had begun. He just hoped all this would not land him with a court martial for interfering in the affairs of other cultures.

Next he had to contact admiral Montrose at Alpha base, to submit his mission report, he informed the Admiral about the discovery of the Eye of the

Dracos, the destruction of the Copernicus, and of the evidence they had found of the systematic hunting down of the scientists through the corridors of the alien facility, and also of the bloody, yet successful rescue of the only survivor, Kathryn Jacobs."

"Do you think these Dracos will return?"

"I would have to say absolutely admiral, and in greater numbers, in fact I would bet my wages on it."

The admiral stroked his grey flecked bearded chin, "what do you suggest?"

"Well, since there are no colony worlds out this far, the threat to E.O.C.A citizens is minimal, however it is still an incursion into E.O.C.A territory, and they have attacked E.D.F shipping. So I would recommend routing patrols to include this area of space, sir. From what we have learned, the Dracos are only interested in this one planet, because of the Eye of the Dracos built on it. From what I have been able to gather they have labelled it as a halo world, a world of special significance to their people, thus it would be a high priority for re-capture."

"So, this Eye of the Dracos is basically an enormous, super advanced geothermal power plant, extracting energy from the core of the planet itself, and then hurling it out into space."

"Yes, admiral."

"Any way we can adapt it, for our own use?"

"Unlikely, from what we have found, the facility used to fire its beam in regular bursts, to a collector stationed in orbit. However, the whole place was shutdown and abandoned some three hundred years ago, as the Dracos fled from Solarian attacks. The collector has since burned up, as its orbit decayed, and that is why the beams are being shot out into space, as the base still *thinks* the collector is there. Plus, we've seen how the Dracos react to anyone studying their technology, they hunt them down mercilessly."

"True, but it's a heck of an opportunity to pass up, captain. A facility capable of producing virtually unlimited energy, that would solve E.O.C.A energy needs practically overnight."

"I agree sir, but at what cost, the facility itself is so far removed from standard E.D.F systems and technology, that we would have difficulty integrating it, and defending it."

"It's a damned shame, all that power on tap, and virtually for free too, what's your plan then, captain."

"We shut the facility down, just as the scientists found it, and then seal it, so that it stays shut. Perhaps in the future E.D.F scientists may be able to integrate into our own systems, and the Dracos may be more amenable to us using it. Until that day however, it is simply too dangerous, and right now beyond our level of expertise."

The admiral sighed noticeably as a few tense seconds passed, finally after seeing that there was no other option, Montrose agreed. "Shut the place down captain, and lock it tight."

"Will do admiral, I have one final request to make, sir. It is one of a more personal nature."

"Go ahead?"

"The survivor we rescued, Kathryn Jacobs, is a former medical officer of the Liberty, and personal friend to me. She had requested some time to be allowed to bury a very dear friend of hers, who was killed by these Dracos, before we arrived."

"You have five hours captain, then I want those ships back at Charlie gamma base for repairs, as well as the final testing of the Liberties new systems."

"Understood, thank you, sir; Alexander out."

Montrose nodded as Michael ended the transmission.

Another intensely bright burst of raw energy, shot forth from the surface of the planet once again, close to the Liberty, it shot past Michaels personal porthole, briefly coating his entire quarters in bright orange glow, "sweet Jesus, that thing's bright," he cursed to himself as he shielded his eyes.

He eventually emerged from his quarters with a new sense of purpose.

"What's the word, cap'n?" Kinraid asked.

"We have to go back down to the surface, to seal off the facility. I don't want to have to do it to her, because Kathryn has had enough of an ordeal already, but she is the only one who can guide us to the central control room in that place, in order to shut it down."

"I hear ya', sir." Kinraid replied, concerned, more for Kathryn than anyone else.

"I also want Lieutenant Logameier to come up with suggestions, as to how he can shut this thing off, permanently."

"I'll get right on it," Kinraid replied.

"I'm off to see Kathryn, hopefully she is awake now and tell her the good news, you're in command until I get back Quinn."

"Understood, sir. I'm sure little Kathryn'll be delighted to find out she's goin' back down the rabbit hole again."

Michael looked at Quinn, "she's one of ours, she deserves better after what she's been through."

"I know, Cap'n, I know."

Michael left the bridge, and entered an adjoining elevator, which deposited him on deck four, made his way through the Liberty, passing various crewmembers making repairs to still-damaged systems, and who all regarded him with the kind of respect one would give a good friend. Eventually he found the temporary inter-connecting corridor between the Liberty and the Eisenhower, he hoped it would be the last time he would have to make this crossing.

As he made his way back to the med-bay of the other ship, he bumped into commander Fontain again; informed her of the new orders and requested the use of a shuttle. The commander duly granted him the request; he also paged Nikolai through his wrist comm. asking if he wanted one last trip down to the surface. It turned out that the colonel was packing ready for the trip back, yet ultimately agreed.

Michael carefully entered the med-bay to find Kathryn awake, although still a little drowsy, he sat beside her.

"How are you feeling?"

"A little sore, and I keep getting this strange tingling sensation in my leg, but I'm okay I guess."

Michael smiled, repressing a slight chuckle, "the tingling is the micro-static therapy working, something you'll have to get used to for now, I'm afraid."

"You mean they put little implants inside me, why I 'oughta."

Michael chuckled again, "well you seem in better spirits anyway."

"I'm just so glad that I'm finally free of that horrible nightmare, I'm glad you came back for me," she reached over from her hospital bed and kissed Michael tenderly on the cheek.

"You are one of ours, as well as one of my closest friends, I couldn't just stand back and let you die down there."

"I know."

Kathryns levity, and emotional state made what Michael had to say next all the more difficult, his face sunk into one of concern, as he struggled within himself how to tell her.

She studied him intently, "I think I know you well enough by now, to recognise that look, what's wrong Michael?"

The Liberty captain grimaced as he realised that there was no easy way to tell her this, "we have to go back down there."

Kathryn recoiled in shock, "No! I can't, I won't, I won't go through all that again, Michael!"

He silently regarded her with patient eyes, "we have five hours Kathryn, in which to bury your friend, and to finally shut that thing down, for good." He looked at her again, and pleaded with her as he whispered, "you are the only one who can end this."

With that, Michael got slowly to his feet, nodded, left the med-bay and Kathryn to think over what he had just said.

Over the next four hours, Michael went through the details of the mission, the team was to be made up of himself, Lieutenant Logameier, Colonel Vargev and four of his commandoes as well as Kathryn, if she was up to it, if not, they would have to find some other way to shut the facility down.

Hopefully, that wouldn't include sending a torpedo straight down the main aperture and destroying its collider.

He spoke to the men arrayed ahead of him, in the briefing room of the Liberty. "So is everyone clear. It's a simple, go in, shut down, seal it off, and get out again."

"Commandoes will be taking the same armaments as before, we did a quick sweep of the base, when we went it the first time. But we could have missed a few, so stay frosty and remember, we are on their turf, comrades."

A loud shout of "Ooooragh!" came back at the colonel.

"Okay let's gear up and get ready; dismissed." Michael said.

Just as the assembled men went to leave, the doors slid open to reveal a lone, dark figure, silhouetted against the bright lights from the corridor to the Liberties bridge behind, and clutching a walking stick.

She stepped through the doors, it was Kathryn, she hobbled unsteadily towards the assembled men in the tiny briefing room, "you'll need me with you, if you want to find the central control room of the base quickly."

Michael gave a broad warm smile, almost wanting to punch the air in delight, she had come around, although in his heart he knew she would. "Thank you so much Kathryn."

"It's time to finally end this," she replied, "besides, I'm a sucker for punishment." A mischievous grin played across her features.

The others, all respectfully filed out of the small room, leaving Michael and Kathryn alone together.

"What is going to happen to Rachthausen, he deserves a proper burial?"

"His body has been taken out of cold storage on the Eisenhower, and loaded aboard the shuttle as promised. As soon as we shut down the facility, we will all bury him with full military honours, you have my word."

"Thank you."

"It's the least I can do, have you given any thought as to your next posting?" He probed gently.

"Not yet; I'm just trying to take things one day at a time right now."

Michael smiled knowingly, nodding, "I understand, take all the time you need, although I'm sure a warship like the Liberty would be in need of a planetary geologist, somewhere down the line." He winked playfully at her.

Kathryn chuckled slightly and smiled in return, "I'll give it some thought."

"Well," Michael said with a little sigh, "I had better get ready for the mission myself." He smiled as he made to move past Kathryn and leave the room, as he did so however, she leaned forward and kissed him tenderly on the cheek, "thank you." She whispered.

He looked down at her tender features, the long dark hair swaying over her shoulders, betraying just the hint of an occasional grey strand. He wanted so much to kiss her back, but it wouldn't have been right, he knew there was a closeness between them, though with what she had gone through he didn't want to pressure her, he didn't know if she really wanted him or not right now, with the burial of someone she loved looming he knew that now was not the best of times, and he did not want to sacrifice what they already had, for one stupid impulse.

"You have nothing to thank me for," he replied with a curt smile as he left the briefing room, for his quarters.

Kathryn headed back to the Eisenhower's hangar bay to join the rest of the team, she knew she was in good hands at last, but was still terrified of returning to those long dark corridors once again.

Michael gathered his belongings, changing into his full military landfall uniform for the first time in five years. Surprisingly it still fit, Nikolai had warned him that the surface of the planet was particularly windy and cold, and that his naval uniform would not be ideal for spending more than a few minutes on the surface at best.. He took a pulse pistol as a sidearm and tucked it into a holster on his hip, as well as his breathing apparatus. Once he was confident he was ready, he left his quarters and stepped out onto the bridge. He felt a little silly, stood out as he was, in his camouflaged combat fatigues and heavy military boots, while all the other officers around him were in royal blue naval uniforms, yet it was necessary.

"Quinn."

The commander turned, and stopped him in mid-sentence, "Yes I know cap'n, I'm in charge until ye' get back."

"Good man."

With that, Michael left the bridge, and quickly made his way over to the Eisenhower also, soon meeting up with Nikolai, Kathryn and the others in the hangar bay, "hopefully this will be last time we will have to go down to Auriga III for a while, has the body I requested been stowed onboard?" He asked as he turned to Logameier.

"Yes, sir. I saw one of the Eisenhower's crew load it aboard not ten minutes ago."

Kathryn hobbled onto the shuttle itself helped by Michael, while Nikolai, his four accompanying commandoes, and Logameier all followed behind.

Michael sat at the controls and began working them, the rear door closed and sealed, and the craft began to power up again, controls and displays all lit up right across the pilot and navigators seat where Logameier was sat. A dull thrumming groan reverberated around the interior of the bay, slowly increasing in its intensity as the shuttle's gravitic engines began to kick in.

Michael keyed in another control, "shuttle alpha-zero-one to Eisenhower, requesting permission to depart."

"Shuttle alpha-zero-one, request is granted, opening bay doors now, happy travels."

Ian J Smethurst

The communications ceased as the giant hangar bay doors slowly opened, once again revealing the starry blackness of deep space.

He increased power to the shuttles gravitic engines, and the craft began to levitate and gently taxi along the wide central aisle of the hangar bay once more, before Michael brought the boosters up to full power, and, with a loud roar, the shuttle shot forth from the hangar bay, and away from the huge form of the Eisenhower.

"You know, sometimes it can be hard to comprehend the true vastness of space," Logameier said, staring out from the shuttles cockpit into the stars beyond. "Just when you think that space, with all the peoples, planets, asteroids, phenomena and everything else is such a crowded place, it shows you something like this, and then you realise that space itself is a whole lot bigger than you ever imagined."

"I agree, Lieutenant, space is wondrous in its vastness." Michael said as he swung the shuttle around, and lined up to take the craft in the channel between the vast bulk of the Eisenhower, and the Arizona again, thereby revealing the dirty beige colour of the planet below, in all its horrible glory once more.

"You know, I think I'm going to miss this world." Vargev said from behind them.

"You have got to be joking!" Kathryn retorted, unamused and finding the colonel's remark in poor taste, after what she experienced on the surface.

"Actually; I am, I hate the place, its cold, windy, there's no breathable air. I have to admit, apart from the muddy, rain soaked battlefields of Gamma IV, this has to rank as one of the worst place I've ever been assigned, the place is one utter shit hole."

"Ditto," Michael replied simply, as he took the craft into a dive as he neared the planets atmosphere. Its hull began to heat up quickly, flames and super-heated plasma began trailing across its bullet-like hull. A thick contrail of smoke followed the craft as it plunged deeper into the atmosphere.

Inside the occupants were jostled in their seats slightly as the craft rocked and shook from the effects of atmospheric entry.

Once the shuttle glided through the thick methane cloud cover, Michael set the craft to atmospheric flight mode, and the ubiquitous delta wings emerged from underneath the main fuselage, the small winglets slid out from either side of the cockpit, the twin tails lifted up and the shuttle gently flew on course for the Eye of the Dracos.

Another beam of intensely bright orange energy surged skywards heralding another release from the Dracos installation, it burst through the cloud cover with ease and careered off into space. The brightness of the energy burst almost blinded the occupants of the approaching shuttle.

The E.D.F craft gently set down gently set down near to the remnants of the devastated Dracos assault landers, its small landing lights illuminating the tagged twisted black metal of the downed craft.

While the shuttle was one the surface, the four Dracos imprisoned within the Eisenhower's brig, had plans of their own in mind. Their suits only had another twenty four hours worth of power left in them, and they did not wish to waste them being confined to this primitive vessel's detention area.

They had lost their A.R. uplink to the blade of Rhovanion when it departed the system, so they were alone, and although the E.D.F guards had removed their eviscerator rifles, wrist blades, and silencers. They were not altogether unarmed, one of them looked up, seeing a small grill supplying fresh air into each of the cells. Using the still functioning magnetic properties of their suits they slowly, quietly crawled their way to this grill, and, taking the greatest of care not to make a sound, opened it. The lone guard hearing nothing untoward, continued to stand with his back to them.

The four Kallan silently crept out from their cells, and made their way along this tiny air duct, barely large enough for them to crawl inside.

Their was an opening to the main walkway of the ship's brig, where the guard, still unknowing, stood below them, weapon in hand.

The Dracos though, had more than just wrist blades, as the guard would soon learn to his cost, one of the warriors flicked out two small, yet incredibly sharp blades from the front of his boots. Waiting for the perfect opportunity, as the guard scanned the walkway and corridor beyond. Waiting for just the instant when the hapless soldier would look away. Eventually he did so, and immediately the Dracos warrior sprang into action, bursting from the grate in a blur of black bodysuit, he swung from it with both hands, before launching himself from it, and slamming his feet hard into the startled soldiers chest. The blades bit deep, the victim hardly had time to even blink as he fell backwards in a spray of blood from the impact.

He took the troopers weapon, sidearm and passkey, while the unfortunate soldier was still convulsing and gurgling on his own blood, much to the delight of his assailant. With a gentle whisper of "shush now." The Kallan placed both hands either side of the man's head and twisted sharply, the sickening crunch of neck snapping rang out, the victim lay silent and the Dracos had found a new hunting ground.

Michael, Nikolai, and Kathryn emerged from the just landed shuttle, complete with full breathing apparatus and flanked by the four E.D.F commandoes accompanying them.

They made it rather quickly to the now blasted open hatch, the wind howled around the giant focusing pylons, the one on the far side of the aperture partially blotted out the sun, casting htem all in shadow. Michael could feel the cold wind through his combat fatigues, he shivered and wondered why in the world would the Dracos build such an important facility on such a blatantly inhospitable world, probably just down to desperate measures, he guessed. The thought intrigued him as he pressed on following the others , down the dark flight of steps and into the bowels of the facility once more.

"Okay comrades, nows the time to remain focused," Nikolai said, speaking into a tiny microphone inside his breathing gear.

The lights were still all cut, and the illumination from their torches cast strange shadows along the length of the dark shaft, just as it did when they first ventured down.

"Kathryn, are you okay?" Michael asked with genuine concern.

"I'm fine." She lied, as she continued to descend, helped in part by Nikolai. No-one wanted her to aggravate the injury to her leg. With each new step she took, she shuddered just a little more. Not from the cold winds blowing in from the surface, but from fear, she was descending back into her nightmare. Both Michael and Nikolai were worried for her, and neither had really wanted her to do this, but she was the only one who new the location of the main control room.

"We have to keep descending, it's on the third floor," she said, her voice betraying only a little of her pent up emotion.

"We're right behind you Kathryn, lead on, we are with you every step of the way."

The going was painfully slow as they descended the long dark steps built into the now defunct lift shaft. After another half hour, they came upon an opening which signified the first of the three floors; pressing on slowly, they passed the entrance to the second floor.

"It's only about twenty rungs to the third floor now." Kathryn announced, her left leg felt painful from the constant stresses and strains the descent placed on her newly operated on leg muscles and Achilles tendon.

Eventually the small group found the entrance to the third and final floor, the howling winds gave off a type of eerie groan to the place, and each footfall seemed to echo into the darkness beyond.

The pain was beginning to get too much to bear for Kathryn, "I have to rest a moment."

"No problem, take all the time you need." Michael smiled through the darkness at her.

Nikolai signalled to his commandoes to fan out, forming a half sphere of protection to those within, while the Russian himself took out a small plastic canteen of water, offered it to Kathryn, who gingerly took a few sips, and the others, before guzzling some himself.

Logameier was perusing the control panels of the security station, as well as the hieroglyphs adorning the walls, "you know for three hundred year old technology, this is remarkably advanced."

"That's what Kalschacht and Gomez thought." Kathryn replied between gasps of pain.

176

"I bet in their day, these guys where a real rival to the Solarians. No wonder their attempted coup scared the bejesus out of them, and they went on to chase them out of their territory."

"What I don't get is; if these Dracos were so powerful. Why didn't they just create their own empire?" Nikolai asked.

"Because the Dracos were already severely weakened by their failed coup, and the Solarians chasing them through their territory made it worse, any empire the Dracos may have made wouldn't have lasted long before the Solarians came calling again. So the Dracos used the only option they had left at the time, they went into hiding."

"It sounds a little like a cowards way out to me," Nikolai replied as he shone his torch over the interior of the security booth.

"Not really, don't forget their entire race was under the threat of extinction, by going into hiding, they ensured that they at least survived."

"I guess so, I'm glad I'm not a president, and just a soldier, I have an enemy and I kill it, nice and simple."

His reply raised a few smiles from the accompanying commandoes who were trained in exactly the same way.

"Okay, I think I'm ready to go on again now." Kathryn said, "at least its level ground from here on in."

The group continued on their long walk through the three kilometre long, third floor, passing the Dracos chief scientists office, now devoid of any kind of life. The gentle tap of Kathryn's walking stick echoed out through the long dark corridor.

They came to the science maintenance stores, where Rachthausen had cunningly rigged up that small laser welder. He was so proud of himself at the accomplishment; the thought gave Kathryn a warm smile. Although it felt kind of strange, almost as if the spirit of Rachthausen was still with her as she soldiered on, willing her to finish this, to put the nightmare to rest. She dismissed it as little more than wishful thinking.

They carried on until they came upon the next room, Kathryn immediately froze, terrified as she relived the horror that went on in there, it was the briefing room. Blood spatter still coated the walls, and stained the floor from the now removed bodies of the dead scientists. The wall directly opposite to the doors was studded with dozens of tiny craters from the pulse rifles and pistols used in the desperate last defence of the men and women inside.

It was almost as if she could hear their dying screams, the swish of a Dracos blade scything down another of her team, her friends. "Noooo!" She cried out, unable to cope with the flood of awful images this horrific place assaulted her mind with.

"It's okay Kathryn, we're here," Michael said.

"No! It's not okay Michael, this is where they died, you didn't hear their screams, the screams of agony as they died, and the Dracos enjoyed it. They fucking enjoyed it! Hacking my friends down like dogs!"

"I know, it must have been horrible." Michael tried his best to comfort her, although he was growing more worried by the second.

"No you don't know! You weren't there! You weren't there……you….bastard!" She sobbed uncontrollably as she thumped Michael weakly on the chest. Collapsing into him, as all the raw emotion came pouring out of her.

"I'm here now Kathryn, I'm here." Michael replied as he consoled her.

The four Dracos warriors continued their silent creeping throughout the air circulation ducting of the Eisenhower, they saw a room that piqued their interest, and using the nearest vent, dropped down into it.

They quickly sealed the door shut, and consulted a computerised layout of the whole ship, they found they were located on deck twenty four of the thirty four deck cruiser.

"We need to retrieve our weapons," one said.

They consulted the deck plan further, "the weapons storage facility is on deck twenty one, three decks above us."

178

"How will we get there?" A third Dracos asked.

"These ships have an elevator system that runs throughout the ship, we can ride it until we reach that deck, retrieve our weapons and then capture the bridge."

"We'll be seen as soon as we exit the elevator."

"Calm yourself Taneth, we are Dracos, the undisputed masters of moving unseen, remember. We can do this."

"We all die if you fail Kallos, remember that." Taneth retorted.

The four Kallan all climbed back into the ducting, and quietly replaced the vent as it was found, they continued on their silent creeping towards the elevator stop, checking to see the corridor below, leading up to it was clear, then one by one, they slowly dropped down into the corridor itself and sprinted into the elevator, lest anyone should see them.

The doors slowly closed around them, sealing them off from anyone who may chance upon them.

"Deck twenty one," Kallos spoke into the elevator speaker.

"Destination confirmed," came the reply from the elevators onboard speaker system as it whisked them onto the next phase of their plan.

Once it arrived the four quickly exited, and dove into a side room, it appeared to be some form of laundry room. There were strange uniforms and camouflaged clothing piled high on the shelves. An attendant whirled around quickly, startled, to face the four intruders. Before the woman even had time to react, two pulse rifle blasts tore a large bloodied hole straight through her chest and flung her into a row of shelving, before she collapsed, motionless.

"Go!" Taneth shouted, as they climbed up through the air circulation ducting again, and began to make their way across this new deck.

A klaxon began to wail loudly, easily audible through the thin aluminium ducting of the ventilation system. As they passed by another venting grille, they saw red flashing lights coat the rooms below in dark crimson, enemy soldiers and naval officers were running hither and thither. The four hidden Dracos all thought the same thing; they must have found the body of the guard.

179

They refrained from quickening their pace however, to the Dracos this was inconsequential, it would not affect their ability to hide, or creep around the ship.

"What the hell is going on! Who ordered a red alert?" Commander Fontain barked.

"The Dracos prisoners have escaped, there are reports that one guard is dead, two stab wounds to the chest. He has also been relieved of his weapons." Maddox replied.

"Damn it! I want a full deck-by-deck search; find them, prepare to seal off the bridge."

"Aye, commander." Maddox replied, as he relayed Commander Fontains orders to the search teams on the other decks.

Despite the constant hurrying back and forth of the Eisenhower's crew below them, the Dracos continued on their inexorable, silent creep toward the weapons storage facility. Two guards were stationed at the door to the weapons room, predictable, Kallos thought, these aliens whom he had come to learn were called the E.D.F from the deck plans he had studied, almost always prepared for a frontal assault.

The problem with that was, the Dracos almost never attacked from the front, not if it wasn't advantageous to do so. He crawled onwards through the ducting, and sure enough there was another vent that provided access to the inside of the armoury, and their weapons.

The four of them gradually climbed down into this room, looking like a maze of weapon racks, ammunition cases, and dusty old grenade boxes.

Taneth switched his helmet to thermal imaging in an effort to see if the guards on the other side of the door had noticed anything untoward, they were stood still guarding the entrance as if nothing had happened, blissfully unaware that their staunch guard had utterly failed, he breathed a sigh of relief.

After a short period of searching, Kallos and the others found their confiscated weapons, there was a crate containing three eviscerator rifles, an eviscerator pistol, two silencers and all their wristblades.

Kallos kitted up with the eviscerator pistol and silencer option he had used on the surface, while the others all held eviscerator rifles, they attached the weapons to the backs of their suits and fixed their wristblades and silencers into position on their arms. Kallos smiled, the second phase of their plan had been successful, now they were fully armed again, and ready. "The hunt must continue." He said to the others.

"I'm okay," Kathryn said as she struggled onward through the gloomy corridor, past the awful sight of the briefing room massacre. Just the gentle tap, tap, of her walking stick kept her company now, as they ventured onward through the dark confines.

They passed Dracos corpses that had fallen, looking like bizarre black mannequins in their environment suits, the red glow of their eye slits, so terrible in the darkness, now long since faded away.

She led them to a small room, its doors once again crumpled and full of blast marks, this was the auxiliary energy monitoring station, the place where they had first activated the station. "This is where it began, perhaps it can be shit down from here too?"

Logameier was first into the room, eager to get to grips with the alien machinery, what he found dismayed him. Much of the delicate electronics and terminals were smashed in the fighting. He looked over the various controls, studying them intently.

"I've had enough experience working on Solarian technology on the Liberty, this is crude, but not too dissimilar, in-fact I recognise many of the controls."

Kathryn's heart leapt with joy, "so you can shut it down, right?"

"Not by the looks of it; not from here anyway, Kathryn this is just an auxiliary control station you see, used to monitor the collider, and the flow of energy from the planets surface, through it. In an emergency it can be used to re-initialise the base, which is likely what has happened. But it cannot be shut down from here, that needs to be done from the primary control station, somewhere else."

"I know where it is, I've been there, follow me." Kathryn replied a little deflated.

The team all filed out of the room, the crunch of broken glass from the various smashed display echoing loudly underfoot.

Eventually they came to a set of giant blast doors, "I had shut these behind me, I guess that alien scum must have opened them again," Kathryn pointed out rather acidly.

The deep thrumming grew steadily louder once again, as the facility prepared to hurl another blast of energy out into space.

The group continued onward, "See how this corridor is semi-circular, it must be following the walls of the aperture, we're not far from the collider itself." Logameier pointed out excitedly to Michael, to him, this was a voyage of discovery, learning about new and alien technology, the secrets it unlocked was all very fascinating.

"We don't need a running commentary Lieutenant," Michael whispered, as he pointed to the forlorn figure of Kathryn trudging ever onward, reliving her own personal torture step-by-step.

Logameier looked at the sad figure, and a profound sense of embarrassment came over him, "sorry, sir." Was all he could think to offer.

Michael nodded silently to him as they walked.

After a slow walk of perhaps half an hour, they had reached the second set of blast doors, this place is incredibly well built, Michael thought, they can section off parts of the base in the event one part is damaged, much like starships can.

They eventually came to a gigantic control centre, light from dozens of consoles flickered off the dark walls. This room at least gave Kathryn a warm feeling, this was where she and Rachthausen had shared that tender moment, when he had kissed her. It was then that she knew the sergeant loved her, and, even though she had been fighting it, loved him too.

The accompanying commandoes took up a guarding position at the doors as Logameier looked over the controls, studying them much as he had done in the smaller auxiliary control station. He watched the power levels build up, in the spinning collider. Incredible, he mused, that collider is spinning at over twenty thousand revolutions per minute. It is spinning so fast, that anything a similar size made by the E.D.F would have spun itself to pieces virtually instantly.

After spending a few minutes hopping from console to console, looking over all the controls, he announced. "Right! I think I have it, with the occasional difference here and there; it is similar to the process used to shut down the Solarian power core on the Liberty."

He eyed a console intently, the language was based upon Solarian script, he had come to recognise many of the flowing, delicate symbols in his time aboard the Liberty, and was able to equate many of them to their English language counterparts. This was somehow different, altered slightly, the symbols instead of depicting peaceful iconography, like the Talula leaf, which symbolised life or beginning in the Solarian language, were replaced with harsher, jagged, aggressive counterparts.

His finger hovered over one of the controls; doubt began to cloud his mind.

Finally, Lieutenant Johnson Logameier bit the bullet, pressed the button, and held his breath.

The station let forth one final, almighty blast of intense energy, bright enough to be seen for miles around, and far more powerful than the previous ones. It was so bright and so intense, that it set nearby plant life alight, creating a number of fierce, yet short-lived wild fires.

This last, furious release tore its way through the planets atmosphere with all the force of a high power sniper round, tearing through a mans body. This was the Eye's swansong, its final farewell to the galaxy that had created it, and what a swansong it was. It shot passed the E.D.F fleet, illuminating every single ship in a bright fiery orange glow.

"Holy mother of crap!" Kinraid replied from the captain's chair of the Liberty, as he had to turn away from the viewer to avoid being blinded by the massive flash of light.

The beam continued past the five ships in close orbit, and shot forth through the Auriga system, then out into deep space on an endless journey into the vast starlit void beyond.

E.D.F Chronicles – Eye of the Dracos

Logameier breathed a sigh of relief, he had chosen correctly, the remaining energy stored inside the collider read zero, it had completely discharged all the energy contained within, and could now be shut down safely.

He made his way over to another complex looking console, discharging the built up energy was just the first part, now he had to shut down the collider itself, if he guessed wrong that enormous spinning structure could very well spin itself into oblivion.

Slowly he traced his finger over a rectangular, touch sensitive control, it was lit up in increments, figuring this was the speed setting for the revolutions the collider was spinning at, he traced his finger along it, the green increments slowly winked out as he did so. Johnson had to do this slowly and carefully, too fast or too jerky a movement could seize the entire thing, tearing it to pieces within seconds, and Michael had told him the E.D.F wanted this thing intact, so future scientists could study it, and perhaps find a way of using it.

The final increment slowly winked out, and gradually the collider came to a standstill, now all he had to do was lock it down, and the shutdown process was complete. He realised he was sweating, not because he was hot, it was warm in here, but more from an intense, nervous concentration.

The weight of responsibility he had felt throughout this process had been huge, akin to the time when he had first took up his chief engineer responsibilities on the Liberty. There was so much at stake, the entire E.O.C.A was counting on him to have this place secured.

If he didn't get this right, not only would the E.D.F lose a potentially vital new source of power; entire star systems rested on this one outcome. If the Dracos did manage to capture this facility, like they are intent on doing, and do become as powerful as they once were, not only were the Solarians at risk, but nearby E.O.C.A colony worlds as well, he was damned if the Dracos would stop here, he had to lock this out and he had to do it right.

He took a breath, swallowed his nerves and calmed himself, walking over to a third console, he found that this was the controls for four giant magnetic interlocks, that clamped to the side of the collider to hold it secure, and prevent it from being activated, even accidentally again. In their haste to abandon this place, the Dracos must have skipped this step all those years ago, just one simple step that could have avoided everything that has happened here.

He punched in the four controls, and slowly four massive twenty metre diameter rectangular clamps, gradually emerged from the aperture wall toward the collider itself, each one must weigh twenty tonnes, and they were embued with a heavy magnetic charge, they extended inexorably outward, until magnetic attraction took over, and they slammed down on the collider with a resounding, dull thud.

Not one man, one single person uttered a word while Logameier went about his work, they simply stood watching in silent awe, as he went about the process, willing him on, because they knew as much as he did, that so many lives rested upon it.

He stopped and turned towards his captain, "Structure shut down, and locked down securely, sir."

Michael smiled with warm pride at his chief engineer, "Good job, lieutenant."

"Thank you, sir." Logameier breathed a sigh of relief as he shook Michael's hand.

"Now let's get out of here shall we, we still have one last task to perform," he said as he smiled in Kathryn's direction.

"Captain, looking at these plans there is a quicker way to the surface, through the emergency hatch," Logameier suggested.

"We tried looking for it, but could not find it ourselves." Kathryn replied.

"Can't hurt to take another look, and besides this time, we are not running for our lives,"

The team slowly walked along the remainder of the floor, eventually coming to the elevator, which had quickly returned to their level after detecting their approach. They all piled in, and were automatically whisked to the floor above, where they disembarked and immediately began searching for the hatch opening.

"It has to be here somewhere, it's noted in the plans," Logameier cursed as he searched about the place.

Kathryn tapped the bottom of her cane on the corridor walls, listening for any hint of a hollow behind the walls, eventually she came across one, "over here!" she shouted over to the rest of the group, all busily searching.

Their collective torchlight illuminated a large panel, certainly large enough to crawl through, slowly Nikolai and Michael unfastened the metal panel from the wall and laid it down to one side.

There were small rungs leading up to an incline all the way to the surface, Nikolai took up the rear and closed the panel shut again behind them, the group all crawled single file up these rungs toward the surface. Kathryn had to stop frequently as the constant crawling was hard on her newly operated on leg, the pain was severe, nevertheless she soldiered on as best she could, as she knew as well as anyone that there wasn't room enough to carry anyone, in the dark cramped shaft to the surface.

Michael was at the head of the line and was first to come upon the hatch, his torch revealed a small two button control panel, he quickly figured that it was there simply as the means for opening the hatch, and, after pressing one of the controls, found he was correct as the hatch slid noisily open, covering him in a thin mist of dirt and the occasional piece of dead vegetation. He wiped the lenses on his breathing mask in order to see properly, and stepped out onto the harsh windswept surface once again.

He helped Kathryn clamber her way up, who took a break as the accumulated pain from the climb had become severe, gradually as she rested, the pain came back down to bearable levels again.

Nikolai, Logameier, and the rest of the commandoes all followed soon enough, and Nikolai sealed the hatch shut behind him.

"It is a shame we had to blow the hatch open in order to get access earlier!" Nikolai shouted over the howling winds, which had picked up somewhat from when they had landed.

"Why!" Michael replied.

"Because we cannot seal the place shut one hundred percent, that's why, not without an engineering crew down here to fabricate a new cover to go over it."

186

"We could ask for a systems engineer to input an E.D.F encryption algorithm into their main computer, so even if the Dracos do try to re-take this place, they won't be able to use it without our codes, and with the language being so vastly different its unlikely they'll be able to break it anyway," Logameier suggested.

"Good idea, I'll add it to my mission report to submit to admiral Montrose, when we get out of here," Michael replied.

He turned to Kathryn, who had now recovered sufficiently to be able to walk "Let's get back to the shuttle, so we can bury your friend, like he deserves to be shall we?"

Kathryn smiled warmly, and nodded despite the pain, and she walked the distance to the shuttle, a little over three kilometres with little fuss. In-fact, other than the bitingly cold winds that constantly harangued this place, the return journey was rather a pleasant one.

The team all took some shelter in the shuttle, and a brief moment in which to warm up a little from the cold conditions outside, took out some rations and began eating while this latest storm surge passed over them, once they were sufficiently warmed up, hunger was staved off, and the storm had largely passed, they set forth to brave the elements again to bury the late Sergeant Rachthausen.

Nikolai, Michael, Logameier, and one of the commandoes bore the zipped up body of the sergeant on a stretcher at shoulder height as they would a coffin. Kathryn carried some of his more mundane personal effects with her, the others like medals, any personal items such as payment cards, would be sent to his next of kin. Kathryn wasn't even sure he had one, he had never even mentioned in the brief time she had known him, E.D.F command would see to that side of things, if he did have a mother or a family she made a mental note to visit them as soon as she could.

The solemn procession slowly marched, without a word, as a mark of respect to the fallen sergeant to a spot Kathryn selected near to the facility. The other commandoes all dug a shallow grave, and gathered together a prodigious amount of rocks, including a giant gleaming boulder of quartz, that would serve as a fitting headstone. The quartz itself was heavy and had to rolled into position, its various facets glinted in the light from the twin Aurigan moons, she smiled as it reminded her of the light that Rahthausen carried within him, the goodness of his soul. Once the digging was finished and the grave prepared, Kathryn began the eulogy, her voice cracked and choked, Nikolai, Michael, Logameier, and all of the commandoes bowed their heads in silent respect.

"Here lies Sergeant Heinrich Rachthausen, of the 69th Sicarian guards infantry battalion, a proud leader of men, who fought with valour and honour, far beyond that expected of him." She stopped to wave away a tear.

"What people didn't know, was that besides his great physical strength, he was one of the kindest and gentlest men I ever knew, always putting the needs of others around him above his own needs, and in the end he made the ultimate sacrifice," Kathryn could no longer hold the emotion within her and she began to break down, tears began to flow, her shoulders dropped, and she began to sob, before with one last ounce of courage summoned up the will to say "so that others may live." She wept openly, finally overcome, her resolve gave out as she remembered his final moments in stark clarity.

Michael took her place, as Nikolai consoled her, "and now we commit this brave and noble soldier to the ground, earth to earth, ashes to ashes, dust to dust, may you rest in peace."

Kathryn planted a kiss on the sergeants personal copy of the holy bible, and rested it onto the chest of the body, "goodbye, my love." She whispered under tear stained cheeks.

They all worked together to cover the sergeants body with the earth they dug out earlier, and then to lay the assortment of rocks, in a simple but fitting tribute to a great man.

Nikolai took out a small piece of chalk, and drew a large white crucifix on the glittering headstone, before placing the blood spattered helmet atop it, Logameier melted the chin strap to the rock so that it would not blow away in the wind.

Finally, Kathryn placed his sergeant's stripes in the centre of the crucifix, and taking great care not to melt the fabric itself, Logameier attached them the same way.

The entire group took a minutes silence, heads bowed low, before stepping two paces backward.

"Present arms!" Nikolai called out.

Snapping into action, the commandoes immediately held their weapons aloft, the muzzles pointing skywards.

"On my mark, three rounds, fire!"

A blast of armschlager fire rang out loudly amongst the desolate, empty surroundings.

"Fire!"

A second blast of gunfire, tore through the silence.

"Fire!"

The third and final blast of gunfire seemed to echo even louder than the previous two over the windswept flatlands, the sound travelled for miles around. The three gun salute to a brave soldier was complete, the arrayed commandoes all stood to attention, clasped their weapons to their sides, brought their hands up and gave a long silent salute.

Nikolai, Kathryn, Michael, and Johnson all did likewise, it was a fitting tribute to such a kind, gentle and brave man, who made the ultimate sacrifice to ensure that Kathryn lived.

Taneth, Kallos, and the other two Kallan warriors, now fully armed , left the armoury as quickly and as quietly as they entered. One, gently shut the metal grate behind them, as they skulked through the air ventilation ducting towards the elevator stop on the Jefferson class heavy cruiser, Eisenhower.

They grinned at the naval officers and soldiers, running to and fro, in a vain attempt to find them, little realising they were passing by right above them.

Kallos and Taneth both knew that the third phase of their plan was by far the most risky, they had to make their way, silently to the ships command centre, a full twenty decks above, which they planned to take over, then fly this crude contraption through the atmosphere, transporting them to the surface, so they could once and for all finish this hunt.

Making it back to a room very close to the elevator itself, the dropped back down inside, surprising a technician in the process, the panicked crewman went to bring up his sidearm, though a casual swipe from Taneths wristblade silenced the man forever, as the young crewman's body fell to the floor, quickly followed by his separated head.

There was a slight, nervous pause, as the four Dracos readied themselves for the inevitable dash toward the elevator.

"Go, go, go!" Kallos shouted, and in one swift movement, all four Kallan sprinted full pelt in unison, out of the room, and into the open corridor.

Their sheer speed surprised two naval officers who were in the process of searching for them nearby. Kallos let loose with his eviscerator pistol as he ran, firing half a dozen of the razor sharp discs at the hesitant officers, trying to bring their weapons to bear.

Three hit home, slashing one of the men's cheek, another embedded itself deep into his chest, and a third tore open his stomach, exposing his flailing bloody innards. He fell in a wet crump to the floor, screaming in agony as the intensely strong acid began to take its effect slowly melting through his face, and eating into his chest and stomach.

The disparate screams were awful to hear, but unfortunately loud. His partner dies quickly as a larger eviscerator disc, fired from a rifle, whipped through the air, and slammed into his forehead, there was little blood, just the nauseating stench of flouro-antimonic acid slowly dissolving his brain matter.

The four warriors dived into the elevator quickly, others would come quickly, attracted by the dying man's scream, they had to get off this deck.

"Command centre!" Kallos barked out his order.

"Destination confirmed." The elevator replied, the doors closed painfully slowly to the sight of three E.D.F soldiers sprinting around the corner of the corridor, seeing the dead naval officers, and then running towards them, weapons raised, the doors eventually closed fully, and the elevator rocketed the inhabitants, at over three hundred miles per hour, to their destination.

"Reports of weapons fire, deck twenty one, two casualties near the elevator stop," Maddox announced turning to Fontain, the commander was worried.

"They're going for the bridge, have all troops converge upon this room, arm yourselves." Fontaine said, nervously brushing an errant strand of red hair from her face.

"Already done, but it's too late, the elevator has already reached this deck."

Fontaine cursed under her breath, sometimes improvements in technology, were not such an improvement after all.

The elevator doors opened out revealing three E.D.F troopers, weapons ready. At close range, the Dracos were far quicker, and leapt gracefully into the air, somersaulting over the heads of the dumbfounded soldiers who desperately tried to track their movements with their weapons. Pulse rifle blasts tore into the walls and ceiling in a neat line following the Dracos's movements. As the Kallan came down, they brought their wristblades down hard on their victims, cleaving through necks, and severing arteries with sickening ease, blood spurted out from the bodies. A vicious kick sent another careering to the ground before Kallos unleashed his silencer, the tiny metallic spike lodged perfectly into the doomed soldier's throat, before the Kallan warrior casually retracted it, tearing the unfortunate victim's throat to shreds within a split second.

They made it to the main entrance of the bridge, but found it sealed shut, two more troopers came charging down the corridor towards them, quickly followed by others behind.

Two of the Dracos took up defensive positions, cornering either side of the 'T' junction that separated the bridge from the rest of the deck, and began laying down bursts of suppressive fire, causing the E.D.F troops attempting to overrun them to dive into cover themselves.

Kallos and Taneth both searched frantically for an air duct, maintenance hatch, anything they could us, as weapons fire began to pepper the walls all around them, they would be dead within minutes if they stayed here.

Finally they found something, they were in luck, it was the opening to a small maintenance crawl space, which ran directly to the bridge itself. If it wasn't for Kallos switching to thermal view, and picking up the heat generated by a small bulkhead light on the other side of the concealed panel, they might never have found it.

Quickly they prised open the panel and dove inside, pulse rifle fire had torn deep blackened gouges into the wall around them. The other two Dracos continued to pour fire into the E.D.F troopers. Three of the soldiers lay dead in the centre of the corridor, riddled with eviscerator discs.

As these last two Dracos neared the entrance to the crawlspace under a withering hail of fire, one of them took a hit in the arm, the force of the impact flung him against the scorch marked wall; three more shots followed it up, two of which slammed straight into his chest armour, shattering the carbon fibre plate into a spray of black shards, the second tore straight into his stomach. The Dracos warrior fell clutching his weapon, as he died propped against the corridor wall in a lifeless sitting position.

With no time to seal the cramped , dingy, confined crawl space shut. The three remaining Kallan warriors shuffled along as fast as they physically could to the other end.

The E.D.F troops all swarmed towards the open end of the tiny crawlspace, yet none dared venture inside for fear of their heads being sliced off.

Another panel blocked the other entrance to the crawl way, which in total was no more than forty feet long, hampering Kallos's access to the bridge itself.

A heavy, swift kick, soon removed the problem, causing it to fall away to one side with a loud clatter; he launched himself out of the tiny hatch, much to the astonishment of the bridge crew who believed their command centre sealed shut.

To all intents and purposes, it was, except to the Dracos, the tiniest crawlspace was a means of access.

Taneth was quickest off the mark, leaping high into the air in an acrobatic flip, his wristblades outstretched, swinging his arm so fast it was barely visible as he quickly decapitated one of the bridge crew.

Kallos sprinted towards a console as the third Dracos warrior peppered the exposed crewmen with razor sharp eviscerator discs, three more fell clutching at bloodied ruined throats, torso's torn open, and severed legs, making them easy pickings for the other two.

In total there were a dozen bridge crew, and they had accounted for four of them at a stroke, there were now eight left, it would be a tall order, but not impossible.

Kallos traded fire with a youngish looking male barking out incomprehensible orders to those around him. Taneth landed from his acrobatics neatly on his feet, and followed this up by with a quick forearm strike to another. The lethal blades sliced deep into the man's face, and he fell back screaming, before he leapt into the air again, adopting a textbook Dracos close combat technique.

Kallos finally dispatched his opponent with a series of well placed shots from his eviscerator pistol, two in the shoulder and a third in the forehead ensured he would travel the hereafter.

The third and final Dracos warrior was darting from smashed console to smashed console, trying to get behind the now pinned crewmen in order to set up a triangular killing field with the other two.

A red haired female was firing back from cover, she was a surprisingly good shot, and one slammed into Kallos's shoulder, blasting apart a fair sized chunk of carbon fibre plate, his pale arm was now exposed and bleeding, the warrior cursed vehemently in his native tongue as he skulked behind cover.

E.D.F Chronicles – Eye of the Dracos

Taneth landed gracefully near the far corner of the circular bridge, to Kallos's right, calmly he put two eviscerator rounds into the back of the head of a male, before taking cover himself.

"Taneth, diversion leap," Kallos spoke into his communicator built into the side of his battlehelm, a silent nod confirmed he had understood the order, as he popped up to spray the surviving naval officers with a burst of Eviscerator rounds.

There were now five left, all in a cluster, defending their captain directly ahead of Kallos. The diversion leap was a risky, yet necessary Dracos technique, used to get in amongst small clusters of enemy troops like this. One would leap high through the air, all the while firing down on their enemy, in order to get them to keep their heads down, while at virtually the exact same time a second Dracos would leap into the air straight at them. The resulting melee was often brief and bloody. It was an incredibly hard manoeuvre to pull off successfully though, requiring exact timing, this was why it was one of the most advanced of combat techniques taught to the Kallan.

"Go!"

Taneth bounded into the air with an immense jump, almost hitting the ceiling. He began pumping fire into the small group as he passed by overhead, catching one in the chest and sending him staggering back crashing into the ships viewscreen. Kallos then leapt straight for the beleaguered group, his and Taneth's bodies missed one another by mere inches, as he landed neatly in-amongst them, sending one sprawling across the ground as he slammed into him.

The two who had been knocked out of the cluster were now right in the firing line of the third Dracos, who gunned them both down mercilessly.

The resulting combat was over in seconds as Kallos tore open the throat of one, while simultaneously spin kicking another.

The female captain broke free, running headlong towards a still intact console smeared with the blood of a crewmate. She frantically stabbed at a control and spoke into the console, all she managed to say was, "all crew, this is Fontaine, abandon shi….."

Three eviscerator discs sliced through her neck, Commander Erica Fontaine's head gradually separated from her body and bounced off the console she was using, her body collapsed onto the hard deckplating in a spray of dark crimson blood.

The Eisenhower was theirs, just four Dracos warriors had taken over control of an entire E.D.F heavy cruiser. The moans of the dying and the screams of agony were a delight to hear, as Taneth and the other Dracos kicked away the weapons of those who still attempted some desperate form of resistance, despite the intense pain of deep eviscerator slashes, and the acid now slowly melting its way into their bodies. Oh to hear their glorious tortured screams that little bit longer, and to revel in the chaos and bloodletting they had caused, they were Dracos, this was their victory.

One by one, the bridge crew slowly expired from their injuries, leaving the room awash with blood, and yet eerily silent, this filled Kallos with a sense of sadness and the very quickly longed to hear those screams once again, such was the life of a Dracos Kallan warrior.

The slaughter had taken a little over three minutes, Kallos approached this third Dracos warrior who had accompanied them all this time, he never actually knew his name, he had fought well, worthy of recognition, as all of them had.

"Kallan! What is your name?"

"I am Aelthris, fourth daughter of Tamrath."

"A female?" he asked almost quizzically, taken aback. Very few females survived for long in the ranks of the Kallan, the vast majority stayed on Corvandris, where they were prized, since the Dracos raced depended upon them for propagation.

"You have fought well Aelthris, daughter of Tamrath; worthy of recognition in the annals of the Kallan."

"I fight only to serve the Dracos, and to hear the screams of my enemy."

"That you have, and there will be more before we are finished. We must continue the hunt, our prey is still on the surface, and continues to taint our world."

E.D.F Chronicles – Eye of the Dracos

All Dracos females had a first name beginning with the letter 'A', it was customary, to honour the first Dracos woman to ever set foot on Corvandris, Alarieth, the sister of blood. She was one behind the original coup attempt against the Solarians, when it failed, she fled to Corvandris and was never found by the Solarians. She also goes by the name of the all-mother now, her age is so advanced many do not believe she has many years left.

Although commander Fontaines warning to the crew of the Eisenhower was cut short, enough of it was heard to start a rush for the escape pods, which began to jettison from the outer hull of the ship in small flurries.

Taneth was sat at the ships pilot's position, the Eisenhower, being an E.D.F ship lacked the sophisticated piloting chairs of the Liberty, Solarian craft or even Dracos cruisers, and instead relied upon the slow and ungainly method of using a console instead. Several stray eviscerator rounds were lodged into the side of the display, and more than once the Dracos warrior came close to being cut by his own ammunition; an occupational hazard for a Kallan, and an extremely painful one.

"Full power to the ship's main engines, head for the atmosphere." Kallos said, as he took the seat once used by the late commander Fontaine.

After looking puzzlingly at the instruments for a few seconds, Taneth finally came across a shiny metallic 'T' shaped handle, and pushed it all the way forward.

This ignited the Eisenhower's twin inter-system boosters with a roar, and the ship began to gradually lurch forward under the thrust of the two gigantic engines, gaining in speed all the time.

The Liberty, still connected to it was being dragged along forcefully by the much larger craft, the small warship started lurching and rocking violently as it was pulled along, crewmen were thrown to the ground everywhere, Kinraid barely managed to hold onto his seat. "What in the name o' god is goin' on!" he shouted over the din of violent shaking, the scream of twisting metal, and the shattering of glass.

"It's the Eisenhower!" Lieutenant Hicks shouted, the relief sensor officer aboard. "She's fired up her main boosters! She's heading straight for the planet!"

"What in the love of Mike for!"

"No idea, but we are being pulled along with her, like a dog on a leash! The stress on the inter-connecting corridor is exceeding design limits! She's going to tear off the ship any minute, and if she does we'll have explosive decompression across the whole deck!" Hicks shouted over the constant barrage of the ship's violent jostling, several other naval officers were thrown forcefully from their chairs.

"Jettison the hatch! Break us free o' the Eisenhower, and then contact that bloody ship, ask them what in god's name do they tink they are doin?"

"Automated docking clamps are unresponsive, attempting to override." Hicks said as he tied in the sensory station with the engineering sub-systems monitor of the ship.

"My station is throwing alerts at me constantly! That section is close to buckling, it'll give way any second!" Logan Jones said as he looked toward Hicks, with panic lined features.

"There, I've got it!" The Lieutenant shouted in triumph as he managed to separate the badly damaged corridor from the Eisenhower, the Liberty floated free as the enormous vessel, five times its size, roared ahead past them.

The heavy cruiser's hull began to heat up, turning a shade of bright orange as it neared the atmosphere.

"Full alert status; follow them!" Kinraid barked.

"commander, our hull won't stand another entry into the planets atmosphere, not with the damage we sustained fighting those Dracos ships." Hicks said.

"Godamnit!" Kinraid fumed, but ultimately knew that Hicks was right, with the pounding they had taken, they would simply burn up trying, the graviton shields would not last for long.

"I've tried contacting them, there's no response, I'm showing a wave of escape pods jettisoned just prior to her firing her boosters."

"What!" Kinraid asked, it was all beginning to make sense now, she's been taken over, had to be.

"Lieutenant, what lifesigns are you showing over there?"

Hicks checked his instruments, three Dracos lifesigns, that is all…." He gasped as the stark reality of what has happened hit home.

"Well if we can't stop 'em, we'll make it bloody difficult! Ready fusion cannon, target their engines, fire when ready!" Kinraid said.

Logan zeroed in on the Eisenhower punching its way ever deeper into the planets atmosphere, flames and smoke trailed off of it, making it difficult to get an exact fix. He pressed the button, and unleashed the full fury of the Liberties largest and most powerful weapon system.

The incandescent electric blue beam of pure power shot from the elongated barrel of the weapon, and slammed home with such force it tore apart one of the Eisenhower's boosters, blasting it clean off the ship, a great black cloud of smoke and debris fragments torn away from the impact, billowed out behind it, leaving a thick black contrail in its wake.

The force of the impact was so great that it caused the giant runaway cruiser to veer uncontrollably off-centre. The massive breach in its rear continued to stream out smoke, as the hull of the huge ship heated up irregularly, glowing red-hot as it pushed ever deeper.

Kinraid could only watch, as the stresses of the ship's hull as it began to list wildly out of control towards the planet grew to such an extent, that halfway along its surface it began to buckle, no longer able to resist the immense forces being subjected to it. It finally gave way; a panel tore open, then another, and another like paper, the ship was slowly tearing itself apart as it hurtled onwards in its suicidal descent.

Support struts, cross-beams, and its internal structural lattice work were all painfully visible as the rear half of the ship slowly tore itself away from the front half in a cloud of flames, smoke, and debris. Miniature explosions flashed across its broken surface like the very fires of hell, swathes of fragments were thrown loose as the latter half of the ship gradually tore itself apart in a giant plume of flame and red-hot hull fragments all streaking toward the planet surface.

Amazingly, the front half of the ship was still intact, and glided haphazardly towards the surface. Now through the upper atmosphere it rushed headlong in its descent to the surface, fire blazed out of a myriad of rents and smoke poured from the torn rear in a thick black trail across the sky. Tiny twisted metal fragments were constantly torn off the devastated structure, like a shower of metallic confetti, before the entire thing smashed headlong into the planets surface with such incredible force that it threw up a great cloud of earth and dust over a thousand metres into the air, before settling into a crater almost a kilometre across. Small fires littered the basin where the remains of the devastated ship lay, and the thick plume of smoke that heralded its arrival seemed to grow steadily wider, before it too began to disperse.

The torn hull fragments of the rear half of the ship rained down through the thick pall of methane clouds, like a plethora of streamers, before they too slammed into the ground themselves.

Kinraid simply watched, as did the entire bridge crew of the Liberty, awestruck. For minutes afterwards debris continued to fall in little black and grey shoots to the ground, he had never seen anything quite like it, it was if the planet had just been struck by a meteorite; to all intents, it had.

Michael, Kathryn, Nikolai and the accompanying commandoes all witnessed the gigantic blast created by the crashing Eisenhower, in fact the shockwave from the impact had blown them all to their feet, as they looked upon the plume of smoke, earth and dust, they could see the bright fiery streamers of falling debris, looking like a swarm of shooting stars.

The three surviving Dracos however had lived through the colossal impact, in fact they had jumped clear of the wreckage several seconds before it had slammed into the ground, using their cat-like acrobatics to literally leap from torn outer hull fragment to torn outer hull fragment, eventually landing hard on the ground itself. The strength of their suits protected them from the worst of the landing, the shockwave of course flattened them all, though they had expected this and so kept their bodies as close to the ground as possible, so that the immense blast passed reasonably harmlessly over them.

Once they had returned to full consciousness several minutes later, they found that they could move easily enough, nothing was broken, and other than a few minor cuts and scrapes, were ready to resume the hunt; and that they did, with gusto as they ran the rest of the way straight towards the Dracos facility.

Michael with the rest of the party on the surface, were beginning the walk back toward the shuttle, the funeral service having been concluded and observed a two minute silence for the fallen sergeant.

He knew that what he saw was no meteor strike, it was an asteroid, the combined firepower fo the fleet in orbit would have either destroyed it or at the very least, diverted it away from the planet. No, that was a ship, but which one? Something had happened in orbit, and he was anxious to get to the shuttle so he could contact the Liberty and find out.

Taneth, Kallos, and Aelthris all sprinted toward the base, then they picked up the thermal signatures of the party, and instantly flattened to the ground, their black shapes virtually invisible as stooped so low. This was it, Kallos thought, the hunt would soon be over, and he would be victorious, he would be the one who claimed the Eye of the Dracos for his people, and rid the planet of this alien scum. He would return to Corvandris a hero, one who had done what that fool Drax, could not. He would have to be careful though, this new species were a worthy adversary, and dangerous, he respected them almost as much as he hated them.

The trio crept closer to the group, which strolled toward one of their own landing craft, it looked a poor comparison to the Dracos assault landers Kallos was accustomed to.

The group was making slow progress, hampered by an injured female with a slight limp, they would deal with her in their own time. This would make the final kill all the more easier Kallos grinned, he was going to enjoy what was to come.

The three Kallan patiently crept to within thirty feet of their target, like big cats stalking their prey, still they had not noticed them. Aelthris readied her eviscerator rifle, Kallos drew his pistol and waited for a clear shot with his silencer.

The time had come, and with a silent nod of his dark battlehelm, Kellos began the assault.

Virtually silenced by the noise of the winds, three eviscerator discs slammed into the back and neck of the closest commando, he fell without a sound as his head was efficiently severed from its body.

The only sound that was audible was the impacts of the ammunition slicing into the fateful commandoes body, a noise similar to a cleaver slicing through thick meat.

Before the patrol had even realised what was happening, Kallos had dispatched another with a well aimed shot to the spine, the paralysed commando simply crumpled to the ground, this however the party did hear.

"Holy shit!" Michael shouted as he whirled around at the sound and saw the two bodies laid infornt of him, not six feet away.

"Get to the shuttle, NOW!" Vargev barked, "We'll deal with this."

Taneth was first into action, leaping high into the air as he fired round after round into the commandoes , one was shot through the leg, another lodged in his upper arm. The soldier screamed as the acid took its effect, yet battled to remain focused despite the acute pain. Unfortunately his focus ended as Taneth landed, blade first, on top of him.

The Dracos warrior kicked out at the other commando almost immediately, sending the trooper clattering to the dirt. Nikolai, however ended his marauding killing spree, by gunning him down mercilessly with his armschlager, the heavy assault rifle bucked and swayed as high velocity slugs tore through the Kallan warrior, almost sawing him in half, at that range Vargev could not miss, Taneth collapsed into a bloody mess yards from the colonels feet.

Michael and Kathryn were nearing the shuttle, he knew Nikolai was in trouble, the colonel could not possibly hope to win alone. He knew he had to help his friend, but also that he could not leave Kathryn either; he was torn, and not for the first time in his life.

"I'm okay, go!" Kathryn said as she hobbled toward the shuttle boarding hatch.

"You're sure?"

"Yes, GO!"

Michael un-slung his own pulse rifle, and charged into combat to help Nikolai, sprinting toward the colonel, there was only him and a badly injured commando left.

Kallos and Aelthris both leapt from their position into action, Aelthris unleashed a fusillade of fire into the already injured commando, a dozen blades jutted out from the soldiers body, and he slowly fell in a bloodied heap to the ground.

She had not, however, counted on Michael now charging into the fray, as right behind where the commando had fallen, the Liberty captain stood. His pulse rifle aimed directly at her, and with her leaping through the air towards them, she could not change her direction. Michael simply squeezed the trigger, and blasted her straight through the mid-riff, she screamed aloud in agony and fury combined as she slammed hard into the ground, another shot silenced her for good.

Nikolai was fighting Kallos, both putting up an even battle, the Kallan swung his wristblades in an effort to behead the colonel where he stood, though Nikolai managed to block with the body of his weapon, though barely. The Dracos then performed a graceful backflip kick, catching the Russian just under the jaw and sending the commando tumbling to the ground heavily.

Kallos though, like Drax before him, had made the same fatal mistake in his fervour for the final kill, and broken one of the fundamental rules taught to every Kallan warrior. He was focused solely on the opponent in front of him, on Nikolai, thus had not noticed that Michael was fresh from killing Aelthris, and was now levelling his own pulse rifle directly at him.

"Hunting seasons over!" He whispered as he opened fire.

Kallos's head was torn apart in a spray of crimson froth, his body crumpled to the ground next to the commando colonel's.

202

With a smile, the Liberty captain proffered an outstretched hand to Vargev, who was still lying dazed, face up after landing hard.

The colonel took Michael's hand and gradually got to his feet, he was bleeding slightly, as the force of the blow, caused him to bit into his bottom lip, the blood stained his chin. He held his breath, as he took off his broken mask, wiped his chin with his sleeve, before putting it back on again.

"Cheap shot." The colonel muttered.

"That's another you owe me," Michael said with a grin.

"Who's keeping count?"

"Time we got off this hellhole of a planet, for good."

"Couldn't agree more, lead the way comrade."

The two of them gingerly made their way to the shuttle, to be greeted by a relieved Kathryn and Logameier, who had already powered up the shuttle.

The hatch slowly sealed behind them, and the gravitic engines kicked into life with their customary whine, gently raising it off the ground, before its main engines took over and the small craft soared skyward.

The colonel took off his breathing mask, relieved at having finally rid himself of the stuffiness inside the cracked apparatus, and dabbed at his no swelling lip as he looked down at the sight of the wrecked craft on the surface, the massive crater left by the Eisenhower, and the enormous focusing pylons of the Eye, and he said, "you know, I'm going to miss it here."

Michael smiled, "we could always set her down again."

"Heck no, besides too much of a good thing is always bad for you anyway."

The shuttle gently raced through the thick methane cloud cover, through the upper atmosphere to the flotilla waiting above, now a ship lighter.

With the inter-connecting corridor so badly damaged, Logameier had to attempt a 'hard dock' with the Liberty, a manoeuvre that was tricky in the extreme. He had to align the rear of the shuttle in such a way as to line it up exactly with the Liberties still functioning starboard docking hatch, taking into consideration the shuttles own engine pods overhang the top of the rear hatch by about a metre. The only way to do this safely, and without wrecking the engines was to dock the shuttle inverted, so that it's engines were clear of the warships hull, and it could still dock.

Lieutenant Logameier, manipulated the controls, very slowly and very gently reversing the upside down craft, metre by metre, inch by steady inch until the rear hatch gently locked into position with the Liberties hull.

With a sigh of released nerves, he magnetised the docking coupling clamping the shuttle secure. "Welcome home," he said as he released the rear hatch with a whoosh of escaping air, revealing the battered interior of the Liberty.

"You know, that was some top notch flying, you sure you don't want to study as a pilot?" Michael asked as he clapped him on the back.

"Nah, I'm happy just tinkering around in the ships engine room."

After a brief walked Michael, Kathryn, and Nikolai made it to an elevator, and was quickly deposited on the bridge. Logameier returned to engineering to help with the emergency repair effort.

"Been having a little trouble with the bad guys, I see." Michael said as he took over the central chair.

"Just a little," Kinraid smiled, "The Arizona managed 't' pick up te' majority of the escape pods, survivors 'ave been distributed amongst te' fleet. We 'ave tree crowded little ships out there, so we 'ave, and we've replaced our own losses."

"Good work commander, have one of the Eisenhower survivors pilot the shuttle back to the Arizona immediately, so we can engage plasma drive and get the heck out of here, I don't want to delay."

"Right wi' ya' cap'n" Kinraid said as he took over his familiar sensory officers station from Lieutenant Hicks, and quickly began compiling a list. Just a single name came up, Ensign Andrews, Quinn contacted the ensign to let him know of his orders.

Michael smiled as he looked toward Eldathar ahead, "Well I believe we should be getting underway, plot a new course back to charlie gamma base, bearing zero-eight-five degrees, elevation minus twenty-one. Initiate Plasma drive as soon as the shuttle is secured, contact the fleet to do the same."

"Understood captain," A relieved Eldathar replied.

"All ships are standing by," Quinn said.

The tiny shuttle successfully detached from the dark outer hull of the Liberty, and Michael watched the tiny craft gently fly out towards the much larger Arizona, waiting patiently.

The first rays of sunlight began to shine out from the edge of the planet below, illuminating the command structure and dorsal laser turrets of the cruiser, as well as the silhouettes of the Ghandhi class destroyers either side of it. It looked almost as if a new dawn had come to Auriga III, and in many instances it had, it was no longer a forgotten world, and the Dracos were no longer a forgotten race either.

"Shuttle is safely secured aboard."

"Then let's get the hell out of this crap hole!" Nikolai said.

"You heard the man," Michael smiled as he looked at Eldathar.

"Goodbye sergeant," Kathryn whispered as she stared out to the planet below, "You will always be in my heart, rest in peace my love."

The fleet slowly came about, and fired their inter-system boosters, before activating their plasma drives and disappearing through the swirling multi-hued morass that was the plasma wake.

The Aurigan sun shone out brightly as they left, a fitting tribute to the brave, gentle hero they had to leave behind.

The return trip to Charlie gamma base had taken two days, for the Liberty alone it would have taken a matter of hours, yet had to keep pace with the slower vessels of the E.D.F Flotilla.

In that time Kathryn's leg had come on a long way, she had took the time to rest, and could walk with only minor discomfort

The majority of the emergency repair work had been completed, although the ship still looked rather battered, the micro-fractures in the ships hull and the great twisted rent near the ships engine would require the services of a major naval yard to fix fully.

Nikolai paced about the ship as usual, being a commando colonel there was one thing the Russian hated, and that was having to sit on his hands, he had been informed that his own Stockholm class lander had been picked up by the Yukon, while on patrol and was being transported to the base, and was pleased to know it be there by the time he arrived.

Michael had a sense of pride at how his ship and crew had performed, they had faced a powerful and relentless enemy, more powerful even than themselves, and defeated it. Though both he and Nikolai had a new found respect for the Kallan's abilities in battle, he wondered how the Dracos would fare, now that the galaxy knew of their existence again. He guessed that they would simply become even more isolationist, than they were before and that saddened him, yes the Dracos were brutal and aggressive and sadistic, despite this the galaxy could still learn a great deal from the technology they employed.

Kinraid had grown in stature immensely, his handling of the incident with the Eisenhower had shown that he was a capable commander, and Michael suspected that his name would feature highly on the list of possible commanders of the future Valley forge.

"Approaching Charlie gamma base, captain." Eldathar pointed out.

"Understood, contact the fleet, tell them to drop out of plasma drive on my mark."

There was a brief pause before Kinraid announced, "Fleet confirms, all ships standing by." He kept and audio-link open so that the other ships could hear Michaels orders.

"Mark!"

At once bright white flashes heralded the return of the flotilla, with the Liberty at its head.

The numerous twinkling lights of the outer structure of the small naval yard and research facility were plainly visible in the distance. A Lincoln class supply vessel drifted out from the station, no doubt just completed its latest supply run. Its inter-system boosters fired up and glowed brightly as it headed away from the station.

"Gentlemen, we've come back home." Michael gave out a slight sigh of relief as he said it, the mission had been a brief but gruelling one.

"Wherever home is." Kinraid replied.

Michael smiled at the sentiment, it was true, the Liberty was one of the most well travelled of all ships in the navy. Home was wherever they happened to be at the time.

"Increase power to main engines, lay in a standard approach vector."

"Aye captain," Eldathar replied, a smile broke out across the Solarians own blue tinged features, he was also relieved to finally leave that place, the whole thing had been a great wrench on him personally.

"Contact Charlie gamma base command and control, and request permission to dock."

"Aye, sir." Kinraid carried out the order with his usual level of light hearted professionalism. "Charlie gamma base confirms, we are cleared for approach, they also say welcome back, Liberty."

"Good to be back." Michael replied, with sincerity.

The battered matt-black hulled warship, slowly glided into the small sub-orbital dockyard, Michael watched as Eldathar expertly guided the ship in, thinking that the small, somewhat cramped interior of the relatively remote facility seemed to close over them, as though protecting them, the thought gave Michael a measure of warmth as he continued to watch.

Interior lights played along the black and silver hull of the Liberty as it gently drifted further inside, highlighting the crumpled twisted port docking hatch, the site of the damaged inter-connecting corridor.

The giant searchlights continued to inspect the flotilla as they all slowly glided inside the facility in close formation, it showed up the horrific jagged rent in the Liberties aft section, a painful reminder of just how powerful those Dracos warcruisers really were. If they could that to the Liberty, a typical E.D.F vessel stood no chance.

Finally the small warship came to rest, as its starboard docking hatch clamped onto one of several terminals with a dull 'thunk', Michael breathed a final, relieved sigh, it was over.

A few hours later after grabbing some much needed rest, Michael returned to the command and control deck of the facility and submitted his official mission report to commodore Valente, who thumbed through the information on the data navigator in his office.

"We took quite a beating out there, fifteen of the sixteen scientists and landing party dead, over twenty commandoes, five on the Liberty itself, another fifteen on the Eisenhower, as well as the losses of both the Eisenhower and the Copernicus."

"Aye sir, total casualty count stands at three hundred and forty five, all told."

"Well at least we managed to drive those damned Dracos back into their own territory again, how is Kathryn anyway?"

"She's pretty shaken up sir, she has been through a lot on this mission."

"I bet she is, poor woman. You've done one heck of a job captain, in very difficult circumstances, once again the Liberty has done us proud."

"If I may sir, I have requested that sergeant Heinrich Rachthausen of the 69th Sicarian guards be honoured with a posthumous citation for bravery. If it wasn't for his sacrifice, and leadership in trying to keep those around him alive, even when faced with such a threat as the Dracos, I don't think we would have found anyone down there, sir."

"Noted, I will take a look through the mission report in more detail with regard to that, but if he fought as you say he did, then a citation should be the least of his reward. By the way captain, Admiral Mason sends his congratulations on your success."

"Understood sir, we've secured what could prove to be a vital facility for E.O.C.A, I just wish it was worth it, because we have more than paid for it in blood out there, commodore."

"Aye, captain, that we did."

A few hours later Nikolai and Kathryn had joined Michael as he sat in the stations restaurant overlooking the various ships berthed in the shipyard beyond.

"Have you given any more thought as to your next posting," Michael asked Kathryn who was sat opposite him.

"Apparently I'm being assigned to the Archimedes as it heads out to study an unusually bright star forming nebula near the Epsilon system." She said with a sigh as she ran her hand through her long dark hair.

"But you don't want to go, do you?"

"The Liberty is my real home, always has been."

Michael nodded knowingly, "My voice carries some weight with the admiralty now, I'll see if I can get you reassigned."

"Would you!" She asked, her face brightened noticeably as a big grin came across her face.

"I can't promise, but I will speak to Admirals Mason and Montrose, see what they say."

"Oh thank you!" She leaned over and gave him a tight bear hug.

Michael smiled, "Hey what are friends for, right?"

Nikolai nodded approvingly as he took a sip of synthetic vodka, the non alcoholic stuff was pitiful compared to real Russian vodka, yet out here this was all there was. "My next stop is back to Alpha centauri, for a full debriefing from General M'cree, the old bull is getting a little long in the tooth now, he's considering retirement, when he does I guess I'll finally be promoted to a full general myself, and be bound to a desk for eternity."

Well I shall have to bid you all a fond farewell, I have some business to attend to with a certain Solarian governor.

They both nodded as Michael left the grizzled commando veteran, and his former medical officer turned geologist to their conversation, and made his way down to his personal quarters aboard the Liberty. It still looked dishevelled from the mauling the ship had taken, and he had to clear several pieces of broken cable and detritus from his cracked glass desk, yet his personal terminal was still functioning.

He contacted Kerulithar again, to update him on the unification process or lack of, to be correct.

"Ah Michael, good to see you again, any news since our last talk?"

"Actually there has, the four prisoners who I had intended for you to use in talks with the Dracos are dead. They hijacked one of our ships and crashed it into the surface, and was killed attacking myself and the rest of my team."

"That is a shame, it would have been an amazing thing if the Dracos and our own people could integrate as one again. It seems like they are just not ready to let go of their bloodthirsty instincts. We will keep monitoring the situation, and at least it is good to hear that our brothers and sisters were not completely wiped out all those years ago, perhaps one day the Dracos will be ready to embrace the galaxy again."

"Perhaps," Michael said, though in truth he had no idea when that day would come. "Thank you for your time and patience with this Kerulithar."

"It was my pleasure, old friend."

With that, he ended the transmission.

Maybe the Dracos could one day change their ways, maybe the Solarians could in future re-unify with a long lost part of themselves, the truth is who knows what the future really holds.

What he did know, was that slowly but surely mankind was becoming an ever-greater presence on the galactic stage, they had now proved that they were not a tiny, weak, backwater empire any more. Through blood, through sacrifice, through pain and hardship, they had finally earned their place amongst the more powerful races of the galaxy, and were finally respected amongst the elite, and Michael smiled with that thought.

The end.

About the author

Ian J. Smethurst is the author of the popular E.D.F chronicles series of novels, now in its third instalment.

Even from his early years in primary school, and later in high school. Ian was always reading science fiction and fantasy novels, his reading age was often far above others in his class, and he possesses an almost boundless vocabulary which he uses to full effect in his novels.

The energy, and imagination that Ian uses in his works are almost without limit, and it is this sense of unceasing energy that is a factor in the success of his novels, although he likes to ground his characters in as realistic environments and scenarios as possible.

He is also a keen historian and was shortlisted for the 2008 writers reign short story contest, and longlisted in the 2011 science fiction review short story competition.

Having now completed the third novel in the E.D.F chronicles series, Eye of the Dracos. He is now working on the grand finale of his much beloved series, entitled The Cyberian menace, due for release in 2015.

www.ingramcontent.com/pod-product-compliance
Lightning Source LLC
Chambersburg PA
CBHW070756280626
47162CB00016B/1073